PRAISE FOR

Faith Bass Darling's Last Garage Sale

"With a big Texas heart, Lynda Rutledge writes of second chances, redemption, what we truly own, and what we must release in this spectacular novel. Faith Bass Darling hears voices, but you will see: the most original of all is her own."

—Adriana Trigiani, *New York Times* bestselling
author of *The Shoemaker's Wife*, *Big Stone Gap*, and the Valentine series

"It's been a long time since I've read anything that let me be a reader again, but this book did it for me. It's a joy to read. I loved every page. Lynda Rutledge has a wonderful, fresh Southern voice to go with her talent, and I predict she'll go far. Treat yourself to this luminous, enchanting story."

—Haywood Smith, *New York Times* bestselling
author of *The Red Hat Club*

"I can't remember when I've enjoyed a first novel so much. Faith Bass Darling will live on and on in each reader's heart. Some chapters made me laugh out loud, some left me with a delicious tear in my eye, others evoked a shiver of recognition at things known but not quite realized. Eerie, charming, heartrending, and heartbreaking at the same time, Rutledge's novel is a triumph."

—W. P. "Bill" Kinsella, author of *Shoeless Joe*,
inspiration for the blockbuster movie *Field of Dreams*

continued . . .

"A small-town novel that asks the big questions of life . . . a heartfelt story about last chances, second chances, and chance itself. When Faith Bass Darling is called to sell all her belongings on what she believes to be her last day on earth, she changes the lives of the townspeople around her . . . and she'll change yours, as well. A most thought-provoking read."

—Tiffany Baker, *New York Times* bestselling author of *The Little Giant of Aberdeen County*

"The town of Bass, Texas, will never be the same after Faith Bass Darling's last garage sale, and neither will the novel's reader. Lynda Rutledge brings to life the residents of this town as they go about their business on New Year's Eve 1999, and in doing so she reveals the tangled histories of an eccentric, loveable, exasperating cast of characters. This book is a tremendous achievement. You won't want it to end."

—Elizabeth Stuckey-French, author of *The Revenge of the Radioactive Lady*

Faith Bass Darling's

LAST GARAGE SALE

Lynda Rutledge

BERKLEY BOOKS
New York

THE BERKLEY PUBLISHING GROUP
Published by the Penguin Group
Penguin Group (USA) Inc.
375 Hudson Street, New York, New York 10014, USA
Penguin Group (Canada), 90 Eglinton Avenue East, Suite 700, Toronto, Ontario M4P 2Y3, Canada
(a division of Pearson Penguin Canada Inc.) • Penguin Books Ltd., 80 Strand, London WC2R 0RL,
England • Penguin Ireland, 25 St. Stephen's Green, Dublin 2, Ireland (a division of Penguin
Books Ltd.) • Penguin Group (Australia), 707 Collins Street, Melbourne, Victoria 3008, Australia
(a division of Pearson Australia Group Pty. Ltd.) • Penguin Books India Pvt. Ltd., 11 Community
Centre, Panchsheel Park, New Delhi—110 017, India • Penguin Group (NZ), 67 Apollo Drive,
Rosedale, Auckland 0632, New Zealand (a division of Pearson New Zealand Ltd.) • Penguin Books (South
Africa), Rosebank Office Park, 181 Jan Smuts Avenue, Parktown North 2193, South Africa • Penguin
China, B7 Jiaming Center, 27 East Third Ring Road North, Chaoyang District, Beijing 100020, China

Penguin Books Ltd., Registered Offices: 80 Strand, London WC2R 0RL, England

This is a work of fiction. Names, characters, places, and incidents either are the product of the author's
imagination or are used fictitiously, and any resemblance to actual persons, living or dead, business
establishments, events, or locales is entirely coincidental. The publisher does not have any control over
and does not assume any responsibility for author or third-party websites or their content.

PUBLISHING HISTORY
Amy Einhorn Books/G. P. Putnam's Sons hardcover edition / April 2012
Berkley trade paperback edition / February 2013

Berkley trade paperback ISBN: 978-0-425-26102-6

The Library of Congress has catalogued the Amy Einhorn/
G. P. Putnam's Sons hardcover edition as follows:

Rutledge, Lynda.
Faith Bass Darling's last garage sale / Lynda Rutledge.
p.   cm.
ISBN 978-0-399-15719-6
1. Garage sales—Fiction.   2. Self-realization in women—Fiction.   I. Title.
PS3619.U476726F35   2012   2011047682
813'.6—dc23

PRINTED IN THE UNITED STATES OF AMERICA

10   9   8   7   6   5   4   3   2   1

To Dad,

for leaving me the rolltop

In my Father's house are many mansions. . . .

—JOHN 14:2

What is this self? It is the sum of everything we remember.

—MILAN KUNDERA

✍ PROVENANCE

LOUIS XV ELEPHANT CLOCK

10˝ x 12˝ gilded automaton elephant clock with moving
trunk • Bronze casting signed by J. Caffieri •
Clockworks signed by C. Balthazar

Circa 1772   *Value: priceless*

---

*In 1772, a time instrument in the shape of an Asian elephant with a
mechanical trunk, whimsically combining the current fascination with
the Orient and the new status symbol of "clocks," was fashioned for the
Countess Marie-Jeanne du Barry, a courtesan of Louis XV's royal court.*

*In 1792, during the French Revolution, in which the Countess du
Barry would lose her head and have no more use for status symbols or
the time of day, the clock was stolen by a seamstress who traded it to a
traveling peddler who in turn sold it on the streets of London.*

*Over the two centuries that followed, it rode in a steamer trunk to
America; survived a fire in Manhattan's Five Points slum; surfaced in a
Washington, D.C., haberdashery; was loaded into a wagon as a dowry
headed for Tennessee; looted by a Civil War carpetbagger and traded for
bordello favors; confiscated in a raid; packed on a train to Texas with a*

mail-order bride; acquired as a defaulted loan's collateral by a storefront bank in a new Texas railroad town; set in the master bedroom of a new mansion by the bank's founder; moved into the bedroom of a great-grandchild named Faith Ann to help her sleep through the night; moved into the bedroom of Faith's daughter to help her sleep through the night; and there it stayed. Until the last day in the Year of Our Lord 1999 . . .

December 31, 1999

PREFACE

On the last day of the millennium, after a midnight revelation from God, Faith Bass Darling had a garage sale.

Considering she hadn't spoken to the Almighty in twenty years, and considering she was the richest old lady in town, this was more than a bit surprising. At straight-up midnight, though, she'd bolted upright in her four-poster bed, certain she'd heard her name called like soft lightning. Yet the skies were calm and the stars big and bright. Figuring it was just one of her moments, Faith had gone back to sleep. A few seconds later she heard it again. But once again she shrugged it off and drifted warily back to sleep.

The third time she heard it, she landed in her bare feet on her hardwood floor with the sound of the gentle thunderbolt still in her ears. And this time she found herself moving through her dark and silent turn-of-the-century mansion, the biggest and oldest in Bass, Texas, gazing at all the antiques in all the rooms of the place where she had lived her entire life. She turned on a room full of Tiffany lamps. She fingered the Queen Anne highboy and Victorian wing-backs. She wandered past the player piano, the Spode china service, the grandfather clock in the foyer, the rolltop in the library, opening every drawer, every closet, every cubbyhole, every cupboard, every nook, every cranny in sight.

She continued this until dawn the next morning, whereupon she surprised all her neighbors on Old Waco Road, the tiny old town's lone strip of mansions built when cotton was king and oil was still gushing, by appearing from behind her big carved doors and hanging a handmade garage sale sign around the neck of her peeling lawn-jockey hitching post. And then—after a last long, strong drag off her first Lucky Strike filter of the day and a flourished stubbing-out of the butt on the lawn jockey's head—she began dragging the contents of a century of conspicuous consumption onto her long, sloping lawn.

Because she knew what this was about. This was about dying. This was about dying and killing Claude. It was the beginning of times; it was the end of times. And for seventy-year-old Faith Bass Darling, it was about time.

BARGAINS

Louis XV elephant clock	circa 1772	Value: priceless
Heirloom wedding ring	circa 1870	Value: $135,000
Deluxe banker's "S" rolltop desk	circa 1869	Value: $8,000
Dance Dragoon	circa 1864	Value: $40,000
Tiffany lamp collection	circa 1925–1939	Value: $400,000
Portrait of Jesus	circa 1960	Value: $10 (frame)
$10,000 bill	Series 1918	Value: $200,000 (mint condition)
Family Bible	circa 1955	Value: sentimental
Love letter	circa 1879	Value: ephemera
19th-century mansion	circa 1880	Value: $750,000

With a rather unladylike grunt, Faith Darling set down the elephant clock on her mansion's wraparound front porch. Then, straightening her sun hat and cocking her jaw in the warm early-morning breeze, she stepped down onto the porch's top step and called the nice, helpful teenage neighbor boys over to her. She had promised to show them the money if they would get started pulling things out of the big house. And so she would. Digging into her sundress's pockets, she came up with a fistful of $20 gold double eagles and held them out to the boys.

Hesitantly, they each took one of the gold coins.

"Something wrong?" the old woman asked.

The boys looked at each other. Until finally one of them, her paperboy—young Eddie was his name—spoke up: "Ma'am, do you have any, like, real money?"

That almost made her smile. "This is more real than you've ever seen, young man."

"Still, ma'am. You can't stick these in a Coke machine."

"No, I suppose you can't," she agreed. "Wait a moment." She went back inside to find her purse. Entering the kitchen, she didn't seem at all concerned with the condition of the room. There were stacks everywhere. Piles of magazines and newspapers she never quite remembered to throw away covered the counters, the floor, even the appliances. A tower of phone books she never quite remembered to clear away stood under the wall phone by the side door. Dozens of Imperial sugar bags, Campbell's soup cans, Heinz ketchup bottles, and Lipton tea tins she never quite remembered she had enough of surrounded the kitchen sink, the only thing in the room that was clean and devoid of clutter, and it sparkled as if it were cleaned every hour of every day.

Faith found her purse perched on months of mail—junk mail flyers, catalogs, and letters she never quite remembered to read—and retrieved some paper money from it.

As she set her purse back on the pile she glanced at the letter on top, almost recalling something important about it. Stamped across its envelope were the words "URGENT" and "OFFICIAL" in red ink. But then the window air-conditioner unit whomped on, rattling and rumbling, cranky as always. So she leaned over and whapped it a good one, the motor hushing as did her thoughts about the letter.

Oh, wait, she thought, I need a cash box for the sale. Grabbing her ornate sterling silverware case from behind the stacks of soup, she emptied the silver onto the counter, half the pieces tumbling to the tile floor, and headed back to the waiting boys.

As she stepped down her front porch steps to where they stood, Faith looked away for a moment. When she looked back, the boys were gone.

And so was the sale. . . .

Faith finds herself walking down the hospital hallway with her doctor.

"Blank spells getting worse?" he is asking.

"Yes," Faith admits, "and I'm seeing people I shouldn't be seeing, least ways as long as I'm still around."

"It's called 'sundowning,' Mrs. Darling," the doctor says. "Try to stay away from visual clutter that can trigger it."

She frowns. "You're not Dr. Friddell."

He is smiling his irritating doctor smile. "I'm Dr. Peabody, remember? Dr. Friddell's been dead ten years now."

"I never liked either of you," she tells him. "Always so damn nice. Makes me cranky. And you both have such bad toupees."

His smile grows and so does his toupee. "Your memories can feel like a shuffling deck of cards as they fade, but reports show some people are happy."

"Is a celery stalk happy?" she asks. "Doesn't a body's soul need a memory? If not, what's all this living for? And if heaven is for the dead, where do you go when you aren't here but you aren't dead? Tell me that!"

"Don't worry, we'll take good care of you," he says, his toupee slowly turning into a black cowboy hat as they float through the long-term care center's doors. "Just like these nice folks."

Faith sees someone she knows—Harold Frudigger, Rotary Club member and Baptist deacon—sitting, staring, twiddling his thumbs. Then she sees his robe and pajama bottoms are open and it's not his thumbs he is twiddling. Horrified, reeling from the twiddling, the care center, the future lying in wait for her, Faith stumbles back out the doors.

I won't be dead before I die . . . I won't . . .

"Mrs. Darling?"

"Holy shit—you think she's about to croak?" whispered one of the boys.

Why, that nice young Eddie, my paperboy, is standing in front of me, Faith realized as she came back to herself. . . . Where am I?

"Mrs. Darling?"

Dizzy, she looked around: *visual clutter.* "How long have you been waiting, Eddie?" she asked, as dignified as possible.

"A couple of minutes, ma'am. Want me to call my daddy?"

She stared at him hard, suddenly remembering that his daddy was her doctor, young Dr. Peabody who replaced dead Dr. Friddell. "No, son," she answered. He already knows.

"Here's some paper money for you." She held out her hand with the dollar bills in it. "And you keep those gold coins. In twenty years, you'll thank me." She noticed something under her arm: her silverware box. She opened it. There was nothing in it. And the sun was hitting her in the face. "Better get my sun hat," she murmured.

"It's on your head, Mom," her son, Michael, said.

Faith's eyes filled up with the beautiful boy, her heart in her throat. "Michael?"

"I said, your hat's on your head, ma'am. And my name's Billy," said Eddie's older brother, the football player.

Ah, yes, Faith realized. Michael isn't here. She swallowed. "Remembering wasn't part of the deal today," she reminded God.

"Ma'am? What was part of the deal?" she heard the nice young man Billy ask her. "You mean you want us to finish bringing out those chairs? We could also come back later. I could get some of my football buddies and pull out the rest real quick."

"That'd be nice. Now go on with you." She waved them away, and with them, the old sadness.

"Hey, lady!"

Faith looked around. A remarkably rotund woman with two ruffian boys was standing by the big armoire, calling to her.

"How much you want for this hutch, lady? I got cash!"

With her silverware case–cash box clutched under her arm, Faith Darling raised her chin, straightened her hat, and went to make her first sale of the day.

Directly across the street, Faith Darling's longtime neighbor Maude Quattlebaum looked out her front window and saw what looked like a wingback chair floating on its own across that brick walkway down from the Darlings' big front porch.

Normally, of course, she wouldn't be noticing what her neighbors were doing, especially this early in the morning. She wasn't one of those nosy neighbors. But she'd woken up in a sweat and there wasn't any going back to sleep. (Hot as H-E-double-chopsticks for December. Everybody's jabbering about it being that Y2K end-of-the-world millennium silliness, but this is Texas, for pity's sake.) So she'd popped in her hearing aid, then headed for the kitchen. And just as she'd taken her first swig of her morning Dr Pepper, she glanced through the front window's venetian blinds and coughed it right up her nose at the sight of the floating wingback chair. When the chair dropped with a plop, who does she see but Faith Darling herself, all dressed up in a starched white summer dress with a matching sun hat, no less, giving commands to the teenage boy lugging the thing.

What the devil is that woman up to? Maude wondered. The Darling place had been so quiet for so long, seeing any sign of life over there was a bit of a shock. Lord only knew the last time she saw her longtime neighbor poke her nose out of those big carved doors. Nothing but a stream of home delivery people and errand boys and cleaning ladies for years now. And lately that fancy yard of hers had gotten so unkempt as to be the topic of neighborly concern. Maude sniffed: Faith Darling always was wound as tight as a clock, all prim, proper, and neat as a pin. Everybody knew she hadn't been right since Claude up and died way back when. Of course, Maude reminded herself, the woman definitely had her trials. Lost that fine son of hers in that awful accident with his daddy and that colored boy. And that daughter of hers was a ring-tailed-tooter even back when Maude had the child in Sunday school, nothing but a pill until the day she ran off. But that didn't make the woman special. "Don't we all have troubles?" Maude muttered into the venetian blinds she was spreading to get a better view.

But then Maude saw the homemade "Sale" sign hanging around Faith's peeling old lawn-jockey hitching post by the curb.

SALE?

And that sent her scooting straight across the street in her slippers. I'm eighty-two years old! she griped. I'm too old to be putting up with such foolishness around here!

Holding up the hem of her bathrobe, Maude stepped onto the mansion's big front lawn. "Faith Darling, have you lost all good sense?" she called across the yard. "Do you know what kind of people this will bring to the neighborhood?"

Faith turned to see her old neighbor heading up the brick walkway in her fuzzy slippers and pink chenille bathrobe. She shot her a sour-milk stare. "What are you talking about, Maude?"

"Only riffraff shop at yard sales—looky-there! That scruffy little urchin just snatched something—I saw you, child!" Maude shrieked at a little girl with a mess of yellow hair in a dirty T-shirt and unlaced sneakers, running the opposite way with a pair of small red cowboy boots. "Where's that urchin's mama? Those dirt-road kids just run wild day and night. And look at that boy!" She wagged a finger at one of the young helpers. "Put that box down right now, young man!"

Faith propped her hands on her hips, already having quite enough of Maude Quattlebaum, still the most irritating woman she'd ever had the displeasure of knowing. "Leave the boy alone, Maude. He's been helping me bring the furniture out, if it's any of your business."

Maude harrumphed, already having quite enough of Faith Bass Darling, still the most infuriating woman she'd ever had the displeasure of knowing. She took a closer look at the boy. And lo and behold, it was Dr. Peabody's youngest child, Eddie, her paperboy. No wonder she didn't get her paper this morning. When she turned back, Faith was giving her that arched-eyebrow look she hadn't missed a bit all these years—a mixture of holier-than-thou Bass and high-and-mighty Darling. She hated that look. "But a yard sale, Faith!" Maude said, offering up her best Quattlebaum glare. "How could you sell your beautiful things? Have you lost your mind?!"

"As we speak, Maude."

As we speak? Maude's eyebrows scrunched up. Now, what did that mean?

"And considering this is my last day on earth, Maude, I don't much care to waste any more of it talking to you," Faith added, walking away.

"Well!" Maude exclaimed, her hearing aid missing the "last day" part. "There's no reason to be snippy!"

"I need a cigarette," Faith suddenly said, stopping in her tracks to pat her pockets. As Maude stared, Faith pulled out a pack of filterless Lucky Strikes and a fancy brass and silver lighter, tapped out a cigarette like some field hand, placed it between her lips, lit it and sucked on the foul thing as she flipped the lighter shut with a click—all in one motion. Like she'd done it all her life.

And that just made Maude throw her hands toward heaven. Claude was the smoker. Faith didn't smoke—no proper Baptist woman smoked. "Sweet Baby Jesus, Faith," wailed Maude, "what is going o . . . ?" But instead of finishing her wail, she all but swallowed her tongue. Because that's when she saw another boy come bumbling down the front steps almost dropping the most gorgeous lamp she ever laid eyes on. And Maude started to wonder whether maybe the world was coming to an end, because she never thought she'd live to see the day.

"You're selling your Tiffanys?"

Without another word, Maude scooted right back home to fetch her purse.

Faith blinked.

Her nose was inches from a closed bedroom door and her sun hat was half off her head.

Oh, for heaven's sake—

She wobbled back a step. Hadn't she just been arguing with her neighbor Maude? But here she was upstairs in front of the master bedroom door—a room she hadn't entered in twenty years. Dizzy, she reached to steady herself and found her silverware box stuffed under her arm. With money in it.

Then Faith remembered: The Sale.

Setting her jaw and straightening her hat, she quickly backed farther away from the insulting door. She would *not* go in that room. "Oh no, no, that wasn't part of the deal. And a deal is a deal," she said loud enough for Midnight Voices to hear, because not even the Lord God Almighty would ask her to do such a thing. Then she rushed through her mental checklist, a litany she always repeated after coming back from one of her moments:

My name is Faith Bass Darling . . . I live at 101 Old Waco Road in Bass, Texas . . . Today is December 31, 1999 . . . My great-grandparents were James Tyler Bass and Belle Bass . . . My parents were James Bass III and Pamela Bass . . .

There. Fine now, she thought, glancing uneasily at the door. This was just a coincidence. And coincidences happen—that's why they're called coincidences. After all, it's not like this was the first time she'd found herself somewhere unexpected. It used to upset her, all this jumping around like a Mexican jumping bean. But it was happening so often she tried to look at such times as, well, surprises. And everybody likes surprises, she groused, letting out a tight-lipped little sigh as she turned toward the stairs.

Faith descended the grand staircase as fast as her old bones allowed, striding through the front doors, down her front steps, and back to the mansion's contents spread from the porch to the curb and back again—armoires, oriental rugs, sideboards, secretaries, china cabinets, chest o'drawers, bookcases, love seats, highboys, lowboys, daybeds, night beds, and on and on.

Finally coming to a stop beside a leather wingback chair to catch her breath, she straightened her sun hat, her sundress, and her resolve. Then, with barely a thought, she passed a massive mahogany dining table completely covered with dozens of antique Tiffany lamps, stopping only to kick a dusty unmarked box aside so she could straighten a sterling-silver tea service on a French maple sideboard.

On some level, Faith knew these antiques had surrounded her throughout her life and that they'd been her only companions for two long decades. But at that moment, standing among her incredibly expensive worldly possessions, as garage sale customers began screeching to a halt by her curb, they were not much different than the broken tricycles and wobbly couches for sale at the other garage sales across town. Faith couldn't remember that she'd once sold the family bank just for the privilege of continuing to own these antiques. She couldn't remember that a century of Bass ancestors had bought, cherished, and handed down these antiques to her. Or that she'd spent her entire life preserving every piece as if they still embodied her family's very souls.

Not even the dusty box at her feet meant anything to her. When the sight of it should have sparked fireworks. Inside were her white baptism Bible, her baby-blue graduation Bible, and the big, black red-letter Bible she'd read every day and twice on Sundays—all now piled in with dozens more, once cherished by pious Bass ancestors. One day twenty years ago, on the day she'd shut the mansion doors on everything, including God, she had stalked through the mansion finding and stuffing every last one of them into this box.

A tiny memory, no more than an echo, forced her to glance at the box, but Faith stuck out her chin and waited for it to fade, as she'd learned how to do. Squinting at the things spread across her yard, things not meant to be hit by the light of day, the scene turned surreal, material mirages dancing on her yellow-dead winter lawn . . . and for the slightest of heart-pausing moments, she almost remembered how she felt about every last possession surrounding her. *Almost.* It had all come at her like a flooding river, right to the edge of her awareness. And then just washed away.

Faith let out her breath, which she only now realized she'd been holding. Her hand went to her heart, sensing something more momentous happening now, her memories moving like a train more than a river, some having taken the last train, never to return.

But the memories she'd wish most to take a last train—the ones that would be a true mercy to never recall again—wouldn't board: that she'd had a husband until she watched him die, that she had a son killed by an antique gun too old to shoot, that she had a daughter who'd run off with the family's heirloom ring, and that she'd believed in a God who disappeared when she needed one the most. A lifetime of fading memories were now bouncing back and forth as half-forgotten echoes—but not those memories. Sooner or later, those *always* returned clear as a damn bell.

Mercifully, for the present moment Faith was not remembering them. Instead, she held herself completely still, waiting for the familiar touch of darn dizziness to disappear. When it did, she sighed slightly, dabbing at the sweat beads on her upper lip. Then she put her hands on her hips and turned back to her God Almighty-inspired sale, the thundering whispered notion she'd heard at midnight still echoing in her ears just like the "still, small voice" her church upbringing had always taught. After all this time—and just in time.

All I have to do is be patient, Faith reminded herself, turning to look up at the mansion. If she could corral her wandering mind for just this one day—if she could keep the pesky memories of all these old things from messing up the sale—she'd make a good and easy ending to it all.

A deal is a deal.

Just then, however, the elephant clock perched on the porch steps struck the hour, and Faith turned toward it. And as she watched its bronze-cast elephant's trunk swaying with each chime, the gilded clock began to slowly shimmer with memory and meaning until it was absolutely aglow with Faith's entire childhood, a childhood full of comforting elephant clock nights. For a breath-snatching moment, Faith Bass Darling, her eyes now locked on the old clock, experienced the comfort as fully as she had as a child . . . clock ticking, elephant trunk swaying, rocking her gently, so very gently, a soothing motherly tick-tock warmth lulling her to sleep. Then, suddenly, she saw it rocking another child to sleep—her daughter—her blond-haired little girl. So Faith rushed over, picked up the elephant clock, and took it back inside.

Dust was already flying at the front of Yesteryear Antique Shop on the town's tiny main street when owner and sole proprietor Bobbie Blankenship opened for business a bit early. The redheaded, thirty-something hometown girl had almost chosen to go to a Weight Watchers meeting instead of opening the shop this morning. Her discount designer-mall pantsuit was beginning to pinch in all the wrong places and she'd just bought it. But she couldn't pass up the chance for a little holiday business.

She, however, never expected this when she opened the doors.

Bobbie hadn't taken her eyes off the Chippendale armoire since it came in the door with roly-poly Mrs. Hackmeyer and her two thuggy sons. "A beautiful piece, truly beautiful," Bobbie murmured. She ran her hand lovingly along the armoire's lines, and then eyed Mrs. Hackmeyer in her print wraparound housedress. Where had she seen this armoire before? Please don't let it be stolen, she thought with a glance at the sons.

"Aren't antiques wonderful? You can almost feel all the lives a piece like this has witnessed," Bobbie said, touching it again herself. "They *are* the past, really," she added wistfully. "To own an antique is to own a piece of the past, the present, and the future, to see things ever so slightly like God surely does, don't you think?"

"Oh, yeah, like God," agreed Mrs. Hackmeyer with a couple of impatient wrist-flips. "So, how much you gimme for it? I paid twenty dollars and I want way more than that," she said, chins up, eyes bright with greed.

Bobbie bit her tongue, trying not to grin at her good fortune.

The armoire was a nineteenth-century antique worth thousands if a penny. "I'll give you two hundred dollars. How 'bout that?" she offered, her best poker face firmly in place.

"Cash?" Mrs. Hackmeyer wagered, one eyebrow low over a watery eye.

"Why, of course, Mrs. Hackmeyer." Bobbie removed several bills from her gilded antique cash register and placed them in the woman's sweaty pink palm. "Wherever did you find this, if I may ask?"

"It was the craziest thing!" she answered, clutching the cash. "I was just starting my garage sale run, heading for the Big Ten Family Neighborhood Garage Sale out in Alamo Heights. When what do I see but a garage sale sign in front of the biggest old house on fancy Old Waco Road! You know, the one built by the Bass guy the town's named after? That old lady's selling stuff like you wouldn't *believe*."

Bobbie's eyes grew wide. A little thrill ran around her stomach and up her spine. Ridding herself of Mrs. Hackmeyer and her offspring, she flipped the "Open" sign to "Closed," grabbed her purse and a cotton jacket to throw over her pantsuit to convey her best professional air, and was out the door.

In five minutes flat, Bobbie was standing at the curb of the Darling mansion, slack-jawed. Except for the parked Chevy pickups and Walmart-clad shoppers, she could be walking onto a lawn in 1900 instead of just a few hours from the year 2000. Before her were hundreds of thousands of dollars' worth of antiques—maybe *millions*—strewn across the long sloping lawn, from Venetian stemware to hope chests to chandeliers to candelabras.

As Bobbie stepped onto the mansion lawn, though, she slowed, gazing up momentarily at the big house she'd worshipped her entire life. She hadn't been this close since she was a little-bitty kid. Then her eyes fell on the dining table right in front of her. Completely covering the long Georgian mahogany table, from one end to the other, was Mrs. Darling's entire collection of authentic Louis Comfort Tiffany lamps.

Bobbie couldn't help herself. She strode over and picked up the closest Tiffany, a lovely lily motif, and held it to her chest as if saving it from the hordes. But then she saw the Tiffany of her dreams: the rare stained-glass fish motif worth more than all the others combined. Why, it was showcased on PBS's *Antiques Roadshow* just the other day—*everybody* might know! Bobbie thought, almost dropping the lamp in her arms, her cheeks flushing bright red with excitement.

She hustled clumsily over to it in her business wedges, and when she couldn't manage both lamps she reluctantly set the lily lamp down and swooped the fish Tiffany into her arms in its place.

Just then, an old woman she'd known all her life walked from behind a Queen Anne secretary. Bobbie hadn't seen Mrs. Darling in years, cooped up as she was in this big mansion of hers. But Bobbie would know her anywhere, the regal way she carried herself, the immaculate way she dressed. As a kid, Bobbie had always stood up straighter in the presence of Claudia Jean Darling's mother, and she felt herself doing it now. From the sound of it, Mrs. Darling had just finished haggling with her neighbor, old Mrs. Quattlebaum, over one of the Tiffany lamps and Mrs. Quattlebaum wasn't happy, stalking off empty-handed.

Bobbie eased the precious fish Tiffany onto the nearest table, one hand poised near enough to claim it, and spoke: "Mrs. Darling?"

Faith turned toward Bobbie. "Yes?"

"Don't you remember me?" Bobbie asked.

Frowning, Faith began arranging sale articles on the table between them. "Can't say that I do."

"Claudia Jean's friend, Bobbie Ann Blankenship?"

Faith's hands hovered over a stack of folded dinner linens. "Claudia Jean?"

Bobbie paused. It was as if Mrs. Darling didn't remember her own daughter. They'd had a falling-out—everybody knew that—but you don't forget your own daughter. How old was the woman now?

As her hands finally landed on the linens, Mrs. Darling said a bit too brightly: "Bobbie Ann Blankenship."

Despite hearing her name said back to her from the old woman's lips, Bobbie had the oddest sensation that Faith Darling had spoken the words like place marks, empty shells she hoped would fill. Faith gazed at her for a beat, then, as if a switch had flipped behind her eyes, she said, "Ah, yes, Little Bobbie Ann. Hello, dear."

Warily, Bobbie watched as Faith began to stack the linens ever so perfectly along the table's edge then restack them again—and again—until a giggling girl in a Dairy Queen uniform with an armload of intricately hand-stitched Spanish lace tablecloths rushed up to hand Faith a single quarter, which, to Bobbie's horror, Faith took. As the girl giggled past, Bobbie resisted an urge to grab the Spanish lace and make a run for it.

"Mrs. Darling, what are you doing?" she blurted, waving an arm.

Faith arched an eyebrow, then returned to the linen stack, inspecting it for perfection. "It's rather obvious, don't you think?"

"But . . . how much are you selling?" Bobbie stammered.

Faith moved to a pile of quilts on the other end of the table and began stacking them perfectly. "All of it, dear."

For a second, Bobbie lost the power of speech. "All of it?" she finally croaked.

"All of it," Faith repeated.

Bobbie took a deep breath and moved around the table, positioning herself directly in front of Faith. "Mrs. Darling, I just bought your Chippendale armoire from a woman who lives in a trailer park. She said you sold it for twenty dollars. Please tell me that's not true."

Faith cocked her head in thought. "I don't quite remember, but sounds right."

Bobbie leaned across the table, quilts scattering. "But Mrs. *Darling*—"

"A deal is a deal," Faith interrupted and began restacking the quilts as if Bobbie wasn't splayed across them.

Hardly able to control herself, Bobbie reeled back on her heels and threw up her hands. "If you don't mind my saying so, Mrs. Darling, you might as well be giving it away!"

Faith paused as if contemplating the concept. "Well, that may happen, too," she said, plumping the quilts.

"Do not do that!" Bobbie sputtered. "If you want to sell your things, I can get you help—an expert, an auctioneer, somebody."

Faith returned to the other end of the table, inspecting the dinner linens for stacked perfection once again. "It's not about the money, dear."

"Of course it's about the money!" Bobbie exclaimed. "Mrs. Darling, are you feeling okay?"

"No, dear. But thank you for asking." And with that, Faith proceeded to the next table.

Bobbie moved in front of Faith again and attempted a professional manner. "In all good conscience, I can't let you do this. What if I take and save everything for you until you've had a chance to think through this a bit? A truck could be here within the hour."

Faith looked indignant. "You can't take it all. There wouldn't be a sale and there has to be a sale." She batted the idea away with a flick of a wrist. "No, no, take one thing or two. That'd be nice. Pay what you can."

Bobbie, desperate now, said the only thing she could think of. "Then could I call Claudia Jean for you?"

This time, at the sound of her daughter's name, Faith winced. It was barely more than a twitch to anyone glancing her way, but Bobbie saw it as big as day. "Well, that's kind of you, dear, except for the small problem of my not knowing where my daughter happens to be," Faith said, her voice suddenly quiet and controlled. "And I doubt if she'd care if I did. No, no, too late for all that."

"*Please*, Mrs. Darling," Bobbie pleaded. "I'm *begging* you."

"Take anything you want," Faith repeated. "Pay what you can." Then she walked away.

Bobbie looked around, her brain whirling so much it was making her woozy. Only her hand firmly attached to the fish Tiffany lamp kept her from swooning. She could probably afford to buy all these incredibly valuable antiques at $20 a pop, but even if Mrs. Darling did let her, she wouldn't be able to live with herself, now would she? She began drumming the fingers of her free hand on the table upon which the lamp sat, a remarkable Queen Anne table with cabriole-paw legs. When she realized her fingers were now caressing instead of drumming, she snatched them back. Oh, how she hated when ethics got in the way of a killing.

All right, just all right, settle down, Bobbie girl, she told herself. She pulled out her cell phone without knowing who to call. The police? But a yard sale wasn't against the law. Maybe 911? This was surely some sort of emergency—an *antique* emergency. Bobbie flinched. Did that lady in the muumuu just buy this exquisite Queen Anne table for $20?

Highway robbery!

Bobbie dialed 911.

As she waited for the sheriff's dispatcher, Stella Stamper, to put down her donut and answer the emergency line, Bobbie watched Faith Bass Darling drift back into the mansion. And she knew there was somebody else she had to call no matter what Mrs. Darling said—a certain somebody who needed to finally get her butt back here, and fast. As soon as she got back to her store, she'd find that last number she had for Claudia Jean Darling.

"That's what I'll do," Bobbie said under her breath, grabbing up the rare lamp once again, "but not before I buy this Tiffany."

Homeless.

Claudia Darling was squeezing her VW's steering wheel so hard her knuckles had turned white as she took yet another curve on the old country road. Grabbing up her cell phone, she dialed Bobbie Blankenship's number for the umpteenth time and got voice mail again: "Helloooo, you've reached Bobbie Blanken—" She dropped the phone back in her lap.

The mind should be homeless . . .

Those were the words playing bumper pool inside her head. They were from a Buddhist saying:

> *The mind should be homeless,*
> *unattached to anything, anyone, any place, or any time.*

She hadn't thought about that saying in over a decade. Yet right now, like some scratchy Zen record, she kept hearing it as her body was headed toward a place she couldn't get around calling "home," eyeing each passing gate, driveway, crossroad like an escape route.

She picked up the cell phone and tried again—but now she had no signal.

Dropping the phone again, she gestured as if pushing the hair out of her face, a nervous tic left over from when her hair was long, and forced herself to take a deep breath.

How do you not go back home for twenty years? she asked herself, studying the familiar flat, scrubby land surrounding her. People do it all the time, don't they? The days go by, simply and safely, with as little drama as possible. Until one day you find yourself driving back home down this weedy Texas road between Bass and Austin that once looked like the yellow brick road to the teenager you used to be.

Slowing to drive onto the first of the slender bridges over the winding Brazos River, she gazed down at the muddy waters that flowed straight through her childhood. The movies get it wrong about Texas, she mused. They always show the tumbleweeds, dust, and rattlesnakes on the West Texas side, the cowboy side. They never show this side, the muddy river bottoms, big trees, abandoned railroads, and rusting oil rigs of Southeast Texas. Her family's Texas. She used to think she was so smart, knowing how to leave it, how not to look back, escaping free and easy from her mother's freeze-dried sorrow and her family's old mansion.

In California, when she'd let it slip how she'd walked out of a mansion at seventeen without a single thing, people would look at her like she was stupid. "But you'll inherit it all and be rich again, right?" they'd always ask. They didn't understand that old things are sponges, soaking up all the living that's gone on around them day to year to century. "You know that sensation you get in an antique store—that musty, brooding, tired feeling?" she'd try to explain. "If you want the definition of a haunted house, that's it." She'd never mention she once loved it all like a gigantic storybook playhouse. Before everything changed.

But as she passed over the Brazos, she found it impossible not to think of the Bass family legend her mother told her like a childhood lullaby. Claudia could almost see her great-great-grandfather James Tyler Bass taming the scrubland with nothing but Texas-sized guts. Fording the Brazos River. Fending off murdering thieves. Bringing the railroad. Founding the town and bank. Building a mansion. Marrying the beautiful Belle with her heart-shaped face and giving her a fairy-tale wonder of a ring inscribed *Love Eternal.* She could still hear the promise, word for word, with which her mother ended each and every story time: "*. . . a ring, young lady, that's been handed down to every new Bass generation's first bride, so someday the ring will be yours.*"

A motorcycle zoomed by the opposite way. Claudia caught herself staring after it for a beat, as if she were seventeen again holding on to Bo Dean, headed toward California. And she was hearing, word for word, the last thing she ever heard her mother say:

"*If your great-great-grandmother Belle's ring leaves this house, Claudia Jean Darling, don't bother coming back—*"

I should have taken it, she thought, cringing at the memory.

But she'd been doing nothing but cringing for miles now at the thought of finally seeing her mother after all these years. She was even having a hard time picturing her mother at all, remembering only the way she began to see her mother after the summer her father and brother died—like the old mansion's antique furniture: dark, looming, brooding, and never moving. And if she allowed herself even a second to think about it, she'd find that too sad to bear.

But I've been feeling rather that way a long time now, haven't I? Claudia admitted to herself. Long enough to have left California and taken a job in a health club in Austin for reasons she couldn't quite name, after she'd begun to fail at everything—being tough, being buff, being young, even being a Buddhist, a practically impossible thing to do. Because she was tired of nothing ever resolving, ever working out right. You can only run so many marathons, teach so many aerobics classes, quote so many sayings of the Buddha, marry so many losers, and talk so much about your warped, angry inner child to people with degrees before you have to stop. If only to catch your breath, she thought, forcing herself to do just that as she took yet another curve.

She'd been less than a hundred miles from her mother for almost a year now. Waiting. For something to show up, something to make sense. For the universe to provide, as she might have said in California. So she'd known the moment the owners of the upscale fitness club had offered her part ownership that she wanted it—just $50,000 for a future, a chance at a normal, stable life, something truly her own to ground her in one place.

God . . . I need it, she thought. Need it in a way she hadn't needed anything since she was seventeen. But there was only one place she could get that kind of money and only one way to get it. Her mother, she knew, would never loan her a dollar or give her a penny. And she'd be damned if she'd ask, anyway. But there *was* the heirloom ring. If the one family possession promised to her since childhood could change her life for the better, then, by God, she should let it by now. Shouldn't she?

Then, just as she was slowly mustering her courage for the return home to claim it, Bobbie Ann Blankenship leaves a message about her mother selling everything. . . . *Everything?* Her mother, who worshipped each antique like a Bass ancestor's embodied soul? Who'd let her teenage daughter walk out the door before she'd let an antique ring out of her sight? *Had hell frozen over and she missed it?*

I could not have heard that right, Claudia thought. Whatever craziness was happening, it didn't matter. I'm just going back for the

ring, that's all, she reminded herself, because if she didn't quit thinking about it, she'd be stomping on the brakes and popping the VW
into reverse. Yet as she passed a highway mileage post announcing
"Bass 29 miles" and dueling signs for the Baptist, Methodist, and
Episcopal churches, all she could think was that the universe *was*
providing—providing a kick in the ass.

Maybe she was still a little bit Buddhist after all.

There's a quality of light in the morning before the Texas day starts its slow burn that once made a younger, sunnier Faith think of old Bible movies, the way it could momentarily give everything on her beloved Bass mansion's lawn a soft, sublime, downright sanctified sheen.

It was still there even though the younger, sunnier Faith was not. And, as the day would have it, an oblivious Faith Bass Darling now stood awash in that morning light, cigarette dangling from her fingers, like some sassy, smoky elderly madonna, her sun hat a straw halo around her face.

"Can you believe this weather? Almost scary, isn't it?"

At the sound of the voice, Faith snapped out of one of her moments to find a pleasantly plump woman talking to her. Quickly, she took a puff of the Lucky Strike, composing herself by running through her mental checklist:

My name is Faith Bass Darling . . . I live at 101 Old Waco Road in Bass, Texas. Today is . . . Today is December 31, 1999 . . .

There. Fine now. Faith took a breath and turned toward the woman. "What?"

"You know. End of the millennium, end of the world, all that?" the chubby woman chattered. "Personally, I think it's the ozone." She shoved a load of leather-bound books and a scalloped chantilly lace shawl into Faith's arms, almost making Faith drop her cigarette, and pulled out a $1 bill from a shirt pocket. "That's what you quoted me a second ago. Deal?"

Faith nodded. "A deal is a deal."

Smiling deliciously, the chubby customer slapped the $1 down on the silverware "cash box" perched on a table beside them, snatched back the antique shawl and leather books before the old woman changed her addled mind, and then hurried away.

Faith slipped the $1 bill inside the cash box and watched the woman flying so fast in the opposite direction that her flabby arms were almost achieving liftoff.

"Hey! Got any children's toys?" asked a bunch-toothed woman orbited by half a dozen children.

"No." Faith grabbed the grubby hands of the woman's toddler from a box.

"Got any children's clothes?" the woman tried.

"No. No children's things," Faith answered.

"Well then, whaddya doing with diapers?" the bunch-toothed woman huffed, pointing at a bag of unopened diapers sitting on the nearby table. "What kind of garage sale is this, anyways?"

Faith gaped at the unopened bag of diapers, seeing what the bunch-toothed lady had not—it was a bag of adult diapers. Horrified, Faith swept them up in her arms so fast her sun hat fell off. Then she rushed back into the house, stuffed them inside the downstairs bathroom's cabinet, and slammed the door.

Where had they come from? Surely she must have brought them home from the doctor's office. Surely she didn't buy them. *Surely!* Faith hurried back to the front porch to scan the lawn for any other surprises to her dignity. Seeing none, she allowed herself to relax a bit. She steadied herself, took a deep breath, regained her famous posture, and returned to the sale.

In a few moments, the sound of a car door slamming made her look toward the street. A police car. She watched as a tall, muscled-up black man in a deputy sheriff's uniform stepped onto her walkway and came toward her with the slightest of limps.

She almost smiled.

She was busy handing the last Tiffany lamp to a teenage girl dressed like a young Jennifer Lopez look-alike in short-short skirt and sassy loop earrings who'd just bought the lamp for the price of $1.

"Much-as grac-i-as," the girl enunciated, flipping her hair out of her face to take the fancy colored glass lamp.

"Angelina," John Jasper said, speaking to the girl and raising an eyebrow at her new purchase. "How's the Spanish coming?"

"Hast-a lueg-o, hasta la vist-a! Ad-ios!" she said to the deputy, wishing she knew the Spanish word for "suckers!" She sashayed by him, then busted some moves in and around the furniture she'd bet even J-Lo couldn't do hanging on to a lamp.

John Jasper watched the dancing Angelina and the valuable lamp until both made it to the street in one piece. Then with a shake of his head, he turned back to Faith.

"Hey, Mrs. Darling." He nodded her way.

"Hello yourself, John Jasper." She placed the $1 in her silverware cash box and then set it down to retrieve her cigarette from a nearby ashtray. "What are you doing here? Seems like today would be rather a big day for law enforcement, even in this town."

John Jasper Johnson stopped right in front of her. "Heard you were having a sale."

She gave him a wry look. "You heard I was having a breakdown."

The big man grinned.

"You look older," she said, cocking her head.

John Jasper cocked his head back at her. "Well, so do you."

A laugh popped right out of her at that. Taking an elegant puff of her cigarette, she rested her eyes for a moment on his fine familiar face.

The deputy sheriff stared. "Mrs. Darling, you don't smoke," he said, noticing the ashtray, where two other cigarettes were sending smoke spirals skyward.

"Don't I?" She frowned. "I have this handsome brass and silver lighter. And there are cigarettes in my house."

The breeze blew the smoke from all three cigarettes toward John Jasper and he batted it away. "Those things'll kill you."

"That possibility, I assure you, is remote." She turned to the ashtray and stumped out the cigarette with a flourish. "Are my neighbors calling you or did you get a message from God, too?"

The deputy did a tiny double take and Faith gave him a flick-away motion with her wrist. "Tell Maude Quattlebaum she's not getting a thing. That busybody has irritated me for fifty years."

John Jasper paused, then took a mint-condition 1901 $20 double-eagle gold coin from his shirt pocket and gingerly held it out to Faith. "Dr. Peabody called. Said you gave this to his son?"

"You've never seen a gold piece before, John Jasper?" she asked, not taking it.

"No, ma'am, I sure haven't. Never seen a hundred-year-old one, either. Dr. Peabody looked it up, said it could be worth a thousand dollars. You shouldn't be giving such things away. They're collector's items."

"The collector is long dead," Faith answered. "They were sitting in a drawer in a sheet of plastic doing nobody any good and I'm not going to need them. So why not?"

John Jasper opened Faith's silverware cash box and placed the coin inside. "The local knuckleheads, you know they're gonna start coming out of the bushes once the word gets around about you giving away gold coins and all," he said. "I'm worried about your safety."

Faith snorted. "That'd be a sight! I can take care of myself, son. Would you like some iced tea? I was thinking about making some."

"No thanks." John Jasper glanced around at the furniture spread from here to yonder. "You moving, Mrs. Darling?"

"Depends on what you mean by moving, I suppose," Faith answered.

"Well, then, are you gonna live in an empty house? You're selling your bed," he said, waving at the four-poster set up in the St. Augustine grass. "Something happen you might want to tell me about? You know I'm gonna keep asking."

"If I said God told me to have the sale, would that satisfy you?" she asked.

This time the deputy shook his head. "Very funny, Mrs. Darling. I'm serious now."

Faith paused. "You wouldn't understand, John Jasper."

"Try me."

Faith leveled her gaze at the big man. "All righty. I'm going to die tonight."

John Jasper studied this old woman he'd known all his life. "That's why you're doing all this? You think you're gonna die?"

"Isn't that a good enough reason?"

Now John Jasper was the one leveling his gaze at her. "Mrs. Darling, are you sick? You know I can help and you know I will. Dr. Peabody wouldn't tell me. Said to ask you."

Faith plopped her hands on her hips. "Dr. Peabody shouldn't be telling you to ask me a thing."

"Yeah, that's what he said you'd say," the deputy answered. Then he placed his hands around his belt.

For a moment, the old lady and the black sheriff, both striking the same defiant pose, stood like two gunfighters in a standoff.

Just then, three junior high boys on minibikes did wheelies in the road in front of the sale, ditched their bikes, and strutted on up the fancy brick sidewalk to see what there was to see. John Jasper stared at them in a way that said: *Don't be messing with this.* The three, making a point to avoid further eye contact with the law, sauntered back toward their bikes as if it were their idea and wheeled away.

John Jasper turned back to find Faith taking a $20 bill for her four-poster bed from a scruffy man now waving over his friends from a beat-up flatbed truck.

The deputy moved in front of Faith again. "Now don't get mad but I gotta ask: Claudia Jean—she know about all this?"

Faith frowned as if she'd just tasted something very bitter. "You know very well Claudia Jean hasn't set foot on this lawn in twenty years, John Jasper. I don't even know where she is," she said, moving around him back to the sale. "My daughter made it quite clear long ago that she doesn't want any of these things. At least the ones she didn't steal. No, no, it's too late for all that."

John Jasper followed. "I think we need to find her, Mrs. Darling. And I think you need to stop selling all your fine things until we do."

Faith whirled around. Any other person at any other time would get his head snapped off with a well-placed "Mind your own blasted business." But she knew this young man was immune to her snapping. Instead, she said, "John Jasper, if you don't remember you ever had the things, why would it matter if you didn't have them anymore?"

John Jasper gestured toward the street. "Because for one thing, you'd still need a bed, and there goes your nice four-poster on a flatbed truck owned by some redneck knuckleheads who know they've just robbed you blind."

Faith sighed. "John Jasper Johnson, you haven't been listening," she scolded, tilting her head his way.

"You really don't remember these things?" he asked.

"Some not for a long time, son," she answered, breathing deeply, softly. Then her gaze wandered away. "Would you like some iced tea? I was thinking about making some."

John Jasper paused, studying her hard. "You are sick, aren't you, Mrs. Darling," he said as if it were fact. He waited for her to reply, and when a little too much time passed in silence, he began to worry. "Mrs. Darling?"

Faith looked straight into the deputy's eyes. "Without our memories, who are we, John Jasper?" Faith's gaze wandered again. "I'd rather not have some of my memories, and God knows it's been a small bit of grace not to remember them for long stretches of time. But good or bad, they're mine, they're who I am. And when the last one goes, what will I be? A celery stalk . . . Mr. Frudigger . . . No, I've wasted a lot of years wishing I were dead. But *that* I won't have. I won't be dead before I die."

John Jasper paused, watching her, letting her words sink in. Then he gestured at the sale. "But, Mrs. Darling—"

Faith sliced the air with a hand to cut him off: Enough! *Enough.*

"I killed Claude, John Jasper," she said, calmly, evenly. "I killed

my husband and now it's time to go." Seeing the stunned look on
the face of the deputy sheriff—her sweet son's football friend—she
softened. "You know how much I like you, John Jasper. But you
need to leave me be now. You see anything you want, you go right
ahead and take it." She began patting all her pockets. "Where's that
nice brass and silver lighter of mine? I can't seem to find it."

Just then, a grimy little hand eased out from under the lion-paw
maple table where the old woman had set the old lighter, closed
sticky fingers around it, and disappeared back under the table just as
Faith glanced that way.

"Claudia Jean Darling!" Faith demanded. "You put that back immediately!"

The big deputy sheriff glanced down, all but expecting to see his
football buddy Mike Darling's kid sister. But what he got was an
eyeful of Faith Darling dropping to her knees, her sundress splayed
around her, and holding her sun hat in place as she craned her
neck under the table. "Come here, young lady. You know you get
spanked for taking and hiding things. You can't have that. You'll
burn yourself."

John Jasper stepped back onto the grass and eased down on his
haunches, putting unsteady weight on his bad knee, to peer under
the table. He was just in time to see something small with a messy
shock of yellow hair in a dirty T-shirt sprint away, vanishing beyond
the house. When he glanced back up, Faith Darling had also vanished. And he felt his knee go. Falling back onto the grass with an
oomph, he just sat there for a minute, arms over his knees, cussing
the thought now rolling through his head:

This—*goddammit*—is gonna be messy.

640,000.

Somebody once told Deputy John Jasper Johnson that was the length of an average life—640,000 hours—and it'd just stuck. He wasn't quite sure why. Maybe because it sounded like a lot. Or maybe because it didn't sound like enough, he was now thinking. Maybe because he'd learned the hard way that a tiny little bit of one of them thousands of hours could mess up every last bit of the rest. Every hour, every minute, every second of the rest of a man's goddamn life.

John Jasper let out a slow fume. A block down from the sale, he sat in his police cruiser watching the goings-on at the Darling mansion. He never thought about his own tiny little bit if he could help it. And he sure wouldn't be thinking about it now except for Faith Darling and what he'd just found her doing over here at this big house of hers. But he'd be lying if he said he didn't think about it at all. Limping around on a gimp knee for twenty years was a pretty big reminder.

Things turn on a dime, he thought. Hair-trigger. If he'd had a lick of sense, he'd have left town after it happened. If he'd had any place to go. But not like I'd be leaving behind the bum leg, he thought. With this kind of memory, the only thing you can hope for is some fading. Like old photos, edges going soft over time. Any other kind was just a fool's paradise.

Besides, after all this time, he'd gotten it pretty much under control . . . but now and then, blips stuck way back somewhere came at him like stray flicks of a knife. From the corner of his eye. Then full-blown front and center. And there wasn't a goddamn thing he could do but take it and wait for the blood-rushing rage of it all to flow over him and be gone.

That's the way it always was when he drove down Old Waco Road by the Darling mansion. He could always find ways to go around the old river bridge road to keep from going by Claude Angus Darling's old oil lease, the goddamn scene of the accident. But not Old Waco Road and that big house—not always. It's a small town. There's only so many ways to get where you need to get. And when he had to pass it, he worked up such a sweat trying not to think about ClaudeDamnDarling—to keep himself from ramming the cruiser into the nearest pole to get rid of the goddamn blood-rush of anger—that he always ended up seeing Mike Darling and that shit-eating grin of his. And what his high school football buddy was always doing was dropping back, pumping twice and hitting John Jasper with the pigskin right between the numbers. And he's feeling the leather and pulling in the pigskin and taking it on in for the TD.

But it never stays that way, right there, right at that fine moment. He can't hold it. Next thing, Mike's always grabbing the ball back and it turns into that rusted-up old pistol John Jasper had found in the oil field's dry creek bed. Then Mike's staring up at the sky from the back of the truck. Bleeding out. Panic pulling at the corners of that shit-eating grin. The rest John Jasper won't let himself go ahead and see—he can't ever stop it from coming but he can stop it right there, right before it all went to hell. He'd gotten real good at it. Had lots of practice over all these years, over these same roads, thinking someday, someday, time'll do its thing and make it not hurt like it was yesterday.

With that, John Jasper flipped on the ignition, threw the cruiser into gear harder than he needed to, and pulled away. One minute you and your rich white buddy are living the Texas schoolboy football dream, headed to signing dates and college scholarships and the goddamn NFL, the next you're just another poor black boy with no prospects all over again and you still got the rest of your life to get through even if your rich white buddy with a shit-eating grin don't. And so every day you do what you gotta do just to keep yourself from going a little nuts like Mrs. Darling all these years.

John Jasper glanced in his rearview. He knew this was a long time coming and he knew he had to do something about it. Considering, he told himself, what the woman done for me.

Across town at the historic little Episcopal church, Father George A. Fallow swung the sanctuary's front doors wide. He needed some air. Morning prayers were over and the priest was fighting a feeling of futility. He'd performed the service every day for over thirty years, but if it weren't for eighty-year-old Mrs. Thistlewaite, bent over like a question mark, he wondered whether he'd continue performing it for just himself. She was the only one who came, for years now. And if he was late, she'd scold him. To which he always answered: "Now, now."

"Little old ladies . . . they'll be the death of me," he said under his breath, far under, to assure that Mrs. Thistlewaite, who still had ears like a hawk, didn't hear as she scuttled toward her big, long Lincoln Continental to drive slowly home. I'm just tired, he told himself, heading across the open-air alcove between the church and his office. The thing was he couldn't remember when he wasn't. Lately he'd found himself wondering what it was that he was really doing anymore besides mouthing ancient, beautiful old words for little old ladies.

He had lived his life in the service of the church like his father before him and his grandfather before him. He'd always loved the order of things, the comfort and safety of words spoken for thousands of years by millions of people. *As it was in the beginning is now and ever shall be. Kyrie Eleison, Lord have mercy. World without end. Amen.* The old and beautiful words were "essential to health as air," his eloquent father used to say. And he had, in no small part, become a priest because of how he longed to say those words himself.

So how does such a man admit that the air has turned a tad airy? That the words no longer fill the holes punctured over and over by the awful mysteries of living this long? That the God of the words was no longer bigger than His contradictions? That now the cadence was all that was keeping him going, like hearing poetry read aloud, the words hardly heard over the inertia of their sound? He could never say any of this to the Mrs. Thistlewaites of his parish. After all, you couldn't have a priest admit that the church liturgy had become little more than a chant, admit that the sound of his own voice had him biting his own lip not to nod along with Mrs. Thistlewaite each morning—admit that he was not even listening to himself for the love of God. But too late for that now, George, old man, he thought. Nothing more useless than a sixty-year-old man of the cloth who's misplaced his calling.

He paused, frowning at his choice of words: Misplaced? Not "lost"? No, "lost" isn't exactly right, either, he realized. Can one lose something by inches? After all, he couldn't point to some traumatic event, the usual scenario for such a sweeping, dramatic statement as the questioning of one's religion. So, the bald truth was he didn't even have the moral authority to make such a statement, did he? Seems there was no perfect word for what he'd turned into. Mediocrity has such a limited vocabulary, he thought with a sigh.

Father Fallow made himself take a deep breath and check his watch. 10:39. He always got cranky before end-of-year budget meetings; the committee would be here by noon. And God forbid the tiny parish's active members, all older than he was now, would miss a chance to talk about what God's will was for the budget even on Millennium New Year's Eve, especially Louise Thistlewaite and her sister-in-law Lula Mae, who believed themselves Divine Conduits on matters of church finance. On top of that, he also had a funeral to perform that afternoon.

All these crankier-by-the-second thoughts were running through his head while he took care to watch his step along the crumbling brick alcove and over his office's broken stone step. It had begun to haunt him, that step. It had been broken when he first set foot on it over three decades ago and it was still broken. If he could at least get that step fixed before he retired, he'd feel he'd accomplished something in this little church. He found that thought so depressing, he had to pause a moment to get his balance. Then he swung the door wide and stepped in. That's when Father Fallow noticed he had a message on his answering machine. He hit the button. And from it came a voice he never expected to hear again.

"Come. Please," the voice said, not even introducing itself. But he would know the voice anywhere. It was Faith Bass Darling.

He realized he was suddenly standing up ever so slightly taller, glancing back out the door toward the broken step where he'd found her sitting one early evening—over twenty years ago now—her crisp cotton shirtdress's hem in the dust. "I need a funeral, George," she had said, ignoring all his attempts to help her to her feet. He'd already heard about the tragic accident that had happened that very morning. And she knew he had; it was a small town, after all. So he had eased down beside her.

"But Mrs. Darling, you're Baptist," he'd said, as soothing as possible. "Shouldn't you be calling Brother Small?"

"I don't believe in that God over there anymore," she'd answered.

As the priest stared at his answering machine, he still wondered what kind of God she thought was over here.

He played the message on his machine again: Come. Please. *Please.*

George fought to stay calm as he sank into the chair behind his desk.

Why did I bend to breaking one of the Ten Commandments for a woman I hardly knew? And a Baptist on top of that? he asked himself. It wasn't even the commandment everyone would think of first. Even his wife, before she left—having enough of the ministry, enough of the old ladies, and, yes, enough of him—wouldn't have thought him capable of any pants-down indiscretion, though he suspected that he might still be married if he had been capable of that sort of passion. No, he'd lived long enough to know that there are other kinds of unfaithfulness beyond the kind that involves zippers and lust in one's heart: his sky-high ideals he valued above all, just as his wife claimed. And that made the whole episode even more of a puzzle.

For the longest time, he waited for someone to notice what he'd done with the best of intentions that day so long ago. He was ready to correct it before it became a big deal. In fact, it was not really that big a thing at all—easily explained away. But he seemed totally unable to do so until someone, anyone, had noticed what he'd done. And remarkably, no one ever did. So he never did anything, either.

George turned toward the large, dusty framed print of a Currier & Ives New England Christmas scene that now hung on the wall behind his desk. He sighed. What came over me? He had no idea—even now as he squinted hard at the wall trying to see what had once been there, what he'd as much as stolen in an attempt to help Faith Darling, but also, he knew, to somehow help himself.

When he'd first come as a young, idealistic rector to Bass, Texas, directly from seminary, a small oil painting that no one knew anything about hung above his desk. That's how long it had been in the rector's study; everyone who knew anything about it must have died and any records of it must have been misplaced. The painting was of a single large water lily at sunset created with broad strokes of thick globs of paint—blues, whites, and golds. It was small and square, maybe 10″ x 10″ at most, an odd shape by today's standards—its frame the kind seen in museums, wide, ornate, and gold-leafed, almost bigger than the painting itself. It wasn't signed on the front anywhere, so he was sure it wasn't all that valuable, but he enjoyed thinking of it as a "treasure" in hiding. Its beauty had begun to give him solace when even stained glass, liturgy, and incense didn't, though he'd felt a little guilty about that fact, still believing God was defined by what was said inside church walls.

He imagined it being hung back before the turn of the century when the church coffers were flush with cash from railroad, oil, and cotton. The parishioners had built an incredibly beautiful church so ostentatious that, here at the turn of another century, the church was continually struggling to keep it from falling down around them—caretakers as much as parishioners. Knowing the church attic was full to the rafters with such old things, he'd had an idea that only a young rector would have, suggesting they sell some of those church's accoutrements to pay for needed repairs. The little old ladies—and there were many, many more of them back then—balked. They would have let the roof cave in, the stained glass crack, and the walkway crumble to dust before they would change a thing, George recalled all too well.

Yet that's how he knew Faith Bass Darling. Of course, he already knew her in the way of small towns; it was hard to miss someone who lives in the biggest mansion on the fanciest road and owned the town's only bank. He knew her Bass family town-founding saga and her husband Claude Angus Darling's rags-to-riches story. He knew of her Baptist piety and his profane charm. The parish's ladies gossiped about the state of their marriage, their money, and their children. The parish's men waxed nostalgic about the better, steadier banking days of her father, bemoaning the young son-in-law's increasingly wheeler-dealer ways. And he'd listened because he was still an outsider with a sense of awe for his standing in this new world that did not seem small to him. And she knew him, too. They spoke when they saw each other around the town, which flattered him beyond words, perhaps even beyond his own good sense. She was a bit older; he was twenty-eight, she was certainly thirty-five, her children still small. The little gossiping ladies called her "plain," but George had seen nothing plain about her. She cut quite a dignified figure. Being born with that sort of wealth and position and history in a tiny town can do that, George mused, especially in the eyes of a new seminarian, full of himself and his new position.

Then, on one of the days their paths crossed, the young priest heard himself gushing about the water lily painting and other interesting effects of the elegant if tiny and crumbling church, believing she might know something about them. To his surprise she volunteered to pay a visit.

Gazing now at the dusty old Currier & Ives print, George leaned back on his desk, remembering that visit as if it had happened that very morning instead of over thirty years ago. Faith Darling had always had that perfect, regal posture that made men like him instantly stand up in her presence. And back then, she'd had a distinctive, somewhat old-fashioned way of wearing her hair with bejeweled hair clips and combs of all kinds; antique ones, no doubt.

They all seemed to match her wedding ring, an exquisite piece of jewelry—a large pear-shaped diamond surrounded by tiny little pearls—that he'd noticed only because she had a habit of touching it as she talked, one slender hand over the other.

"Please. Call me Faith Ann," she'd told him, and he wouldn't.

They'd spent a pleasant afternoon in the wake of vases and lecterns and silver candelabras, and the small water lily painting that she seemed to appreciate as much as he did.

"What an unusual painting for a minister's office," she'd said as they sat down in the two chairs in front of his desk to look at it. She sat with her hands in her lap, her eyes transfixed on the little painting. "It's very soothing."

"Yes, that's what I've always thought," young George had gushed as she continued gazing at the painting, seemingly unwilling to pull her eyes from it. And he so enjoyed her enjoyment.

"I marvel . . ." she'd finally murmured.

"Excuse me?" he'd said, noticing a sudden melancholy tone in her voice.

She shook her head slightly. "I was just thinking about the differences between our churches. Our pastor's office might have a simple cross on it or some such thing, but a modern painting of a water lily? Never." Then she'd confessed—as if it were a tiny sin—that she always preferred the Episcopal church's beauty to the plain Baptist sanctuary where she said even stained glass was somehow made plain. "You Episcopals revel in your beauty. You feel the spiritual tug in it, too, don't you?" she said, pointing at the oil painting and looking his way. "Basses have always been Baptist. But I wish someone would tell me what Baptists have against beauty. Our preachers worry about worldly possessions as if they were golden calves tempting us to worship them, for heaven's sake," she said with a flip of her ring hand, the pearls and diamond and gold filigree swishing the air. "They think they'll somehow stunt the soul when it seems the very opposite to me—if they are beautiful."

As her hand landed back in her lap, she must have noticed George's eyes lingering on the ring, because she'd said: "This ring is a perfect example. Do you know it's been worn as a wedding ring in the Bass family for four generations? Isn't it beautiful?"

"Very beautiful," he agreed. "So you'll hand it down to your daughter?"

"Oh yes," she said. "It's mine only until she marries. Family tradition." She then told him the story behind the ring—how the town's namesake had it specially designed for his wife and how its beauty had inspired the love in every new generation's marriage. "Look, you must see the inscription," she said proudly, taking it off and leaning near to show him the message etched gracefully inside: *Love Eternal.*

Then Faith Ann Darling began chatting animatedly about her pious father—a man young George knew had been the richest Baptist deacon in this entire part of the state when he was alive. Who loved beauty so much, she recounted, that he'd bought a roomful of Tiffany lamps for her mother. Whose favorite Bible passage, she proudly stated, was "What profiteth a man who gains the whole world and loses his soul?" And she told it to the young priest without the least hint of irony. (It was the way of the pious rich, Father Fallow had come to understand, to believe it is entirely possible to have both world and soul if one is careful—and that went, it seemed, for Baptists as well as Episcopals.)

And while she'd known little about the church's possessions, she regaled him with a dozen stories handed down from her long-gone relatives of fortunes made, world wars fought, Spanish flu epidemics survived, and electricity brought to town. She was a keeper of some personal family flame that lit up her face in the most marvelous way. "We're lucky to have you in Bass, George," she'd said as she left. And for a blessed moment, a young Father George had felt a sort of seamless, soulful, God's-in-his-heaven-and-all's-right-with-the-world feeling that he hadn't felt since. He'd been schoolboy charmed. Faith Ann Bass Darling became all things right about the past surrounding him in his new church and new little town. And that feeling returned, embarrassingly so, with each sight of her around town for years. Despite the fact he barely knew her, with her every nod and smile his way, he felt she saw him the way he saw himself.

Ah, me . . . the old priest thought, shaking his head, amazed he could ever have been that painfully young.

As the years passed, things had grown cruder. Or perhaps it was just the tarnish of time, George pondered. History was always more appealing from the long view, he knew, and small towns, by their nature, had a way of making all things, from one's sins to one's soul, smaller as well. He rarely saw or even thought of Faith Darling, his own life's pomp and circumstance seeping steadily away with the daily humdrum of the church and his own sudden marital struggles. He'd begun to face his own pastoral mediocrity, yet his wife's suggestions of another career seemed almost sacrilegious to a son and grandson of priests. He could not imagine doing anything else.

Then one day, there she was.

Father Fallow sighed again, this time long and slow, wandering back to look out his office's open door: he had found her just sitting on that damn crumbling office threshold. *Faith Bass Darling sitting on my broken step,* he thought, remembering the embarrassment of it. He could still hear her voice hardly more than a whisper asking him to perform a funeral; he could see her in silhouette not even turning his way. And after a few moments of sitting with her on that crumbling step, he'd finally helped her inside and eased her into one of his two office chairs, sitting down beside her in the other. He knew there were no words for what had happened to her precious son and so he'd offered none. Not yet.

Instead, he'd waited and watched as she gazed for the longest time at the bright little water lily painting behind his desk. Trying not to stare, he couldn't help but see the changes in her appearance since the last time she'd sat in that very chair. No longer did she wear jeweled hair clips in her now hairdresser-styled hair. Nor was she wearing her heirloom wedding ring she'd been so proud of. A simple, large solitaire diamond wedding ring set had taken its place. Then he noticed the tiny spatter of blood on the hem of her starched shirtdress, and he stared transfixed—wondering how it got there, wondering what horror her eyes had just seen, wondering why someone had not helped her to change—until he forced his eyes to look back at the calming beauty of the lily painting. With her.

She was in shock, no doubt, but she gazed at it like no one had since her visit years before. He was already deeply moved with pity for this woman he still admired perhaps a bit too much, but that gaze ripped his heart asunder. Perhaps it was because his own wife had left him that year. Perhaps the sight of Faith Darling and all she once symbolized overwhelmed him in the face of her tragedy, making him want to recall her as she was then—so happily chatting with him about beauty. But for whatever reason, her gaze seemed to show she was finding the same small solace in the painting that he still did, a kind beyond any solace words could give.

The priest in him knew it was time to say something, offer some words of comfort. But they would not come. In the presence of a grief that would forever change Faith Darling, he found himself completely unable to talk across the emptiness between them. He didn't talk about the accident. Nor her son. Nor her grief. Nor even God. It was his job to do all of the above. Yet he felt, for all the world, mute. Not the prerequisite prayer book words or even one comforting Bible quote was George able to conjure. Something in her face kept him silent. He was failing her. And himself. Why couldn't he come up with anything? How useless was he? Just say something, he berated himself. Anything, for God's sake! An old painting is ministering to this woman better than I am, the priest realized.

And with that thought, Father George had felt an overwhelming urge to give her the painting.

Surprised by the impulsive thought, so out of character, he sat up to wonder: Could I? Surely his vestry board could see how sharing one small piece of parish accoutrement might be a form of ministry. It was not his to give but perhaps to loan?

Of course, George knew better. No, not even a loan, he'd reminded himself. They'd never allow it. Yet the urge was so strong, he could barely contain himself as he continued to gaze at her gazing at the painting.

Until she sensed his gaze and looked back his way.

Staring straight into Faith Darling's grief-stricken eyes was like nothing so much as a fist to his own jaw. George felt helpless, utterly powerless; it was how he'd felt every day since his wife's departure but now magnified beyond what he could bear. He had to do something and do it right then. . . . Yet again, he fought the impulse to give her a gift that was not his to give.

But suddenly she was sitting up no-nonsense pencil-straight to say: "Will you do it?"

"The funeral? Yes, yes, of course," he'd answered, shooting up straight himself.

At that moment big Belva Bowman and a younger, more erect Mrs. Thistlewaite barged in on church committee business, eyes popping at who was sitting there, making apologies and trying not to miss a thing.

And just like that, Faith Bass Darling was gone.

So he'd officiated at Michael Darling's funeral, one of the saddest he'd ever performed, the crowd overflowing the funeral home's chapel. He'd leaned on the beautiful words more than ever before: *Ashes to ashes, dust to dust . . . In my father's house are many mansions . . . Kyrie Eleison, Lord have mercy. World without end, Amen.* Afterward, he kept planning a pastoral visit to the Darlings, hoping for a second chance at finding his tongue. But after hearing that Faith had opened the door to Reverend Small only to slam it in his face, he kept finding reasons to wait a bit longer.

Then suddenly Claude Angus Darling died. And Faith Darling did not appear to ask George to bury him. The priest heard through his church ladies' grapevine that, after Reverend Small put Claude in the ground, Faith Darling had gone back inside the mansion and closed its big doors to everything and everyone, including poor, persistent Reverend Small once again, slamming door and all.

So Father George Fallow knew there would be no more doorstep visits from Faith Darling. And perhaps it was better. He'd done all she'd asked of him as a priest, even though she wasn't a church member. The truth was he barely knew her, not even enough to be called a true friend. Yet he continued to feel compelled to do, to be, something better for her—as a priest and a friend. He just could not decide exactly what the correct thing might be. He'd already discovered he was not a gifted man nor a brave man. But now he began to wonder what kind of man he really was.

Days passed; still he fretted and stewed. He tried gazing at the

water lily painting for solace, but now it only reminded him of
Faith's grief-stricken face and his own abysmal failure to help beyond
his rote words spoken over her son.

Until one drizzly morning, he—for once in his life—quit thinking and just gave in to the impulse that would not let him go. Jumping to his feet, he took the water lily painting off the church office
wall, taped some brown paper around it for protection, and put it
under his arm. Then he went to see Faith Ann Darling.

He'd strode up the walkway clutching the painting under his
arm, stepped onto the wraparound porch, and rang the mansion's
doorbell.

No response.

He rang it again, shifting the painting from one arm to the other.

Still no response. So he knocked. Still no Faith.

He didn't know quite what to do; he'd never considered she
would not come to the door. He knew she was at home. She hadn't
left since Claude's funeral—everyone knew that. So he'd taken out a
pen and scribbled in large letters on the brown paper covering:

MAY YOU FIND SOLACE IN THE BEAUTY.
KEEP IT AS LONG AS YOU NEED.

FR. GEORGE

Then he'd leaned the gift that was not his to give against the
carved front doors and stepped back into the rain.

Returning to the church, he'd filled the empty place above his
desk with the dark Currier & Ives print of a nineteenth-century
Christmas scene from the rectory. Then he'd sat down to let his actions sink in, and the second thoughts came dancing.

I just gave away church property, which was the same as stealing it, he realized, and to a Baptist . . . just because the Baptist happened to be Faith Bass Darling. Back to his proper rule-abiding self, he cursed under his breath and resolved to wait for the deserved hailstorm from his church members. Then he'd quickly right it all.

But when no one ever noticed the oil painting's absence—not one little old lady, not the church sexton who cleaned his office, not a single person of the dozens who traipsed in and out of the office—his resolve oozed away. Instead, it made him wonder what his parishioners did see each week. It made him wonder what any of them truly sees at all.

And, most of all, it made him wonder what they saw, if anything, when they looked at him.

That prickly memory made the old priest lean even heavier back on his desk, hand to his heart, recalling his sudden awful longing for the painting: wanting it back on the wall where it belonged. Wanting for things to go back to the way they were, even if he was the only one who noticed. As if that would give him back his highminded young self who first met and was charmed by Faith Ann Darling. Who saw himself as he felt she saw him—confident and capable—not the least bit mediocre.

But she never called.

And neither did I, George mused with the slightest of sighs as he looked back toward his answering machine. No, neither did I . . .

He'd retreated into the liturgical order of things, into the comfort and safety of the old, beautiful words that still held power and solace for him back then. Yet he often caught himself glancing with the old fierce longing toward where the painting once had hung, the entire episode growing, as such things often do, into something that never quite went away. The church ladies continued to talk about Faith

Darling: sightings at the grocery store, at the hairdresser, in her front yard. They talked about how unpleasant she was turning, and, after her daughter ran off, how reclusive she was becoming by herself in that big, big house.

"How far the mighty have fallen." Mrs. Thistlewaite tsk-tsked. "So sad, don't you think?"

"So, so sad," Belva Bowman agreed, shaking her big head.

The priest recalled doing his duty and telling the ladies: "This is what happens in tragedy—it propels us toward God or away. This is the ultimate question of the soul. And this is how Mrs. Darling can instruct us."

But the young man he once was—that man knew better. That young man had seen something else, had bent to breaking a commandment over it, and perhaps had broken something else.

And the old man I am now still doesn't quite know why, Father George Fallow pondered, his fingers poised over his answering machine where her voice waited to be heard again. But he did know this: there rarely had been a time throughout these last two decades that he had not thought about it when he'd driven by that mansion, rarely a time he hadn't contemplated knocking on the big carved front doors—as if he had not just left some church property on her doorstep, but also the man he once believed he could be.

And now, Faith Darling has finally asked me to come, Father Fallow thought as he listened to her message again. And the man I am now will be going.

✿ PROVENANCES

HEIRLOOM WEDDING RING

3-carat pear-shaped diamond ring • Seed accent pearls •
White gold filigreed setting • Custom-designed by
L. Francois of New Orleans • Inscription: *Love Eternal*

Circa 1870   *Value: $135,000*

DELUXE BANKER'S "S" OAK ROLLTOP DESK

M. L. Himmel & Sons of Chicago • 50″ H 60″ W 34″ D
• Large locking side panel and 2 custom secret
compartments • 1 niche drawer/1 letter slot

Circa 1869   *Value: $8,000*

In the spring of 1869, the brand-spanking-new Texas Brazos Valley rail-road line unloaded a deluxe rolltop desk special delivery at a new little whistle-stop called Bass, Texas. Young James Tyler Bass had purchased it for his fledgling storefront Bass Bank across from the one-room train depot. There it occupied his office as the town sprang up around it, until thirty years later, when it was moved to his Waco Road mansion, where it would stay for the rest of the twentieth century.

Throughout the next four generations, its cubbyholes filled up with the ephemera of life—inkwells, fountain pens, old wallets, money clips, tie clips, pocket watches, old checks, and such—until it was only disturbed now and then by James Tyler Bass's little great-great-granddaughter Claudia Jean. Fascinated with all its wonderful cubbyhole "treasures," she discovered one of its two forgotten secret compartments, a sliding niche inside the middle drawer, and often hid some of her own little treasures there.

Years later, the girl's mother, Faith Bass Darling, after locking a small, 10" x 10" golden-framed little oil painting in the desk's large side panel and returning the key to the middle drawer, rolled the S-curved rolltop down permanently.

Or so she thought.

It was opened once more when the seventeen-year-old great-great-granddaughter Claudia—before leaving "for good"—hid one last thing in her discovered secret niche compartment: an heirloom pearl-accented three-carat diamond ring in a black velvet ring box. Then she rolled down the top to stay.

Until the last day of the twentieth century, when the desk was moved out onto the mansion's lawn.

"You can know all about a person from the things they collect, the books on their shelves, the chairs in their parlor," Bobbie Blankenship once heard an auctioneer say. "Let me into your house; I could write your life story." As she careened back toward the sale, Bobbie was thinking how true that was. With just one childhood peek inside the Darling mansion, her little Bobbie Ann imagination had written volumes about the Darling family life among the antiques, which grew into the life story of her own mansion dreams. And a little girl's dream was not a thing to mess with.

Jolting her Yesteryear Antiques minivan to a halt at the mansion's curb again, Bobbie dropped her fancy new flip cell phone from her ear, popping it shut. All this telephone tag with Claudia Jean Darling was driving her nuts—was she coming? Bobbie glanced at the sale and a tiny moan escaped her lips. She *had* to come—every second could be another precious antique gone!

Bobbie gazed longingly at the Darling mansion, and for a moment she was ten years old again. That was the age she discovered that Claudia Jean Darling was the sixth-grader who lived in the biggest house on the fanciest street in town. Little Bobbie Ann followed her around like a puppy dog all through her fourth-grade year, and if Claudia Jean ever minded, she never let on.

Bobbie's family lived around the corner from the Darlings in a small frame house on a nice little paved street—not one of the dirt streets beyond the Old Waco Road mansions, a distinction Bobbie Ann always made crystal clear. The dirt-street houses, built for the mansions' servants long ago, were mostly unkempt shacks of unkempt people popping out unkempt children, wild and running loose. That wasn't her house. But it wasn't the Darling mansion, either. And while she'd imagined a childhood chockful of invitations from Claudia Jean Darling and her mother, Bobbie had really only been inside the mansion once. She'd trailed her grade-school idol into the mansion one day after school, sneaking big-eyed peeks at the beautiful lamps and tall clocks and life-size portraits—at all the fancy things that were everywhere she looked. Until she followed Claudia Jean up the grand staircase to Claudia Jean's bedroom where they stayed just long enough for little Bobbie Ann to revel in the pink canopy bed and the elephant clock before following Claudia Jean back down toward the kitchen for a snack.

But she never made it that far. As Claudia Jean disappeared into the kitchen, little Bobbie Ann had slowed to stare again at the wonders surrounding her. That's when she noticed a sparkling crystal dish full of penny candy on a table. Up to that moment in her short life, the penny candy would have been all she saw. But now she couldn't take her eyes off the sparkly dish. It was the most beautiful thing she'd ever seen, even prettier than the candy. Hurriedly, before Claudia Jean looked back, she grabbed a fistful of the candy and stuffed it into her pocket. Then she touched the sparkly dish. Then she picked it up. And then, looking around again to see Claudia Jean coming back her way, she dropped it.

Bobbie could still see the look on Claudia Jean's face seconds after it hit the parquet floor and shattered. "Quick! Get lost! *Go-go-go!*"

she'd hissed as they heard Mrs. Darling coming, pushing Bobbie's frozen little self past the sparkly crystal shards, candy falling from her pockets, and out the big carved front doors, never to be invited in again.

But that one visit had changed her life. Little Bobbie Ann had seen enough wonders that afternoon to jump-start her lifelong love affair with antiques, an obsession that wouldn't take a psychologist to connect with her fantasy of living in that mansion on the hill.

After grammar school, things changed as they do, but not Bobbie's adoration of all things Darling. It hadn't taken little Bobbie Ann long to grasp she was never going to be a Darling and live in the big mansion, but grown-up Bobbie discovered she could make a living from the love of such things she'd seen there. And she never quit believing her grade-school idol would one day be back to take over the mansion and be forever Claudia Jean Darling of Bass, Texas, and forever inviting her inside those big carved doors like the childhood friends they once were.

You begin to own such a dream, if you dream it long enough, Bobbie realized, and that's why, a lifetime later, she now sat in front of the mansion worrying herself sick. Her plan was to try one last time to talk some sense into Mrs. Darling and stop this hometown travesty. In case that didn't work, she had a Plan B, her pantsuit pocket full of $20 bills.

Slamming the door behind her, she straightened her pantsuit and strode again into the sale. Marching up the walkway, she zeroed in on Faith Darling, who was now opening the silver box to stash the single $1 bill she'd just been handed by a hairy-necked old guy wearing a "Miller High Life" T-shirt for a Dresden porcelain cake plate with reticulated floral border. Bobbie heard herself moan. She could not bear to see this glorious mansion's things vanish one piece at a time to people who'd set beer bottles on them, fill them with pennies, or plop a TV set on top of them. It was a *sacrilege*.

Just then, somebody elbowed her. It was Bobbie's second-grade teacher, mean old helmet-haired Mrs. Hitt, waving a $20 bill at Mrs. Darling.

"SOLD!" she screeched right by Bobbie's ear, pointing at a gigantic banker's rolltop with one hand while depositing the $20 bill in Faith Darling's palm with the other. "I'll be right back to pick it up with my husband and his pickup!" she said to Faith, hurrying off. "Don't you forget now!"

Good luck with that, Bobbie thought, waggling a finger down her ringing ear canal. That's when her antique-dealer eyes landed on the box Faith Darling was using for a cash box. *Uh-oh.* Bobbie gasped. "Mrs. Darling, where's your sterling silverware?"

Faith placed the $20 bill inside and looked down at the cash box in which her silverware would logically have been. "Why, I don't quite know. But it doesn't really matter."

"Mrs. Darling . . ." Bobbie said between gasps, "is everything in the mansion really coming out?"

"Everything's got to go," she answered.

Bobbie stared up at the big house. How much was still inside? She *had* to see. Bobbie sneaked around the side of the mansion. She opened the kitchen screen door, turned the wooden door's brass doorknob until the old door squeaked open, and then sneaked inside, shutting it firmly behind her to make sure no one got any funny ideas about following her.

When her eyes adjusted, Bobbie froze at the sight: piles of newspaper and phone books and mail and stacks of soup, sugar, ketchup, and tea. The clutter was astounding. And the possible meaning of the mess for her beloved mansion, not to mention Mrs. Darling's mind, almost brought tears to her eyes.

But then she spied the heap of antique sterling silverware on the floor and dropped to the tile, testing the limits of her snug pantsuit's stitching as she began scooping up the spoons, forks, and knives, all monogrammed with a curlicue *B*, counting as she went. She rescued the entire twelve-place-setting set—(the *exquisite* Tiffany & Co. "Vine" pattern worth a thousand a setting, if a plug *nickel*) from salad forks to fish knives to sugar shell—all except one missing tea-spoon. Bobbie pulled herself back up on her business wedges to cram the entire lot into the nearest kitchen counter drawer, but then thought better of it, worrying somebody would give Mrs. Darling a quarter for the whole shebang.

She emptied a grocery sack full of more canned soup, tea, ketchup, and sugar, and crammed all the silverware into it before stuffing it securely under an arm. Then, heaving a big sigh, she wound her way through the piles to the door that led to the rest of the mansion, and reverently stepped into the foyer. It was exactly as she remembered, the portraits, the parquet floor, the grand staircase—a majestic view from out of a movie and her dreams. But the foyer was the only room untouched. The rest of the downstairs had already been cleaned out, the empty rooms giving off the sad feel of echoes and disturbed space.

Bobbie stomped her foot on the empty foyer's parquet floor. "This can't be happening!"

Frantic now, she gazed up the grand staircase. Up she shuffled as fast as her sensible shoes would take her to the only room she'd seen on the second floor, Claudia Jean Darling's bedroom, hoping against hope to find one certain object still there. Glancing over her shoulder, Bobbie turned the room's brass doorknob, and the moment the door creaked open, her eyes locked like a missile on what was still sitting high atop the room's fireplace mantel:

A Louis XV gilded bronze elephant clock.

The hair on the back of her neck stood straight up. For years now, Bobbie would see pieces at high-end auctions and even museums she was sure she'd seen in the Darling mansion—every antique glimpsed on that long-ago visit etched indelibly in her mind—and she'd ache to tell someone important about what might be right down the street, especially a type of eighteenth-century French automaton elephant clock she once saw in a flyer about lost objects of French antiquities. But the urge created a bit of a Bobbie conundrum. While she always dreamed of making a name in the antique world by being the one to discover some great find, she also felt comforted by the idea that the Darling mansion's antiques would never go anywhere, would always be forever a part of her little-girl mansion dreams.

Still, Bobbie couldn't help herself. She scooted toward the clock until she was close enough to touch it. Then she reached out and did just that. Setting down the silverware sack momentarily, she took both hands and inched the heavy clock sideways, peeking at the back's clockwork innards, searching for a special lever that just had to be there:

Yes!

She flipped it. And like magic, the elephant trunk began to sway.

With a guilty glance back toward the door, Bobbie whipped out her cell phone and her fingers began to fly.

Outside, Faith was rearranging a stack of Spode gold-edged china serving plates that were precariously leaning off the side of a buffet table. In fact, the entire fine china set, which spanned the entire length of the buffet, needed a bit of work.

"Mrs. Darling—"

Faith glanced over her shoulder. A plump red-haired woman in an unbecoming pink pantsuit was calling her name as if they were acquainted. Now the woman was buzzing around her like a darn honeybee.

"Mrs. Darling!"

Faith frowned, then remembered. Ah, yes, little Bobbie Ann Blankenship. With a sigh, Faith went back to rearranging the china spread out before her. "I do hate to break up this set. Would you be interested in the entire thing?"

Bobbie lost her train of thought a moment, contemplating the "entire thing." (The Spode Gloucester Blue & Gold design worth even more than the sterling silver, lordgawd*help*me.)

"Here, hold these a moment, will you?" Faith held out four serving dishes.

Bobbie obeyed, setting down the silverware sack and her cell phone on the buffet table to take the stack of century-old Spode china plates Faith was shoving into her arms. She gazed an admiring moment at the gold-rimmed plates. "This is just wrong," she muttered as Faith took the china one piece at a time from Bobbie's grasp. "Mrs. Darling, this is wrong! I'm begging you—let me take everything. I can sell it all for you. We'll talk through the value of these things, maybe even get an auctioneer—"

"No, no, dear," Faith responded. "You can't take it all. There wouldn't be a sale. And I have to have a sale."

Bobbie set the gold-rimmed serving dishes down dramatically (but carefully) on the table and took a professional posture. "Then I just have to talk to you about the Louis XV elephant clock up in

Claudia Jean's bedroom. I hope you don't mind, but I took the liberty of going up there, because—"

"May I help you, young lady?" Faith interrupted, her sun hat dipping a bit toward Bobbie, which made Bobbie completely lose her train of thought.

For a beat, Bobbie stared at Mrs. Darling staring back at her.

"It's me. Bobbie Ann."

"Oh, hello, dear. You still here?" asked Faith.

"Uhm, yes, I am." Bobbie forced herself to focus. "I was asking you about the elephant clock, remember? This is *very* important."

But Faith turned and strode away, leaving Bobbie Ann in midsentence. Out of the corner of her eye, Faith had once again seen the mess of blond hair, little red cowboy boots, bulging pockets, and sticky little fingers, now hiding in her favorite place in the opening under her great-grandfather's rolltop a few feet away. "Are you hungry?" Faith asked, leaning down and smiling.

The little shoplifter snapped her head around at the old lady who was looking at her like she knew her. Then she sprang from under the sold rolltop and scampered off. But not before she circled back behind the red-faced pantsuit lady and palmed the shiny cell phone the pudgy lady had left on the buffet table.

Bobbie stepped back in front of Faith. "Mrs. Darling, *please* listen to me. We must talk about your elephant—"

"It's not for sale," Faith answered, straightening up.

That stopped Bobbie cold. "But I thought everything was for sale."

"Not that."

Bobbie fanned herself with her hand, thinking hard now. "Not for sale."

"Not for sale," Faith repeated.

"Okay-okay. I don't mean any disrespect, Mrs. Darling, it's just that I'm a bit worried that it may not stay that way considering the sale's . . . dynamics. See, I don't want to get your hopes up, but I am relatively positive, almost certain, pretty darn sure, it's museum quality! The provenance on it could be mind-boggling! Why . . . why . . . it could go all the way back to Louis XV *himself*!"

"Take something else," Faith said, returning to the Spode china.

"Mrs. Darling, did you hear me? It could be a museum piece! It could be priceless!"

Faith gestured at the Spode set. "Would you like this nice china set?"

Bobbie paused, a wave of lust for the set distracting her. "Yes, of course."

"It's yours. Pay what you can. But the clock is not for sale."

Bobbie blurted: "But there's one just like it in the Louvre in Paris!"

"And your point?" Faith asked.

Bobbie quickly changed tactics: "Okay-okay. Then how about I hold it for safekeeping for you? Until all of this"—Bobbie paused to wave a frantic hand around the sale—"is over. Again, no disrespect, but I'm really afraid it'll sprout legs and wind up in somebody's double-wide trailer when you're not remembering, uhm, looking."

But Faith, having forgotten she was talking to someone, was now preoccupied with the cotton sash belt that had come undone on her sundress.

"May I help you?" Faith said to her. Again.

Bobbie once more found herself staring at Faith Bass Darling as Faith stared back, the old lady's hands poised to return to tying and untying her cotton sash. "May I help you?" she repeated, irritated at this big-boned young woman in an unflattering pink pantsuit who would not state her business. "I said, may I help you?"

For another frozen moment, Bobbie studied Faith Darling's eyes before the old lady went back to worrying with her sash, tightening, loosening, tightening. Then with a glance over her shoulder, Bobbie cleared her throat. "How much for the elephant clock?"

"Elephant clock?"

"Twenty dollars?"

Faith walked away. "Pay what you can."

Claudia Darling was working very hard to get a handle on the moment. Frozen to the piece of asphalt under her running shoes, VW door open wide, she stood at the mansion's curb, gaping at the surreal sight spread across the lawn.

"Claudia Jean, you got my message!" Someone was yelling from behind her. "It's me! Bobbie!"

Claudia turned to see Bobbie Ann Blankenship jump out of a minivan and rush over to give her an awkward hello hug.

"You haven't changed a bit! I really like your hair short! And I love your hippie jewelry!" Bobbie babbled while Claudia was still working to find her tongue. "How have you stayed so skinny? I bet you jog—those are fancy jogging shoes, aren't they? Oooh, is that a silk camisole? Love it."

"B-Bobbie Ann . . ." Claudia stammered, gesturing helplessly toward the yard. "What . . . ?"

"I was just about to call you again, but I've misplaced my cell phone. Can't find it anywhere." Bobbie heaved a big sigh. "But I'm so glad you're finally here—you have *no* idea how painful it's been watching this debacle. I've been back and forth over here all morning. Rest assured I've taken as much as I could. Hey, you don't look so good."

Claudia couldn't stop blinking. It was as if someone had picked up her mansion, shaken it, and poured her entire childhood out the front doors spewing onto the lawn. As kids, Claudia and Mike were never, *ever* allowed to touch any of the old things that seemed to fill every inch of the mansion, for fear of their mother's having a meltdown. And here they all were being touched. By strangers. *Lots* of strangers.

Only inches from where she stood was the nineteenth-century china cabinet once full of hand-blown Vienna crystal, now standing empty, leaded glass doors flung wide.

To her left were her mother's froufrou Madame Alexander dolls that once perched like stuffed royalty atop the parlor's tall secretary, untouchable and unreachable, now piled up together by the brick walkway. A woman was holding one upside down, petticoats flapping, checking its underwear.

To her right were a dozen tiny figurines—Italian porcelain angels from a locked glass display case in her mother's bedroom—even more untouchable than the dolls (but obviously not unreachable since she remembered a chipped, and quickly hidden, cherub). Now they were all bunched together on a tabletop like plaster of Paris knockoffs.

Her eye caught on something under the table she'd never seen before: a dusty box marked "Bibles." Claudia pushed back the box's flap and her mind almost refused to believe what she saw: it was jammed full with the familiar worn holy Bibles that her mother had treated like holy relics, reading daily from whichever was at hand and drilling her children in memory verses from them every Sunday night. The sight of the Bibles thrown carelessly into a box was so unthinkable that Claudia momentarily wondered whether her mother had died and Bobbie just hadn't gotten around to telling her.

But just then, Claudia saw her mother, unmistakable in that same old sun hat, pinched-faced and pencil-thin as ever, her posture still as perfect as could be. Even her gestures are exactly the same, Claudia thought, watching her mother take money from a balding man and then hand him an oversized portrait of a nineteenth-century woman with a heart-shaped face.

"My mother sold *Belle*?" she gasped, watching the balding stranger grab up the oversized portrait of her bustle-clad great-great-grandmother Belle Birdsong Bass, star of her childhood lullaby, and head directly toward where she and Bobbie stood.

"I like the frame," the man said proudly to the two women admiring his new purchase as he lugged it between them.

Bobbie grabbed the balding man's arm and whispered something in his ear. The man shook his head. She whispered again. The man shook his head again. Bobbie whispered again, this time pulling out ten $20 bills and thrusting them at the man, whereupon the man happily handed Bobbie the big portrait, pocketed the cash, and strolled away. With a harried glance back at Claudia, who still had not moved, Bobbie pivoted and marched the portrait right back up the steps to its rightful place inside.

Claudia collected herself. Pushing her way into the crowds of strange people looking hungrily at the things she knew as intimately as her own skin, she charted a double-time course through the rows of bookshelves, around the antique wicker, and by the massive lion-claw buffet to stand directly in front of Faith.

"Mother—" she began.

"Hello, dear," her mother answered ever so casually.

Claudia opened her mouth and then realized she was about to hyperventilate. She couldn't believe it. She hadn't had an anxiety attack in years. She was too tough for this now! But there was no stopping it. Cussing herself, she sank onto a brocade love seat behind her and threw her head between her knees.

"Breathe now," she heard her precise, infuriating mother's voice say. "Still doing this, I see."

Claudia took a deep breath, coughing and waving as her mother's cigarette smoke surrounded her. (*My mother is smoking?*) She felt Faith's hand on her head and then felt a sharp "That's enough" pat as her mother turned back to a box she was unpacking. "Perhaps you should take up smoking, dear. Calms the nerves."

Claudia raised her head from between her legs and gazed at the ash smudge on her eternally immaculate mother's cotton sundress, at the clutter strewn across her mother's eternally immaculate lawn, at the cigarette in her straight-back Baptist mother's hand, at the homemade sale sign around the old paint-flecked lawn jockey's neck—at all the things that were wrong with this picture. She forced herself to take a practiced calming yoga breath, in, out, hair to toenails. Then with heroic effort she got to her feet to try again:

"Hello, Mother—"

Faith barely looked back. "Hello, yourself. I'm a bit surprised to see you, but that seems to be the order of the day. So I suppose I shouldn't be surprised to be surprised, should I? You're looking older, dear. What are you doing here, I wonder? Bringing back our ring, perhaps?" She sighed wistfully. "Now that I'd truly love to see again."

Claudia threw up her hands. "What are you talking about?"

"The ring you stole, dear." Faith paused, her face mellowing momentarily as she looked Claudia up and down in the way one might a portrait-in-progress. "Ah, Claudia Jean." She sighed. "How I wish you hadn't."

"Mother, that ring never left this house—and you know it!" Claudia said, setting her jaw.

"I certainly do not."

"You certainly do—" Claudia countered. "And how could you sell Belle!"

Faith frowned. "Who?"

"Belle!" Claudia answered, gesturing toward the mansion. "Great-great-grandmother Belle! Her portrait, Mother!"

"Oh, was that the woman's name?" Faith shrugged. "The man wanted a big frame, so I went in and got one. For some reason, I keep leaving those big pictures inside on the wall."

"Is that your idea of a *joke*?" Claudia found herself sputtering again. "Have you lost your mind?"

"Now, dear, I don't see how that's any of your business," Faith responded. "And watch your mouth. You'd think I'd not imagine you so rude, my goodness."

Claudia turned red. "You will not make me yell at you. I am not going to yell."

"Well, I certainly hope not," Faith said, picking up a box.

So Claudia yelled. "You haven't changed a bit! What have you been doing for twenty years?"

"Not seeing you, certainly," Faith said, over her shoulder, setting the box on a chair. "So I'm rather certain you're not here."

Claudia paused at that. "What?"

"You're not real," Faith responded, looking into the box. "That's been happening lately. Usually closer to sundown. And mostly people not among the living. But for all I know you aren't among the living anymore yourself." With that, she paused to glance again over her shoulder at Claudia, softened by the thought. "But obviously I do wish I could see you one more time," she said, under her breath. "I suppose it's why I have you here today of all days."

"*'Have me here'*?" Claudia repeated.

"Yoo-hoo, lady!"

At a table a few feet away were two matronly black women with French-twist hairdos and matching tailored outfits—one sea-foam green, the other firecracker red. The twin in green was waving a hand full of ornate jewelry as she headed Faith and Claudia's way: "How much for this costume jewelry?"

"That gaudy stuff?" sniffed the twin in red, following behind. "I wouldn't be caught dead in that."

"Well, it's not for you, sister. It's for Aunt Velmena," snapped the twin in green, coming to a stop in front of Faith to drop an ornate diamond-and-coral necklace with matching brooch and ear clips into Faith's hands. "Aunt Velmena's ninety-nine years old, you know. Turning one hundred tomorrow—if she makes it, poor soul," the twin added, shaking her head mournfully.

Her sister joined in, French twists swaying in unison.

The twin in green then brightened. "Will you take twenty-five cents for it all?"

Claudia choked. "Twenty-five cents!"

The twin in green cocked an eyebrow, now in bargaining mode. "Okay, fifty cents, but that's my final offer."

For a beat, Faith gazed down at the Victorian jewelry in her hands as if she'd never seen it before. Then she held it back out. "Why don't you take it as my gift to your sick aunt."

Gasping, Claudia scooped the jewelry out of her mother's hand. "Mother, my God—they're real!"

"Real?" guffawed the twin in red, slapping a thigh. "Well, we must be at the Queen of England's yard sale! C'mon, sister." She grabbed her twin's arm, pulling her in the opposite direction, the two sisters bickering as they went.

Faith leveled her gaze at Claudia, who was staring at the jewelry she was holding, just as stunned at what she had done as what her mother had almost done.

"You know, dear," Faith snapped as she retrieved the jewelry from Claudia's hands and plopped it unceremoniously onto a nearby table, "if I want to give away my own jewelry, I will do just that. Now, excuse me, dear. I'm sure you have a vanishing schedule to keep. The others at least had the courtesy not to stay so long."

Others? Claudia watched her mother turn and stride toward the mansion.

"You're going to stop your mother, right?" Bobbie was asking, tugging at Claudia's sleeve. But then she noticed Claudia's blank face. "Uh-oh, what'd she say?"

"I'm not real," Claudia responded, still gazing after her mother.

Bobbie screwed up her face. "What does that mean?"

"I have no idea," Claudia murmured.

"I think she may be sick, Claudia Jean," Bobbie hazarded, glancing toward the mansion's kitchen.

"She's not sick." Claudia frowned, slowly shaking her head. "She's just twenty years more herself."

Bobbie took her old friend Claudia Jean by the arm. "You better sit down again. You're looking rather pukey." Bobbie eased Claudia back onto the brocade love seat.

Claudia shook her head again. "This was a mistake."

"What?" Bobbie plopped her hands on her hips. "Get a grip, girl. This is all yours!"

Claudia gazed her mother's way for another lingering moment. She knew she should have feelings for her mother. She should have missed her in some way all these years beyond the blame and the anger and the grief. But her mother had left her nothing to miss. Bad enough she lost her big brother, and even her father, no matter how she might have hated him by the end. Yet the truth was she lost her mother, too, long before she ran away.

Bobbie all but stomped a foot. "Claudia Jean Darling, did you hear me? This is yours. Don't you care?"

"No," Claudia answered. "I don't. I can't." Then she ran her hands through her hair, trying to get ahold of herself. "I thought I could handle it . . . her . . . but I really can't."

"What if she's going crazy?" Bobbie countered.

"Especially if she's going crazy," Claudia answered.

"But it's your inheritance," Bobbie cried. "Claudia Jean, the Tiffany lamps are going like hotcakes—your Louis Comfort Tiffanys! I'll sell it all for you, I swear—but right now just save it, for the love of All That's Holy. You can't tell me you don't at least need the money."

Claudia paused at that.

The ring.

But what was all that about Mother missing it? And me stealing it? Claudia suddenly wondered, glancing back toward Faith.

As the obvious answer sank in, she felt a shiver flit up her spine. "Mother really does think . . . Oh dear God." Jumping to her feet, Claudia scanned the lawn for her great-great-grandfather's rolltop desk. She scanned it again—and again. "Bobbie Ann, where's the rolltop?"

"Sold quick, like I've been saying! It's *gone.*"

Stop this now! Faith told herself, striding to a halt on the porch and squeezing her eyes shut. That's quite enough—you don't have time for any more such nonsense!

Behind her eyelids, though, she could still see her daughter, no matter what she did. But it wasn't today's grown-up figment daughter she saw. It was her daughter at seventeen, the way she looked the last time Faith ever saw her.

Faith opened her eyes to find that her hands were younger . . . that the white cotton sash in her hands had turned to red satin . . . and her sundress is now a red satin robe she hasn't worn in twenty years. . . .

It's dawn, and she's thrown on the robe to rush down the hall.

Her wild seventeen-year-old daughter, who has been threatening to run away with her motorcycle thug of a boyfriend, has finally done it.

Claudia Jean is gone.

And Faith now stands in Claudia Jean's room, grasping that she may be gone for good—because the family's heirloom ring is missing from Faith's bedroom dresser. Her daughter has taken it despite being told not to come back if she did. Faith can only stare. She's numb and has been for so long she does not know what to feel. Strangely, all she can think is how she should spank her daughter but good as she'd done the last time she'd taken the ring—when her daughter was barely four. But that only makes Faith cringe, remembering how horribly angry she'd been, how close she'd come to actually hurting her own child, and Faith quickly pushes it from her mind.

Suddenly trembling—worse than she had since her son's accident two years before—Faith sinks onto the canopy bed for support. For a few moments, until the shaking subsides, she sits gazing at the elephant clock on the mantel. Then she's no longer thinking of the heirloom ring. She's thinking of her daughter, seeing little Claudia Jean at that age, her tiny sticky fingers on everything. She sees the child in Faith's bedroom staring wide-eyed at the elephant clock on Faith's mantel as its trunk moves with the sounding chimes. Every hour on the hour, for days on end, she'd hear her running footsteps and find little Claudia Jean watching the elephant swing its trunk to the striking hour. When she'd caught the four-year-old in her pajamas climbing the dresser to get to the clock, Faith spanked her and sent her back to bed across the hall.

Soon, though, the sound of her little daughter's muffled sniffling had made Faith recall how it felt to be a child crying in the dark. She knew what a good mother should do. Her own mother had given the clock to her at the same age to help her sleep through the night—one of the only memories of her mother Faith had. But she feared she was not a good mother, not to this difficult child who so favored Claude it was as if she'd shaped her face by naming the girl after him. Her son, Michael, was easy to love, so much like her own dear father. But she didn't seem to know how to be a mother to a little girl so unlike herself. Faith had lost her mother too young, raised neat and quiet by housekeepers. Her own little daughter was such a wild thing. No matter how meticulously she dressed her each day, she'd be filthy by noon. But most upsetting was the child's sudden snatching of the mansion's precious things, some of which Faith never saw again. If the elephant clock wasn't so heavy, Faith was certain she would have snatched it, too.

"The girl is just trying to get your attention, Faith Ann," Claude had laughed. "Let her have the antique baubles! God knows you've got a houseful of them." Her husband seemed to enjoy this side of their daughter, at least until his coin collection's buffalo nickel jar went missing. Still, Faith tried to be calm about it. But then the child somehow snatched Grandmother Belle's wedding ring—right after she'd brought it home from the safe-deposit box to show little Claudia Jean on her birthday—and Faith had spanked her daughter so long and so hard before the child returned it that she had scared them both. After that, she had prayed daily that her little daughter would be a darling girl . . . just as she'd prayed daily that her daughter would not remember her frightening loss of self-control.

As the child's sniffling grew louder now, Faith kept thinking back to the childhood night her own mother had given her the elephant clock. The clock was the first antique she'd ever loved, its ticking like a mother's heart long after her young mother's heart had stopped. It had always been there stitching together time with its ticks as if it were keeping things together—keeping her together—from tick to tock to tick: after her daughter's difficult birth, after her marriage ended in all but name, after she moved out of the master bedroom and took it with her, when she and Claude began their separate peace in separate ends of the mansion.

How could she ever give it away?

But then Faith pictured little Claudia Jean whimpering under her pink chenille bedspread and something deeply maternal welled up in her, flowing past all her conflicted feelings. In its wake, she'd grabbed up the elephant clock, rushed it across the hall, and set it high on the room's mantel out of harm's way. Then she had leaned over and kissed her little daughter gently on the forehead, her hand lingering on her mess of blond hair for the briefest of moments as her daughter, sniffing happily, watched the elephant clock move its trunk her way.

It's just a loan, Faith had told herself as she left. It's just across the hall.

But crumpled now on her runaway teenage daughter's bedroom floor, staring at the elephant clock exactly where she'd placed it so many years before, Faith feels things shift. With her daughter's vanishing act and her own screaming ultimatum over the ring, whatever was holding everything in tenuous place had vanished, too.

Fumbling for her red satin sash, Faith collects herself and the elephant clock, returns it to its old place on her own bedroom mantel, and then goes back to bed. Covers pulled tight, she watches the elephant clock's trunk move and the sun move and the morning move, chasing the light along her bedroom wall. And she stays that way as day turns into night, the ticking of the elephant clock once again keeping things, keeping her, together.

And she feels her solitary silence deepen and settle in to stay. . . .

. . . Faith jerked back to herself. Blinking the familiar dizziness away, she saw her hands were still on her sash—her plain white cotton sundress sash.

She was no longer on the porch. She was upstairs again, this time standing exactly halfway between the master bedroom and her daughter's bedroom. Grabbing for the wall to steady herself, she rushed into her memory litany:

My name is Faith Bass Darling . . . I live at . . . I live at . . . at . . .

But she couldn't think straight to finish. Upset and breathing hard, she whirled her old bones toward the stairs to run away. Then she forced herself to stop, but it wasn't because of those confounded doors or whatever all this boomeranging might mean to her midnight deal.

She stopped for the silence.

Her breathing slowed as the mansion's silence settled around her, calming her down like the old friend it had become since she'd closed bedroom and mansion doors against all the noise and pain. Since she'd begun desiring it above everything because it was the only answer that wouldn't remind her why it had become what she most desired.

There, Faith finally thought. Fine now.

Feeling something heavy and metallic under her armpit, she noticed the silver cash box lodged there and remembered she had a sale to run.

So Faith Bass Darling once again headed down the grand staircase and out the front doors, but slower this time, moving as if wading, as if the old silence itself held the weight of muddy water, wishing to sweep her back inside to stay.

Bobbie, Claudia, and the Yesteryear Antiques minivan bounced to a halt in front of a small pink brick house, the home of her mean old second-grade teacher Mrs. Hitt, who'd all but knocked over Bobbie buying the desk not an hour before.

Under its semi-attached carport, Geraldine Hitt, self-proclaimed garage sale aficionado extraordinaire, was happily looking through her new $20 purchase right where her husband, Hiram, had unloaded it.

"Look, Hiram!" Geraldine said, holding up a dry inkwell to show Hiram on the other side of the carport. "Remember these? Sure brings back memories." She placed the inkwell into the small cardboard box already full with the rolltop's contents. "And look at this tiny old key," she went on. "I wonder if it fits this little door on this side of the desk."

She turned the key in the lock and the door swung open. Out fell an old ledger book and some yellowed bank receipts. But something else was still in there. Reaching in, Geraldine carefully inched out something small and square, no bigger than 10″ x 10″.

"Look, Hiram—it's a painting," she said. "But such an odd size." And the fancy golden frame was almost as big as the paint-blobbed canvas. She held it at arm's length: *Oh. A water lily.* She made a face, not caring for globby "modern" art, her taste being more traditional, like the Thomas Kinkade Limited Edition *Bambi's First Years* framed print she'd just bought on the Home Shopping Network, complete with certificate of authenticity. Now *that's* art, she thought. But the little globby painting was free. And free is free, she reminded herself as her attention returned to the rolltop. "I better get a bigger box," she announced and hurried inside, painting still in hand.

Hiram grunted, his head poked under the truck's front seat, having more important matters to attend to, what with Y2K upon them. His stockpile was good-to-go: water jugs, propane stove, shortwave radio, canned goods, flashlights. But he couldn't find his sackful of batteries he *just* bought at Walmart on the way to get the rolltop (plus the jumbo bag of M&M's and 50-percent-off Y2K manual). And batteries could soon be like gold. Where the dad-blamed devil did that sack go?

Across the street, Bobbie turned off the minivan's engine. "Let me do the talking," she suggested, but she was talking to herself. Passenger-side door yawning wide, Claudia was already sprinting toward the desk.

Oblivious to Hiram Hitt's yelp of surprise as he hit his head on his truck's dashboard, Claudia grabbed the desk's middle drawer, pushed on a hidden side slat, popping it open. In her hand went. And out it came: empty.

Bobbie appeared. "Hello, Mr. Hitt! I'm Bobbie Blankenship. Your wife was my second-grade teacher. Hot enough for you?"

By this time, though, Claudia had sunk slowly to the Hitts' concrete driveway, the middle drawer still in her hand.

Bobbie mustered her best smile. "Mr. Hitt, might I ask if you happened to find a large wedding-type ring as you were looking over this wonderful new purchase of yours? In an old black velvet ring box?"

Hiram found his tongue. "Well . . . I dunno. Geraldine's the one to ask. GERALDINE!"

"What!" Geraldine stuck her head out the side door.

"You find a ring in this desk?" Hiram asked.

"No, no ring," Geraldine said, and then suddenly suspicious, added: "Who wants to know?"

"It's me, Mrs. Hitt. Bobbie Blankenship? This is Claudia Jean Darling," Bobbie said with yet another gum-busting smile. "You just bought this desk from her mother. Might we look through the contents? I'm sure you won't mind. It's rather important."

Geraldine narrowed her eyes. "I suppose not." Moving over to the desk, she pointed to the box full of the rolltop's contents.

Bobbie leaned near as Claudia plunged her hands into the cardboard box, sifting through the bank stubs, tie clips, paper clips, staples, business cards, receipts, old ledger books, labels, loose change—all strangely intimate. But no black velvet ring box; no *Love Eternal*–inscribed diamond and pearl antique filigreed ring. Then she noticed several unopened letters and stopped. Slowly, numbly, Claudia closed her fingers around them and got to her feet to walk away.

"Ex-*cuse* me?" Geraldine called after her.

Claudia leveled her gaze at the woman, and then handed the envelopes to her. Geraldine took one look and handed them right back. "Oh. Of course. Take them. My pleasure."

Grasping the letters, Claudia strode away.

"Sorry for the bother," Bobbie said. "You certainly made a fine purchase." Then she handed Geraldine her business card. "When you're ready, I'll make you a good offer," she whispered.

Claudia was waiting in the minivan.

Bobbie eased into the driver's seat. "What was that about?"

Claudia handed her the envelopes. Bobbie saw that they were very old letters. From Claudia Jean Darling. To Faith Darling.

And they had never been opened.

❧ PROVENANCE

DANCE DRAGOON

Civil War–era .44 caliber Colt pistol • 14″ with 8 ³⁄₁₆″
barrel • Obscure Texas-made weapon • Extremely rare
in any condition

Circa 1864   *Value: $40,000*

*In 1864, during the last days of the Civil War, J. H. Dance and Broth-
ers of Old Columbia, Texas, on the Brazos River, designed a revolver for
the Confederate Army called the Dance Dragoon, of which only 330
were made before the federals captured and burned the factory. An ex-
perimental low-back-hammer Dance, shelved due to potential misfiring,
was happily found in the rubble by a ne'er-do-well named Moses Tur-
nipseed, who used the purloined revolver in a string of robberies up and
down the river for four thieving years.*

*In the spring of 1868 during a downpour swelling the riverbanks, a
liquored-up, cranky, and drenched-to-the-bone Moses pointed it at a
passing young settler named James Tyler Bass, ordering him to hand over
his sturdy leather overcoat, then deciding just to shoot him for it instead.
The Dance, however, chose that moment to misfire. A struggle ensued,*

landing both in the swirling waters of the Brazos, James alone surfacing to the sight of his thwarted murderer's body washing downriver. Deciding this was his lucky day and his lucky spot, James Tyler Bass decided right then and right there to settle on those very banks and make a life.

While the Dragoon disappeared.

Until the day, over a century later, a teenage oil field worker spotted its handle poking up from a dry backwash of the same Texas river.

There's always one funeral director in the lone funeral home in every tiny little town who is silent witness not only to the last act of the town's citizenry, but also to their entire lives. They know everybody's business—living and dead. And, as was the case in Bass, Texas, sometimes that mortician himself is not really the silent type. Which was what Deputy John Jasper Johnson was counting on as he pulled the patrol car up to the Anderson–DuBois funeral home.

He parked, walked around to the back, and tapped on the metal door's windowpane. A wrinkled, string bean of a bald man with a set of Dumbo ears pushed open the door with his elbow, his rubber-gloved hands being occupied with a brush and a towel.

"Earl," John Jasper acknowledged with a nod.

"C'mon in, John Jasper," the mortician said, waving him in, as he turned and started back toward the funeral home's inner rooms. "I'm preparin' Eloise Tuttle. Passed this morning, and the family's coming over to see her first thing this evening, smack dab on Millennium New Year's Eve. The woman's ninety-three years old with a face that'd stop traffic, and her kin's gonna be expecting Sophia Loren. And on top of that, we got Belva Bowman's full-blown funeral in a couple of hours," he said, slapping the towel to rest over a shoulder as the deputy followed him past the viewing room full of floral arrangements. "I tell you what, preparin' her took it outa me. Swear to God, that woman just let herself go—three hundred and fifty pounds if she was an ounce. Whew! I'm gettin' too old for this." He waved him into the preparation room. "You don't mind if I keep working, do ya? Almost finished. And that gol-dang family of hers is gonna be here any minute."

They walked into a small room where a tiny, hollow-cheeked, thin-haired old woman was laid out in a rosewood coffin dressed in her Sunday best with heavy makeup to match. "Here, hold this." Dropping the brush into the coffin, Earl handed John Jasper a blue-silver wig, then grabbed some casket pillows and stuffed them under Eloise. "What can I do ya for?"

John Jasper held the wig as if it might bite him. "I got a thing going on over at the Darling mansion."

"Just heard! Ain't that something? The woman finally comes outa that house after all this time and brings everything with her." Earl took the wig from John Jasper and began fitting it on Eloise Tuttle's head, moving it around until it was straight. "This ain't been a good week for old ladies 'round here, has it?" He shook his bald head. "But that's the way it is with old folks. Some don't take bad times so good. They can't change, so they break. Others, like Eloise Tuttle here, they got it good for ninety-three years and then die in their sleep, leaving a gaggle of relatives without the sense God gave a goose. Hell."

"Earl," John Jasper interrupted, "you do Claude Darling's funeral?"

"Sure did." Earl nodded as he retrieved the brush and leaned in to make slight wig adjustments. "Now, that's been a while."

"You knew the Darlings pretty well. That right?" the deputy went on.

Earl shrugged. "Much as anybody. Back then you made sure to

watch yourself with the owner of the only bank in town, and that went double for Claude Angus Darling." Earl thoughtfully scratched a big earlobe with his free rubber-gloved hand. "Now, he was a case. When that man first started out, he could charm the flies off a cow paddy. Later on, you never knew who was at home. Peaches and cream one minute; hell on wheels the next—even with all that Bass money and big house. Always felt kinda sorry for Faith, matter of fact." Earl rested his rubber-gloved hands on his hips. "What's on your mind, son?"

"Died of a heart attack, right?" the deputy went on.

Earl nodded. "Sure did. And it sure wasn't his first. Thought I was gonna see him in here after his second one and dead sure after his third. He had a temper. A nasty combination when you got yourself a bad ticker, and that man was always on a slow burn. So after what happened to you and his boy, wasn't much of a surprise a fourth one finally got him, the ol' sumbitch." Earl paused, glancing down at John Jasper's knee. "How's that leg holdin' up? Damn shame. You were greased lightning on a stick."

John Jasper realized he was favoring his knee and stopped. "Was there a coroner's report?"

"Sure was. I'm the coroner. Don't mean to be rude, but Mrs. Tuttle's waiting. That all?"

As John Jasper steered his cruiser away from the mortuary, he started working the situation over in his head.

The thing about ClaudeDamnDarling, he was the kind of man you could see somebody killing, John Jasper pondered. That white man was a piece of work. There could've been a truckload of people from both sides of town lining up for the privilege. It was just like Earl said, the man was permanently pissed off about something and taking it out on the world.

The town used to be busting with men just like him. People had forgotten and maybe that was a good thing, made a deputy's job easier, John Jasper mused. But he sure hadn't forgotten. The town had Football Almighty to thank for keeping the peace back then. Hell, who knows what would've happened without football.

Look at me as a good for instance, John Jasper thought. Raised up by broken-down grandparents who never knew nothing but cleaning white women's houses and doing white men's gut-busting farm work. Yeah, except for football, it could've been me, easy, standing in a ClaudeDamnDarling-killing line.

So when his football buddy Mike got them both summer work on his daddy's oil rig, John Jasper wasn't surprised the old guy was in his face. He just didn't expect him to be in Mike's. But that's the way it was the whole time. Talking about making men of them, toughening them up. Pushing Mike around, calling him soft, girlie, a spoiled mama's boy.

"If he'd done that to me, he'da been sucking through a straw," John Jasper mumbled, the whole thing still able to piss him off. But Mike just took it. Blew it off. And that just made ClaudeDamnDarling even redder in the face. Mike Darling was a lot of things but one of them sure wasn't girlie. Playing ball with a guy tells you all you need to know about him, and he knew for a fact that Mike Darling was crazy fearless. First varsity practice scrimmage, John Jasper had been lined up raring to butt some white boys on their asses—and Claude Angus Darling's rich white son was right in front of him like it was John Jasper's birthday. So all he wanted was to mow that white boy down like a field of hay. And he did. Again and again. Until it wasn't any fun anymore, because the guy never cared. Never slowed a step. But that was nothing to watching him in a game, hanging back in the pocket with the coach yelling, "Dammit! Protect yourself, Darling!" But Mike just did his thing, John Jasper recalled, unable to keep from smiling at the memory. Waited till the second he was gonna be hit and then he'd let that ball fly. Perfect. Everybody knew he'd be smiling that shit-eating grin while the other team's linemen were pretty much taking his head off. And everybody knew he'd be the first back up on his feet, ready to go again.

So there was something else going on with that SOB of a daddy of his. Like he was trying to get a rise out of Mike, like he thought being a man meant having a goddamn temper like his. Or something worse, like being jealous of his own son and having to keep him down to keep feeling good about his own screwed-up self.

John Jasper knew to keep his mouth shut. He was just the football buddy with the split-end hands that made his son look good under Friday-night lights whether the bigot liked it or not. Besides, when you're seventeen, you *want* to work on an oil rig—making big money moving around big machinery—even if it's on land leased by a piece of work.

We were nothing but studs and nobody alive was gonna tell us any different, John Jasper remembered, shaking his head. We had time to burn. College ball—hell, pro ball—was waiting, and when you know you got it made, you don't do what you want to do when somebody calls you "boy" when the whole world knows not to do that anymore. Even if you are a boy, you know you ain't no "boy," not his kind. No, you act deaf when you hear him slip in a "nigger" here and a "nigger town" there. You know he ain't gonna change and you know he can't stand that his own boy has. So you know to stay patient. Last thing you want to do is cause trouble with a town big shot when you're on your way to leaving him way behind.

So, yeah, I could've put him out of his ClaudeDamnDarling misery, John Jasper admitted to himself. I could've been the one to kill him off that summer when I was pointing that rusted old pistol I found at him. But I didn't kill him. And Mrs. Darling didn't kill him. Nobody killed him. No matter how much he had it coming.

Bobbie kept glancing at her childhood friend in the passenger seat as she maneuvered the minivan away from Claudia Jean's great-great-grandfather's rolltop. She had a million questions, but Claudia Jean hadn't moved a muscle since they left the Hitts', just kept staring at the unopened letters in her lap. And Bobbie had no idea what to say about that. How could a mother not open letters from her daughter? She just could not wrap her mind around the idea. But she had to say something to her friend, didn't she?

"Well," Bobbie began, "she kept the letters. I mean she could have thrown them away. That's something, isn't it?"

Claudia didn't answer. Instead, she turned over the top letter, eyed the unopened seal, and closed her fingers around it, crushing it slowly in her palm.

Bobbie noticed and began to babble nervously. "Want me to turn on the AC? I think you could use some air. I'll turn it on. Want to go look at the things I bought from your mom down at the shop? You've never seen my antique store. Hey, remember the time I came over? And I dropped that crystal candy dish and you took the heat for me? Boy, did your mom get mad. I was like a little bull in a china shop, but I'd never seen such wonderful things. You know, it wouldn't be out of line to say I got my inspiration for my entire antique career from you and your mom's wonderful antiques. No, not out of line at all," she went on. "Why, I should thank you!"

Claudia closed her eyes and began breathing slowly, in and out, deeper each time.

"Are you okay?" Bobbie asked.

But Claudia was deep in thought, attempting to understand what she'd just lost, what she'd just found, and what it all meant.

The ring is really gone and it's my fault, she kept thinking, her mother's screaming ultimatum now like a broken record in her ears: *You'll lose it . . . you'll sell it . . . we'll never see it again . . . if it leaves this house, don't bother coming back. . . .*

All through her senior year, Claudia had threatened to run away, trying to make her mother hear her, see her, stop being the zombie she'd turned into since her father and her brother died. "It's been two years!" she'd yell at her mother. "Two *years!*" But her mother would respond only by looking at her with eyes so dead they could still give Claudia shivers.

If she could have pulled herself together, even just a little, to somehow save me from myself, like mothers are supposed to do, Claudia suddenly thought. But then she paused, still seeing her mother's eyes. And all the sorrow that had once seeped from the mansion's very walls, the hovering sadness that forced her to run away and stay away, came rushing back to Claudia as she sat in Bobbie's van squeezing her old letters. She remembered why she wanted so desperately to stop being either a Bass or a Darling, why she wanted nothing from the mansion that had turned from a childhood wonderland into a depressing old place full of dead people's things— except the one thing she'd been promised since birth. But when she'd asked for it and got her mother's ultimatum instead, the lingering fear she'd pushed away all her life had seemed true: her mother cared more for an antique ring than she did for her own daughter.

So at midnight, on her way finally out the door, she slipped into her mother's bedroom and snatched the ring from where it perched on the dresser like some shrine ever since her father was buried and her mother brought it home from the bank. She'd tried to take it with her, tried hard. But despite her hurting teenage self, she'd known her mother was right—something *could* happen to it—and she couldn't take that chance with the one piece of family she'd allowed herself to still feel something for. But she was not going to give it back to her mother—not *yet*. Instead, she'd quickly hidden it. She remembered the feel of the ring box's worn black velvet in her young grasp as she rolled back her great-great-grandfather's desk, opened the sliding middle drawer niche she'd discovered as a kid, placed the ring inside, and then rushed toward Bo on his motorcycle waiting down the block.

And she remembered how she'd regretted the stunt even before they'd hit the state line, and how, that very night, she'd written her mother a letter on cheap motel stationery to tell her where it was.

This letter, Claudia thought, gazing at the unopened letter clenched in her fist. Then she dropped it onto the others in her lap—every letter she'd written home, all sealed like the day they were sent. "I should go home," she said under her breath.

"This is your home," Bobbie pointed out, taking her eyes off the road.

"No," Claudia answered, "not for a long time."

"But you just got here!" Bobbie exclaimed, swerving to avoid hitting a parked car.

"Maybe I'm not meant to have the fitness club partnership this way. Maybe I'm not meant to have it at all." Claudia's eyes moved back to the letters. "Maybe it's finally time just to let it all go."

"Let what go?" Bobbie asked, now thoroughly confused. "You're Claudia Jean Darling! That's the Darling mansion! Those are the Darling antiques! All you have to do is stand up to your mother to save it all. You cannot let it all go!"

Claudia glanced Bobbie's way. "I just came back for the ring. I don't care about all those other things in that house. I can't."

Bobbie was at a loss for words. How could a Darling not care about her antiques? Doesn't she know their value, their importance? Why, why, she might have had a museum piece in her bedroom her whole *life!*

What Bobbie hadn't told Claudia Jean—what she hadn't told anyone—was that the call she'd made the moment she saw the elephant clock was to a museum curator in Houston she'd once met. The man had dropped everything to come all the way out here to Bobbie's shop not an hour ago and got so excited he took it back for authentication. Who knows what else could be in that mansion!

"You don't understand," Claudia went on. "I'm not my family and I'm not my family's things. I haven't been for a long time. I can't be."

Bobbie pulled the minivan to a halt at a stop sign. Her head was beginning to hurt. "What are you talking about?"

"It's hard to explain," Claudia began. "I'm sort of a Buddhist. At least I was. . . ."

Bobbie turned all the way around to give her old friend a dead-on gape. "Buddhist!" she erupted, narrowing her eyes. "C'mon, you don't fool me. You want all your family's wonderful things. You're a Darling!"

"Didn't you see my *mother*?" Claudia answered. "I can't be like her—I *can't* want them."

"Aha!" Bobbie exclaimed. "But you didn't say you didn't want them. I tell you what you sound like. You sound like a chicken! Are Buddhists chickens?"

Claudia looked blankly at Bobbie and then burst out a dark laugh. It was a sound that made Bobbie feel like the little kid from down the block, which made her furious and desperate not to show it.

Claudia stopped herself, smiling tentatively, apologetically. "I didn't mean to laugh, Bobbie Ann."

Bobbie jutted out her chin. "The Claudia Jean Darling I knew stood up for herself," she muttered. "That's all I'm saying. You never backed down."

Claudia studied the plump redheaded neighborhood girl who was now the plump redheaded small-town woman in the tight pantsuit and business wedges gazing so earnestly back at her, as if the years had only been minutes. And she was strangely touched. "I'm not that girl anymore, Bobbie Ann," she said, softly. "Everybody changes."

"No, you're wrong—nobody really changes," Bobbie spat out, shaking her head. "We're just like the antiques. We grow old and get scarred and beat up along the way, and the only question becomes whether we're going to make it until we realize what we already have is valuable. So you need to snap out of it and take care of your valuables!"

Claudia's eyebrows rose. "Is that what is bothering you so much? That my family's things I won't stop Mother from selling are worth a lot?"

As Bobbie jerked the car back into gear and goosed the minivan away, her chin went even higher. "Maybe. Maybe something I know to be worth thousands of dollars is more beautiful to me than something that isn't. I'll admit to such thoughts, all right? Yes, I know the best things in life are free—you don't have to be a Buddhist to know that. But what if the free things also happen to be the expensive things and they're yours just by being born?" Bobbie went on, hand flying off the wheel. "Don't you see, Claudia Jean?" She glanced her way. "The best things are free—for you! And it's just a . . . a . . . sin to turn up your nose at them!" Bobbie stuttered, throwing up both hands, momentarily forgetting she was supposed to be steering. "You can't be like 'one with the universe' if you won't accept what the universe has already dropped in your lap! And if Buddhists don't know *that*, they can go sit on a rock and be one with their own blind selves."

Claudia stared a little slack-jawed at Bobbie's diatribe, blinked, and then instead of responding, she gazed out the window again, which made Bobbie lip-chewing livid. And just as Bobbie was about to loudly articulate the feeling, she heard Claudia say something.

"What?" Bobbie asked.

"Stop the car, Bobbie Ann," Claudia quietly repeated. "Please."

"Huh?"

"Stop. Let me out—"

Bobbie reluctantly pulled to the curb.

Claudia got out and began to walk.

Bobbie rolled down the window, leaned out, and yelled: "I'm sorry, Claudia Jean! I'll see you back at the mansion. Right? *Right?*" But Claudia had already stepped onto the nearby sidewalk and was striding quickly away.

When she turned the corner and disappeared from sight, Bobbie glanced down to see the old unopened letters lying in the floorboard.

Ever so carefully, Bobbie picked them up, staring at the amazing things, completely unable to fathom the fact of them, how something written in the past by Claudia Jean Darling to her own mother could be here in the present—unopened. To say that she felt torn was not only an understatement but also a description of what she literally wanted to do to each envelope. The only thing stopping her was her respect for the past . . . her past. Because she couldn't help but feel these letters were somehow part of her personal past since the Darlings certainly were. She held up the top letter to the sunlight. Then with a weary glance back at where Claudia Jean Darling had just disappeared, Bobbie Blankenship leaned back in her minivan seat and sighed a long, hometown-girl sigh.

There's always one person in every high school who's the keeper of the flame, and Bobbie Ann Blankenship knew that was her. She'd once heard a famous psychologist on TV explain that the past is a place we visit every day and that most people never understand they do it. But not Bobbie; she'd always understood. "Bloom where you're planted"—that was her motto. She even had a memory room in her house—a 1920s bungalow, authentic to the period, wainscoting and the works that she totally rehabbed all by her lonesome.

And since she knew everybody and everybody knew her, she didn't mind planning all her tiny high school's reunions, keeping everybody's addresses up to date. She'd always get a band out of Austin and reserve the rumpus room of Del's Suds Shack down on the river. Nobody had come home famous so far. But it almost happened back when they were state champions courtesy of Mike Darling and John Jasper Johnson, she thought, sighing at the memory. Everybody was betting the farm John Jasper was going to be their Dallas Cowboy, and nobody would have bet against Mike going places his own hot-shot self.

At the thought of Mike Darling's death, Bobbie paused, momentarily feeling his loss as if it had been her own big brother, not just her friend's, who'd died so young. The whole town had felt it and kept on feeling it for a long time. And everybody still loves John Jasper, she mused. Not a reunion goes by that people don't ask if he's coming, which he never did. But not for want of her trying.

No, Bobbie was well aware she was the "go-to hometown girl." And while she liked to think Claudia Jean Darling called her out of the blue last year when she moved back to Texas because they were still friends, Bobbie really knew why. If Claudia wasn't going to call her mother, well, she knew little Bobbie Ann Blankenship would still be there to call. Because Bobbie knew that people might leave home and not talk to their mothers for years (and never return phone calls to hometown friends who call them back), yet people deep down, even people named Claudia Jean Darling, have a need to be connected in some way before all is said and done. Even if it's just that somebody has a phone number.

Bobbie allowed herself another little sigh, gazing again where Claudia vanished. So this is what I want to know: What happened to my Claudia Jean Darling? And what do I owe this new one? she wondered. Why should I give her back all her beautiful things I saved—the Tiffany, the china, the silver, and especially the elephant clock—if she doesn't give a flip about what God gave her?

Her eyes dropped to the letters in her lap.

And how can someone like me not read old letters left in my car written by someone like her?

"I mean, for crying out loud!" Bobbie yelled. "What is this? A test?"

Claudia had already sweated clear through her camisole and blouse, walking fast, putting one foot in front of the other along the sidewalks of her run-down little hometown, not exactly knowing where she was going, not going anywhere at all. Just moving.

What am I doing here? she kept thinking. If I were near my car, I'd just get the hell out of here. Go. Be *gone* . . . just like the ring.

She stepped off a curb.

A car tooted.

Claudia spun around to see an oddly familiar face—some now-wrinkled somebody from somewhere in her childhood—behind the wheel of an ancient Buick. The old woman waved her across; Claudia obeyed. "Watch yourself, honey!" the woman called as the old sedan puttered away.

On the far curb, Claudia placed her hands on her hips and forced herself to settle down—to watch herself. Don't think, she told herself. Just walk.

She looked around to see exactly where she was. Like most small railroad towns, she could see half the town from every curb. And this particular curb, she knew very well. A block down was the Baptist church where her mother dragged her and her brother every time the doors were opened; directly across the street was the tiny historic old Episcopal church, and behind her, a few blocks toward the railroad tracks, was the little city park, home of the rickety chain-linked high school stadium. From where she stood, she could even see someone on the field. So she headed that way.

Two boys—one black and one white—were throwing around a ball inside the little stadium. They had taken off their shirts and were hooting and hollering, high on being teenage and alive. She could smell the manicured grass as she got closer. The place had not changed in the least—the same signs, the same goalpost, the same scoreboard—as if it had been frozen in time the year she'd left. Maybe it had, she thought, in the way small-town football fields are after their glory years. Wasn't this why she'd so dreaded coming home again? The fear that she'd find everything the same, everything exactly as it was the moment she'd run as fast as she could from here?

Despite herself, her eyes and ears full of the boys on the field, Claudia had a sudden pleasant memory of a Bass, Texas, Football Friday Night. Since leaving Texas, she'd forgotten all about what football had meant. It was like some Greek production, pomp and circumstance on the plains. If you were a quick-as-a-buck variety of scrubby good-looking Texas boy, you were born to play, and an entire culture orchestrated around you. Girls vied to cheer for you. Marching musicians showered your actions with horns and cymbals and put on a show in your absence. Queens were crowned for you. Adults were hired and fired around you. If you were good and golden, you could write your own ticket. And her brother had been good and golden, he and John Jasper both—so very good and golden.

Claudia had now come to a dead stop, leaning on the stadium's cyclone fence, staring out at the boys on the lush field looking so much like Mike and John Jasper. *John Jasper Johnson.* She felt herself soften as her thoughts lingered on the name.

Newspapers as far away as Dallas had written up Mike and John Jasper. She could feel the metal stands groan under the weight of the cheek-to-jowl crush of fans coming to see the black-and-white lightning. And she remembered watching her brother becoming buddies with John Jasper, the photogenic, incredibly gifted black boy from across those tracks, defying their father and most of the town's white adults by running around with him all over both sides of town, nobody saying a thing because everybody knew who they were. At first, she hadn't been quite sure what to think about it, watching her big brother with a black friend from across the tracks. Then as the victories began to pile up, she found herself worshipping John Jasper Johnson along with everyone else on both sides of town. It had made football seem a bit like magic.

But the magic had its limits. She turned her head to gaze behind her toward the other side of the railroad tracks, toward what even the church people of her childhood called "nigger town." Through the leafless December trees and dead scrub bushes, she could see it was still there down to the same shacks backing up to the tracks with clothes hanging on lines and dogs on chains barking at everything that moved. And even if her sheltered fourteen-year-old self had been more than a bit clueless, Claudia knew full well that some of the same limits were still in place, despite the boys playing on the field so free and easy. It was one thing for sons from different sides of that track to be friends. But no black sons had better look twice at any white daughters, football be damned. And that had included "JJ" Johnson.

But that didn't keep the white daughters from looking at him.

As she began to walk again, along the stadium fence, Claudia felt a marvelous warmth flow over her, something young and sweet and thrilling, full of hero-worship innocence. John Jasper Johnson had never quite vanished from her thoughts for more reasons than his being forever linked to their family tragedy. Her first few years in California, with every wide-eyed sight of a mixed race couple, her mind would find her first forbidden crush. She closed her eyes, her head tilting ever so slightly toward the memory of her freshman year, before the wild and angry Claudia, before all the death and sadness.

John Jasper Johnson.

Claudia tried to hold on to the surprisingly nice feeling for just a little longer . . . but then another memory blindsided her: there before her mind's eye stood her sudden sprouting self at fourteen, breasts as big as melons ripening overnight like black magic. Big, bulky things in the way, throwing her tomboy-self off-balance, they were suddenly so big—so there—years before she had a chance to grow into her looks. She was the daughter of a father who didn't see her anymore and a mother so religious she couldn't even say the word "breasts" to her daughter much less explain their sudden *there-ness* and what it all meant. But at fourteen there was no stopping those melons from popping or her world changing because of them, boys she'd played tackle with now tackling her just to cop a feel of them, girls she barely liked comparing their own to them. And just like that, through the magic of breasts, she found herself popular. And "beautiful." And just like that, she wasn't just Mike's kid sister anymore. She was an attention-starved little girl at a feast, noticing boys noticing her, including her brother's buddy, the football hero, who happened to be black, who, unlike all the other boys, looked at her eyes instead of her chest.

Claudia paused, feeling anxious, knowing what was waiting

down this certain memory "lane." Her hall of shame with the boys in backseats down country roads after her family's world spun out of control. The angry, crushing longing of it, the sex-as-love-and-death of it, the way-too-early, fuck-the-world reality of it.

She had to stop. She froze in her tracks, directly across from the stadium's locker room entrance, and put her hands to her head.

Stop!

But as she focused all her energy on halting the wild-child memories, she was suddenly blindsided by an earlier teenage memory, triggered by the stadium surroundings, that came rip-roaring back in all its Technicolor chagrin and pain:

She was once again fourteen, hearing the sound of her brother's Grand Am out her bedroom window on a cool autumn day between her sprouting summer and the summer of the accident. It was the afternoon of a big game, although they were all big since her brother and John Jasper Johnson were the football heroes. From upstairs, she heard Mike come bounding through the mansion's big front doors with—for the first and last time—John Jasper Johnson. She'd rushed to the upstairs landing in time to see John Jasper following Mike in agile slow motion, taking in the foyer and the grand staircase and the big portraits of all the Bass ancestors lining the walls. To her freshman mind, it was like having a celebrity in the house, and her heart was pounding out a tune. She ran down to the kitchen.

"Hi," she'd said upon hitting the door, suddenly cool, so very nonchalant.

"Hey, CJ," both of them said in unison, John Jasper calling her by the same nickname as her older brother, which gave her a little thrill.

"Mother's still down at the church," she informed them. "I can help." And she'd never had a better time making a sandwich.

After they gulped down the food and left, Claudia remembered drifting out the open doors behind them to watch John Jasper Johnson lope down the front brick steps toward Mike's brand-new Grand Am—just as her father pulled up the driveway in his pickup.

Claudia saw her father glance her way, gesture Mike over to him, and then talk low and furtive, both of them glancing back up at her on the porch. She ran down closer to hear, but Mike was already marching back to the Grand Am. Claudia stepped in his way, waiting to be told what was going on.

Mike glared at her with his "clueless baby sister" sneer. "Leave it alone, CJ," was all he said, pushing past her to jump in the car with John Jasper and roar away.

So she followed her father into the kitchen. She watched him hang his Stetson on the peg, noticing he was even more preoccupied than usual, his shoulders hunched, his office dress boots shuffling across the tile. She knew better than to talk to her father when he was like this. But before she could turn to go, her father looked straight at her, really looking at her for the first time in a long time. For an instant, she saw the softly exasperated look he used to give her back when she was a little tomboy, back when he used to smile, when he was sometimes fun. But the look vanished into something else, as if he were just noticing how very much a teenage girl she'd become.

And then he said: "I want you to stay away from that boy."

Claudia frowned, confused. "What? . . . Who?"

"You heard what I said."

And she knew who. "But that's John Jasper Johnson!" she'd replied.

"Just do as I say."

Stay away from John Jasper? He's Mike's football buddy. She sees him every day at school. How was she going to do that? "That's stupid!" she'd said, as only a fourteen-year-old can.

Something darkly furious passed over her father's face. Something sad, conflicted, hard, old, like some personal memory of his own. It was an expression she'd never seen before, would never see again, and one she'd never forget, because that's when her father had slapped her with the back of his hand.

She stood there shocked right out of her outrage and into a whole new one, hand on her cheek, her mouth dropped open. Waiting for the next moment. And when it came, her father was speaking.

"Don't talk back," he said, his voice low as dirt. "Stay a good girl. And don't ever make me slap you again."

Suddenly, her father was a mystery. Until that moment, he was just her father in the way that fathers were fathers: he went to work at their bank, he collected guns and coins, and he did "oil speculating." He wasn't home much, and when he was, he was grumpy and distant, reading westerns in his bedroom at the far end of the hall. He and her mother didn't seem to get along, but he never cursed, drank, used racial slurs or any un-Christian thing her mother did not allow in the house.

And never, ever had he slapped her.

She stood stunned, holding her cheek, watching her father walk into the rest of the mansion.

The next moment Claudia remembered for its lack of oxygen. She had suddenly forgotten how to breathe. She was hyperventilating, but never having done it before, she panicked, stumbling out the kitchen screen door to stand dizzily under the sycamore tree, certain she was about to die. She felt her knees wobble. She bent over, waiting to fall to the ground. With her head below her knees, though, she'd accidentally done the right thing and her lungs filled with air again. She fell to her hands and knees. In a moment, she sat back on the grass. In another, she was standing up. And in another, she began to run. She ran across the front lawn and down to the street. She ran as hard and fast as she could and soon found herself on the highway; she rushed across and ran along the railroad tracks. She spied Mike's Grand Am returning over the next crossing a block away. So she went running toward it, but it had vanished. Catching her breath, she stared down at the tracks, which good girls did not cross.

And she crossed.

Even though she had no idea where John Jasper might live, she suddenly had to find him. She asked a dried-up old black man sitting on the steps of his little house who acted as if he had white girls asking him for directions every day. He just pointed at the house directly behind him, one street over.

In a minute, she was knocking on his door, a door attached to a ramshackle unpainted shotgun shack she barely noticed, because John Jasper Johnson appeared suddenly with no shirt on, staring at her as if she had landed from Mars.

"CJ? What the . . . ?" he sputtered, eyes darting behind her.

Her teenage self had lost all powers of speech. She wasn't quite sure why she was there, except that it would piss off her father. This daring thing, propelled by a slap, was probably how it all started, she now realized—her being the bad one, the wild one, the runaway—even before Mike died. But at that moment, she was just a hero-worshipping fourteen-year-old, feeling all arms and legs and sprouting breasts. Before she could say a thing, though, John Jasper was throwing on a shirt and herding her back toward the street.

"I'm walking you back right now," he said. As dogs began to bark from beyond the darkening shadows of the setting sun, they set out for the railroad track, John Jasper constantly looking over his shoulder. When they arrived, he gave her a slight push on her way over the tracks and stepped back. "Don't come over here again, CJ, you hear?" he said. "I ain't telling Mike."

Claudia remembered breathing hard but only from excitement. She was going to tell him she was a rebel, that she hated her parents, that her father had suddenly slapped her when she'd said his name. Instead, as he jogged quickly back into the shadows, his open shirt flapping behind, she stood there watching. For that instant, she'd forgotten the slap and her anger, feeling only the pure hormonal rush of her first crush. It was the single most thrilling experience of her short life—and it would last exactly four hours, when thrilling would turn mortifying.

She didn't go home. She went straight to the stadium and hung out until the game started. But she had no memory of the game at all, because of the moment afterward. As the stadium's parking lot emptied, she stood by her big brother's Grand Am waiting to catch a ride home—her heart pounding, her hormones bubbling. Because waiting with her was John Jasper Johnson fresh from football glory, who'd wandered out ahead of Mike. She hadn't noticed how he'd slowed when he saw her; she hadn't noticed how awkwardly he'd acknowledged her, glancing nervously back toward the locker room. She hadn't noticed because she was fourteen and alone again with her brother's famous, now forbidden black friend who was her friend, too.

So, mistaking John Jasper's awkwardness for the intimacy of secrets as a warm breeze blew over them both, she had dreamily leaned over to touch his hand. And to her horror John Jasper Johnson jerked back, glancing all around with a revolted look she could still see to this day.

But now, through the lens of a lifetime, Claudia saw the look for what it had truly been: kindness studded with absolute fear that had everything to do with train track boundaries and white men's daughters and nothing to do with her. Yet for a mixed-up fourteen-year-old white daughter, nothing had registered but rejection. And, just like that, Schoolgirl Adoration turned into Schoolgirl Hate. A hate that festered until everything went bad, with antique guns and brothers dying and fathers dying and mothers drying up and only John Jasper left to blame: *"You killed my brother—"*

She desperately wanted to believe she hadn't said that to his face the last time she ever saw him. But she knew she had, because she could still *see* his face. . . .

"Stop-*Stop!*" Claudia commanded herself, and by sheer will or some small cosmic mercy, she did. But she knew those images were back to stay, and for that, she cursed herself: "You idiot! Haven't you got enough to handle?"

She began to jog away from the stadium through the city park in the direction of the mansion and the reality of right now, but not before her mind wandered one last time to John Jasper Johnson—who should curse the day he ever met her family—wondering where he was and how life had turned out for him. But Claudia quickly steered her thoughts away from that, too, because she knew the answer could be heartbreaking and her heart could only take so much in one morning.

Reaching the other end of the park, having now sweated enough to be miserable in the unusual December heat, she slowed to wipe as much as she could from her face and neck, jiggling both her camisole and her blouse to help dry herself out. When that didn't work, she took off her blouse for a moment and waved it to create a breeze, fighting an urge to keep stripping right down to buck-naked crazy and be done with it.

Noticing a police cruiser passing up ahead, though, she stifled herself. As her eyes followed the slow-moving police car, they landed on the man behind the wheel and stuck, because the driver looked exactly like—John Jasper Johnson.

Claudia gave her head a shake, certain all the old memories were messing with her mind. She just stood there staring as the cruiser vanished in the direction of the mansion.

Then she was no longer staring, she was running. Claudia made it to Old Waco Road in record time, and as she rounded the corner of the mansion's lot, the voices of the teenage helpers on the lawn floated toward her:

"Dude, check out this old football in this cruddy box."

"Oh, man. 'State Champs.'"

"Look at all the teammate names on this thing! Hey, John Jasper! Catch!"

Claudia stepped onto the grass in time to see her brother's old football fly straight into John Jasper Johnson's hands.

And as she drank in the incredible sight, some young, long-gone reflex made her look back to see if her brother, Mike, had thrown it.

At the same moment, Faith also looked back from where she stood at the bottom of the front steps, a piece of hand-blown Venetian crystal in her hand. But unlike Claudia, Faith Darling saw what she was hoping to see.

"Michael?" she whispered. "Is that you?"

"Yes, ma'am."

Her son took a few steps toward her and stopped. Faith stared at his sweet face, his dark hair's cowlick, and his crooked grin, as he picked up another ball out of thin air and began twirling it, just as she remembered.

". . . How are you, honey?" Faith whispered.

"It's okay, Mom," he said. "It's not like you think."

"It isn't?"

"No, ma'am. Time's gone and all, but you can find yourself in between here and there if you start remembering things. Like what's happening right now with that ball over there: I'm throwing it and I'm waiting for JJ to catch it. And oh, man. Time, Space, Infinity—all Hallelujahs and Hail Marys and Roger Staubach—are in that perfect spiral on its way to his hands," he went on, twirling-twirling the ball. "That's a memory. That means something. It's hard to put into words. Harder all the time."

"You get to remember?"

"Yes, ma'am. But only if you want to. And only if you can find the words. See, what you do here is you work yourself away from words, slowly shedding them until there's no more need of them, because you're them and they're you—*wordless words*. And then, what you want, all you want, are the slow silent white fireworks of Who-What Made It All, calling it whatever you want to until you don't call it anything at all because you don't need to, you just don't need to anymore. . . ."

Her sweet son stopped twirling the thin-air ball, stilling it between his hands to look at her thoughtfully.

". . . But Mom, you've got to let go of things first. Understand? And those things are still all mixed up with words. I could find the words to tell you the way it felt when what happened that day happened. To tell you of the heat and cold and fear and blood. I could tell you the way it sounded. And looked. The sounds of my own dying; the very last thing, last face, I saw. I could do that. I could even probably tell you the reasons behind it all if I cared to reach back for them, Mom. But not so much anymore. Because I'm slowly getting rid of the need. Or the want. That's how it works. But that's also how people get stuck. Like . . . Like . . ."

"Like who, honey?" Faith asked.

"Like . . ."

"Your father?"

"Yes, ma'am," he said as the football vanished from his hands. "But, Mom, about me? It's really

okay.

Faith heard something break. Venetian glass shards were on the sidewalk, in the grass. And her hand felt sticky.

. . .

John Jasper Johnson, meanwhile, having just realized what he'd caught, barely glimpsed the white woman in jeans and running shoes before she was hugging his neck. He started to pull away from such a woman in such a place, considering he was still on the job and still on Old Waco Road. Not to mention that he didn't know who the hell she was.

Then—suddenly—he did know. He felt himself surrender to Claudia Jean Darling's embrace, his knee giving a little. And as Mike Darling's kid sister hugged him even tighter, he tucked the moldy old championship-game football in the safe crook of his arm.

John Jasper and Claudia stood about a foot apart, both working hard to find something to do with their suddenly empty arms, Claudia crossing hers, John Jasper resting his hands around his belt, both smiling self-consciously. They had just that moment stepped back a little from each other after their spontaneous hug, both full of the itchy, intimate awkwardness of time and circumstance.

"Sure glad you're back," John Jasper said, breaking the silence. "Got a call this morning and found your mama doing this." He waved an arm. Just then, the police radio in the cruiser squawked and kept squawking. He sighed, then headed toward the police cruiser. "Gotta go. Sure damn glad you're back," he said again over his shoulder.

Claudia, awestruck at the way this day was going, could only watch him vanish back into the cruiser and disappear down the street.

Inside the mansion's kitchen, Faith's hands were still trembling. She couldn't seem to stop them.

She pulled a small metal box of Band-Aids from the kitchen cabinet drawer, somehow separated a single Band-Aid from its wrapping, and applied it to her palm. And still her hands wouldn't stop trembling.

She kept thinking of her son, thinking that it didn't matter that he wasn't real. Because he was. In a way Faith had longed for. She must have some power over this . . . thing . . . happening to her that she didn't understand, something she might be controlling right along with the Almighty.

Then she reminded herself: "I'm just 'sundowning.' Like the doctor said. It's not real. Nothing is real."

Fighting for the old Faith Darling resolve, she took hold of the counter. But it was all too much. Michael *was* real.

"Can't this be over?" she gasped. "If I'm losing memories, then let me lose them, for God's sake—"

Faith sank onto a kitchen stool, tried to light a cigarette with still-trembling fingers, and then gave up, lowering her head to rest on a stack of magazines atop the kitchen counter. For the first time in years, she wished that she could cry.

Outside, Claudia was still staring down the street, where John Jasper had just disappeared. *John Jasper Johnson . . .* her mind kept repeating, as if convincing herself she hadn't just hugged a ghost.

She wiggled the neck of her damp shirt and sighed. What she'd hoped for after jumping out of Bobbie's van was some enlightenment. Instead, she'd sweated big, fat underarm rings and all she could think was: Had John Jasper noticed?

Claudia blushed at the ridiculous teenage thought. Then she cringed, suddenly realizing what was really bothering her—those last words her teenage self had said to him. And all she could think was: *Did John Jasper remember?*

Claudia gave herself a moment. It was all too much. Then, pursing her lips, she pushed her thoughts away from John Jasper Johnson's appearance in the middle of her mother's mess and forced herself back to the grown-up problem at hand.

What was she going to do now that the ring was gone? What was she going to tell her mother? And what about the fitness club? Whatever dim plans she had for coming back here were now shot to hell.

She glanced up at her VW by the curb, past all the antiques and sale customers between here and there. Should she let it all go and just leave? She knew the normal thing to do would be to try to stop these people from walking away with her inheritance. But, even needing money, Claudia couldn't do it. Her family's possessions were not good for her—never were and never would be. She couldn't explain something like that to someone like Bobbie. Part of Claudia, the best part, was pleased with this enlightened, rather Buddhist response. Yet she sensed the longer she stayed, the more her nicely detached feeling would begin to dim. Her jewelry-saving grab from her mother was proof of that.

Just then, somebody bumped her elbow. "Oopsie," said a petite woman apologetically, her hands full of tiny statuettes. Claudia saw that they were the delicate Italian porcelain angel figurines from her mother's locked curio case, and the woman was stuffing them all into a Safeway grocery bag. "Ain't these gorgeous?" she purred, now digging into her coin purse and scanning the lawn for Faith Darling, who wasn't even around to take her pennies on the dollar.

So Claudia turned toward the mansion, knowing she had to go in sometime, and headed inside to find her mother.

Taking the front steps slowly, she approached the carved front doors even slower. Then pushing them open, she strode in, instantly feeling a dozen eyes on her—the painted stares of all her Bass ancestors' portraits surrounding her like a painted welcome home party. But that was a familiar after-school childhood feeling. It was the echoing, empty foyer that was weird, spooking her ever so slightly.

Claudia had thought there was nothing more unmoving on the earth than the antique furniture in her mother's mansion. As a kid, she could run through the entire house with her eyes closed and never stub a toe. She thought the musty, brooding, haunted-house feeling she remembered, the way she'd always explained the mansion to friends, came from the antiques. Now, all she could think as she stood in the empty foyer was that her mother had moved out the antiques but that sensation hadn't budged an inch.

Claudia forced herself back into motion. "Mother!"

When she got no response, she headed toward the kitchen—and the sight waiting for her there made her forget all about the foyer. Claudia gaped at the piles of yellowed newspapers, junk mail, circulars, magazines, and mail—some almost as high as she was tall. She could barely see what was right in front of her, much less across the room, except for the sparkling-clean kitchen sink lined with perfectly arranged stacks of tea-bag tins, soup cans, sugar bags, and ketchup bottles, eight or nine deep.

Something is wrong, very, very wrong. . . . For a moment, that thought was all her mind could handle.

Winding her way through the kitchen, she passed the drawer her mother had left open. She saw the Band-Aid box and wrapper lying on the counter's edge with some tea bags and her mother's sun hat. She noticed an oven burner was on, the gas flame flickering for no reason at all, and she quickly turned it off. Then, feeling a breeze, she saw the door to the outside was wide open, her mother's circular trail as clear as bread crumbs. With another bewildered look around her, she grabbed up the sun hat and followed it.

Rounding the corner of the house, Claudia slowed, looking closely at everything. For the first time since arriving, she gazed beyond the antiques arranged so neatly across the lawn to notice the thick dust everywhere on everything and the unkempt look of the mansion's yard. She spied Faith standing quietly in the middle of the brick walkway, gently holding her bandaged hand to her chest. Her mother's face in direct sunlight without her sun hat showed all the wrinkles and creases natural for her age, and Claudia was startled by the sight. Only now did she truly study her mother for the passage of time: her mother's posture, the first thing she'd noticed when she'd arrived, was still too perfect. And yes, her figure was still just as thin and that jawline of hers was, still as ever, raised and proud. But now Claudia saw that her posture seemed all angles, bony, brittle, the skin of her jawline had more than just a slight sag, and the quality of her mother's "thin" now held a hint of "ill."

She began to call to Faith. But something stopped her, something about how her mother stood staring at nothing, her face empty of expression, empty of everything.

Something is very, very wrong, Claudia thought again. "Why didn't I see it before?"

As she made her way toward her motionless mother, her mother's empty face did more than scare her. It was now slowly squeezing her heart as she caught a glimmer in it of the young forgotten mother from her childhood. Then Faith began to stir, to come back to herself from wherever she'd been, and her face was once again that of the mother from whom Claudia had run. For the oddest moment, Claudia felt caught between the two faces. She watched her mother steady herself, take in where she was, check for her cash box under her arm, and, at last, slowly move up the walkway as if this happened all the time.

"It's in your bedroom, Claudia Jean. I told you," she said Claudia's way, as if she were finishing a conversation started somewhere else.

"What is, Mother?"

"The elephant clock, dear."

Claudia once again felt a squeeze around her heart. She watched her mother veer away to refold a stack of Turkish towels. Then she watched her mother glance back her way to ask: "May I help you?"

"Mother . . ." Claudia said quietly, "you're sick, aren't you?"

Faith's face changed, memory returning. She looked away. "I don't think the word 'sick' is really quite right," she said, hands paused in mid-fold. "No, I don't like it all that much."

"I'm calling Dr. Friddell," Claudia said.

"That should be interesting," mused Faith, back to plumping the towel stack once again.

"And why is that?"

"He's quite dead. My paperboy's father took his practice. Pea-something." Faith paused to wipe daintily at the beads of perspiration that had formed on her upper lip. Then she glanced back at her daughter and murmured to herself: "Look at that, she's cut off her long hair. Interesting I'd imagine her that way."

"Why are you talking as if I'm not standing in front of you?" Claudia asked.

"Because you're not. Don't feel bad, dear, it's been happening to me all day." She sighed. "Probably because it's my last day."

"Your last day of what, Mother?"

"My life, dear." Suddenly Faith yelled toward the sycamore. "Come back here, young lady! I want my nice brass and silver lighter back now! You're going to hurt yourself!"

Claudia set down her mother's sun hat on a table, moved up the front steps and back into the house to use the kitchen phone. She needed to call this new doctor.

Once inside, though, with the foyer's painted portrait eyes trained on her, she instead headed up the grand staircase to her old bedroom, taking the steps two at a time. She threw open her bedroom door and was stunned yet again: the room was a museum of Claudia Jean Darling, circa 1978. It hadn't been touched. Her Pat Benatar and Kiss posters still on the walls, her paperbacks still on the desk, her canopy bed still covered with her pink chenille bedspread.

But one thing was different. Her mother was wrong—the elephant clock was not in its place on the fireplace's mantel. As she stared soulfully at its empty space, a surprise wave of emotion she couldn't quite name whipped through Claudia, so pure. And sad. And personal.

How often do you dream of elephants? a therapist had asked her long ago.

"I don't know. A lot," Claudia answered.

"Interesting," the therapist had said. *"Wild animals can reflect a feeling of being out of control and an elephant can sometimes symbolize a large burden. Different cultures have different symbols. Hindu mythology has an elephant-headed deity of wealth. Western cultures, of course, associate elephants with memory. So a dreamed elephant could be an effort to remember something important, or, depending on your exposure to other cultures, a mixture of all of the above. Does any of this sound right to you, Claudia?"*

Faith stood in the middle of her sale arguing with herself about this daughter situation that was not going away. These Claudia Jean sightings felt different from the rest of her moments—and she wondered why. Only a few seconds had passed, but Faith had no idea how long it had been—being outside of time more and more as the day wore on. Still, she was certain that her mind had seen fit, in the last few hours, to give her two versions of the daughter she'd written out of her life. There must be a reason.

Hesitantly, she looked around to see if either daughter was still "here." The older Claudia Jean had vanished. But the younger one, the messy-hair little Claudia Jean in her little red cowboy boots was back.

Why, yes, there she goes right now, snatching things again with those little hands of hers and scurrying away, Faith thought. She took a step toward her child now sitting cross-legged under an upholstered chair, examining her new stolen treasure in her dirty little fists.

Faith felt an urge to hug her. Why had she been stingy with such things with her daughter but not her son? Yes, Claudia Jean had been a handful from the moment she was born compared to Michael, who was such a joy. But what kind of mother does not love her children equally? What had changed in this house between the two births of her children? What had changed inside her? Faith couldn't quite recall and she had a sudden overwhelming feeling she didn't really want to . . . something about Claude, something about her great-grandmother's wedding ring, something that had turned her sour and begun her slow unraveling long before her sweet son's death. . . .

Right now, though, watching her little Claudia Jean manifestation, Faith Darling wanted more than anything in the world to put her arms around the dirty little girl and hug her hard. But when Faith bent close enough to touch her, she'd wiggled away and vanished from sight just as she'd been doing all morning, leaving Faith wounded by the fear she saw in the little girl's eyes.

A new, old ache sat square on Faith Darling's chest. The truth was she had forgotten she still felt this way about her daughter—or about anything at all. She was certain such feelings were over long, long ago.

Straightening up, Faith placed her hand square in the middle of her chest right where it hurt, and begged for the fading to come over her again.

The little shoplifter peeked out from behind the big sycamore to spy on the old lady. She'd almost caught her this time. As soon as the coast was clear, she scampered again for the safety of the backyard shade courtesy of the mansion's other big tree—the centuries-old live oak that had been there long before there was a mansion or a town or a railroad or even a road.

Of the thick nineteenth-century Texas forest grove covering the small rise where the Bass mansion stood, only the big oak and the front yard's sycamore survived into the twentieth century. The two trees now draped the Bass/Darling mansion, front and back, like leafy sentries. The sycamore, with its beauty, size, and longevity, was the pride of Old Waco Road. The live oak, with a trunk bigger than a man could reach around, anchored the back edge of the mansion's lot. So even though it towered bigger and broader than the sycamore, nobody much noticed it since the dirt street it faced was lined only with beat-up bungalows full of wild, dirty kids raising themselves and wandering where they might. The only adults who might have noticed such a tree were busy with the rocky things of dirt-street survival that made a tree unimportant, even a big tree, even a big tree with a small secret known only by one Darling daughter of a generation ago: the musty hobbit-like hollow that had formed in the oak's trunk. Thanks to a long, prolific lineage of raccoons and squirrels, it was an opening big enough for a child to wiggle in. Big enough for a little Darling girl to have had her own secret world, to hide in and hide her treasures in.

Right now, a current young darling girl, a dirt-road wild-child in frayed T-shirt and stolen red cowboy boots, was curled snugly inside the hollow surrounded by a pack-rat heaven, sitting in a rusted-out stadium seat with the tips of her red cowboy boots poking out the hollow's hole. Off in the distance, coming from the dilapidated bungalow a block away, she heard a familiar sound. It was nothing important, just one of her worn-out mama's screeches for all her "little hellions"—the little shoplifter and her stair-stepped brothers and sisters—to get theirselves on home. Ignoring it like she always did until dark, the little shoplifter settled in.

Scratching her nose, she surveyed her finders-keepers domain with all the dusty, cobwebbed treasures she'd found there: a headless naked Barbie, embroidered hankies, a Mason jar of mint-condition buffalo nickels, a tarnished monogrammed silver teaspoon, a chipped porcelain cherub figurine, and a silver music box she opened just to hear it play (contents: three mismatched sterling-silver cuff links, two tie clasps, a cameo brooch, and a golden hair clip). Then, careful not to disturb the daddy longlegs or the roly-poly bugs going about their lives in the dirt and dust and tree grunge surrounding her, she pulled from her pocket a fancy flip cell phone and a polished silver and brass lighter.

She opened and closed the silver and brass lighter to hear the sound of its *clinkclinkclinkclink*, and then placed it inside the music box by the golden hair clip. She opened and closed the fancy flip cell phone to watch it light up and flash numbers, and then placed it on a gnarly root by the headless naked Barbie (pushing aside the

Walmart sack of batteries and the now empty peanut M&M's package). The cell phone suddenly began to *buzzbuzzbuzz* and *ringringring*, vibrating right off its perch into the dirt. She picked it up and held it in her grimy little hands, enjoying the feel and sound very much. When it hushed, she placed it back on the big root by headless Barbie.

Then she emptied her pockets of the last of her loot—a tiny black velvet-covered box with rounded corners. She ran her fingers over the little box's cat-furry velvet and then opened it to gaze at the shiny ring inside, brushing her finger over its funny-shaped diamond and little-bitty pearls. She eased it from the box and ran her finger over the curvy carved markings inside the ring:

L-o-v-e E-t-e-r-n-a-l

She tried the heavy ring on every one of her little fingers, even on her thumb. Too big. So she put it back in the velvety box and with a satisfying snap, she closed it. After opening it several more times just to hear *snapsnapsnap,* she carefully placed the tiny black velvet box on the big gnarly root beside the Barbie and the cell phone. Then she sat back.

With another scratch of her nose, the dirty little shoplifter nodded approvingly; it was good. She felt safe and snug and perfectly content in her own little hand-me-down world, feeling just like the tree-hollow world's creator had once felt. Because worlds you create are much nicer than the worlds that create you.

And such worlds are worlds never, ever truly forgotten.

TIFFANY LAMP COLLECTION

44 authentic, signed, stained-glass electric table lamps
designed by Mr. Louis Comfort Tiffany of Tiffany
Studios, New York, New York

Circa 1925–1939   *Value: $400,000*

---

*In 1925, James Tyler Bass III of the prominent banking Bass family of
oil- and cotton-prosperous tiny Bass, Texas, who now ran the bank his
grandfather founded, financed a generator that brought electricity to the
town. Upon converting his mansion's gas lines to electric ones, he immediately bought a signed dragonfly-motif Tiffany lamp for his new
bride, Pamela, delivered by rail, direct from Tiffany Studios, New York.
She liked it so much, he bought her another one, and another, until it
became a tradition with each passing prosperous year. With each occasion, anniversaries, holidays, birthdays, in they came—in all shapes and
sizes and colors, acorns, grapevines, butterflies, amber, iridescent, geo-
metric, opalescent—always signed by Louis Comfort Tiffany himself.
Until his wife told him to stop since she had no more places to put them.
He just smiled and bought her another. And he continued to do so, right*

through the Great Depression, which barely touched the town because of the East Texas oil boom, right up to the day his beloved wife died on her thirty-fourth birthday. And on that day, after placing drapes over the clocks in the house, he and their only child, nine-year-old Faith Ann, carried each lamp from all over the house to the formal dining room, where they placed them in perfect rows on the vast dark mahogany table, turned them all on, and left them on until dawn. And then, one by one, James Tyler Bass III turned them forever off.

In my Father's house are many mansions. . . .

. . . Faith Ann still has on her best Neiman Marcus black funeral dress and high heels, even though it's been hours since they buried her dear father, the preacher's familiar funeral scripture still echoing in her ears. She has just put her toddler son, Michael, to bed and kissed his little face, and now she is standing in the room she most loved in her father's entire mansion—the Tiffany lamp room.

One by one, she turns on every lamp covering the massive dining table and stands back. They are all brilliant and beautiful, and she's overcome with a brilliant, beautiful sadness. The lamps have not all been on since her mother's death so very long ago. Tonight, though, she is awash in her parents' love burning bright. And from the shadows, she imagines her father appearing, smiling through his tears at this beautiful shrine to his love for her mother, Pamela. Then her father vanishes and in his place stands her young husband, Claude Angus Darling, handsome in his black funeral suit, tie askew, a Lucky Strike dangling from his lips. He is smiling, too, sweeping her into his arms to sweetly dance her around the lamps. Faith Ann, the good Baptist girl who does not dance, is caught up in the moment— her inner light aglow with her parents' love and all the love of all the generations before them in this mansion, their mansion, her mansion—and the moment is so perfect, so full of love that, as they dance, she tells herself that she will leave the lamps on forever—

—until her husband stops, takes a slow, satisfied drag off his cigarette, and, still smiling, begins to turn all the lamps off, one by one. . . .

"Excuse me, ma'am?" someone was saying behind Faith. "Do you have any more of those beauuuutiful lamps?"

With a jolt, Faith returned to her sale from another of her moments, which seemed to be coming more frequently now. Dizzy, she put a hand on the long dining table that had been covered with Tiffany lamps only an hour ago, sagging from the weight of it all, the feeling like a poker to the pelvis each time she came back to herself.

No, this time it's different, she realized. It's more a burning. In my fingers. Faith dropped a cigarette that had just burned down to her knuckle and stood there staring at her raw skin.

"Oh! My goodness!" exclaimed the lady behind her who was holding a woven handbag as big as she was. "Did you burn yourself?"

Faith glanced down at the cigarette ash smear on her pristine white dress as she felt her fingers burning. Bright. And she forced herself to repeat her memory litany:

My name is Faith Bass Darling. I live at . . . at . . . at . . . 101 Old Waco Road in Bass. Today is December 31, 1999 . . . My grandparents . . . no . . . my parents are James Bass III and . . . Pamela. . . .

"Hold still, sugar." The skinny woman with the huge woven handbag was now standing in front of Faith, eyeing her burned finger. "I carry aloe vera in my purse; it's just the best stuff for burns. Let me dab a little on it. Ooh, you've got a Band-Aid on your palm. Did you cut yourself, too, sugar? You've got to be more careful!"

But Faith, her time and space scrambled, was still caught in the latest wave of her mind's softly shuffling memories, neither hearing the woman's chattering nor feeling the green goo. And as she continued to lean dizzily against the now empty dining table, the last of Pamela Bass's Tiffany lamps arrived at its new home.

At a tidy bungalow among the scruffy dirt-street houses beyond Old Waco Road, Angelina Lopez swiveled a hip, practicing a J-Lo dance step as she sashayed up to her frame house's front door after a morning of garage-sale hopping.

"Me, I got the style. I'm one hot *chiquita bonita*. You can call me A-Lo!" Angelina told herself as she opened the screen door, sassy loop earrings swinging, her arms full of her beautiful lamp from the big house. "I gonna be hot, hot, *caliente mucho mucho*," she said as she bopped into the kitchen to show off her *muy bonita* purchase to her *mamacita*. "And when I am, I'm gonna come back to this cowboy *barrio* and buy that old *gringo* lady's big *casa*. And *mi casa* not gonna be you *casa*."

"Talk right, crazy girl," her mother ordered, not even looking up from the dishes she was washing in the sink.

"How can I talk right when my own Mexicana mama never taught me *español*?" Angelina answered, setting Faith Darling's last Tiffany lamp down on their rickety kitchen table. "I have to get my native language from Telemundo?"

"Talk right! Talk English!" her mother went right on grumbling. "That's your native language, crazy girl! You are never going to get ahead in America unless you speak English. I taught you better."

Angelina cocked a hip and spun around, practicing a new move. "English has no melody, Mother. It's ugly, all angles. But *español*, off the tongue it rolls: 'Lamps. Slow. Crazy. *Lamposa. Poco. Loco!*' Which ones sing? Which ones are *muy* boring-o? I'm the *opuesto* of boring, *Mamacita*, I got style, *estilo*. See?"

But her *mamacita* wasn't listening; she wasn't even looking. "*Mamacita!* Turn around! Look at what I found at the sales this morning!"

Her mother made that disrespecting noise with her lips Angelina hated. "You just wasting my money on people's trash," her mama griped, refusing to look.

"Well, then, I'll just sell it for *mucho-mucho*," Angelina tried. "Then I'll go to Miami. Or Hollywood. I'm not gonna be Mexican-American, I'm gonna be Puerto Ri-can-American like J-Lo. Or maybe I'll be Cu-ban. And I'll say like a *bueno cubano, SOLA VAYA!* GOOD RIDDANCE to *Tejas!* I go where d'respect be!"

"Now you sound like those hip-hops," her mother answered. "One thing you're sure not, crazy girl, and that's black."

"If I'm a crazy girl, then call me *loco, Mamacita*—loco motion! Look!" And when that didn't even get her mama to look, she knew it was time to make nice. So she picked up the lamp and set it right on the sink, right under her *mamacita*'s nose. "Mother, look what I bought for a buck! A dollar! It's worth a whole lot more. I heard the people talking. Now I've got my own colored glass lamp! Maybe better than your Walmart lamp. Look, *Mamacita!*"

Her mother was not only looking, her mother was staring. Angelina had never quite seen her mother stare like that before.

"Where did you get this?" her mother demanded.

"At the rich old lady's big house—'*La-grande-casa*,'" Angelina proudly pronounced.

With that, her mother's head almost twisted off looking around at her. "'Rich old lady's big house . . .'?"

Flicking a wrist, Angelina gave the words a little snort: "Listen to that, Mama! This Latin *chiquita bonita* can't samba to 'rich old lady's big house.'"

But now her *mamacita* was looking at the lamp like she was seeing the Virgin of Guadalupe, and that scared her back into English: "Mom?"

Suddenly her mother was scooping the lamp into her arms and rushing out the door.

"Hey, that's mine!" Angelina yelled. "You got your own lamp!"

The screen door slapped shut behind her mother. She's taking it back? She's taking it *back*!

"Oh, that's the way it's gonna be?" Angelina yelled. Pivoting, she grabbed up her mother's Tiffany knockoff lamp from the living room, ran out the door, and hopped into the back of her mother's pickup just before she drove away, thinking: she takes my lamp, I take hers. It's a sale, no? Maybe I'll sell her *lamposa* for *mucho mucho* and keep the money myself! *SOLA VAYA!*

With her crazy girl bouncing around in the back, Juanita Lopez steered her little truck toward the mansion on Old Waco Road, deep in her own thoughts.

You come to America, she was thinking. You wade across the Rio Grande and you find a way to come as far as the fields of this town. And you only know dirty Rio Grande *agua* and the gnaw at your stomach's pit. You see these big houses and you don't know beauty. She glanced at the Tiffany riding in her floorboard. No, you don't know beauty. Then you go to work with your cousins cleaning those big houses and you walk into rooms full of dust and you make the dust vanish. It is what you do; it is what you are; what you must be. One day you walk into the biggest house in town, the house of the *señora rica ermitaña*, say your cousins—the "rich hermit lady"— who lives alone with only her old fancy things. The lady's big house has more rooms than you've ever seen in a house, all filled with the old fancy things that are all filled with dust. And you are warned that only God can help the help that moves—much less breaks— something in these rooms. Your cousins tell you they quake in their sandals each time they come to the big house for fear of such a thing. But not you. You are good, you will use your mind; everything has a place and everything in its place.

Then you walk into a room that is full of lamps—more lamps than you've ever seen—and you make the dust vanish in that room, too. And when you do, you are surprised by the sudden beauty surrounding you, beauty and light like the holy glass of churches. These you clean with your heart. Your rich lady sees your good work and soon you are in charge of keeping the holy glass beautiful. For no one. Not even for the rich, lonely lady who never turns them on. This you cannot help but notice. You wonder: Where are all the people to see this beauty? Where are the magicians who made these? And what is it that is giving these things the power to make you feel the beauty? They are somehow speaking to you and for a few moments the constant gnaw in your stomach's pit turns to thrill.

So after you make the dust go, you begin to close the door and turn them all on for a few moments. Just for you. And you stand in the room filled with colored, beautiful light and you are filled with the beautiful, as if you are seeing it with all the eyes of all the people who are not. And you are beautiful, because the light surrounding you—polished to sparkle by you—is beautiful. And you, the cleaning lady, feel somehow privileged more than the privileged lady who no longer sees it. And even now you are moved to tears by the memory and you cannot express why. All you know is that it is a feeling you've never known without priests and nuns to tell you what it is.

But then you worked on your English and you saved your money and obeyed the American law and dreamed your dream of a good American job and a good American life. And you stayed longer vanishing the dust of that big house than you'd planned, not just because you among all your cousins are the only one the rich lady did not fire. But because you felt you owned that moment every week and it owned you and you couldn't bear to leave it . . . that moment of lamps lit like colored music.

Then one day you did. You took a job at Walmart and you worked your way up to bookkeeper and every day you passed the aisle full of imitations of the beauty. Until one day you missed the memory of the room of beauty so much you bought an imitation beauty, hoping the colored music would once again thrill your stomach's pit. And you rushed the imitation beauty home to your little dirt-street house and plugged it in. But it only made you sad.

Before you came to this country, before you stepped into that big house, before cleaning all day to deserve the moment you spent with such beauty, the imitation of beauty would have been enough and you would have never known the difference. But now you do know. Your hands and your eyes know, even if your mouth cannot express it. And you wish that you didn't. But you are proud. And you say to yourself: *Juanita, you have a good job and a good American life and a beautiful family. You are living your Rio Grande dream. And it is real; it is not imitation!* And you keep the imitation of beauty to remind you.

Then this day, fifteen years later, your daughter Angelina brings into your little house a real lamp of beauty. From that room. From inside that big house. And your crazy girl says, "I bought it! For a dollar! At a garage sale! From a rich old lady!" And now, just like that, you own it? Did you die and go to heaven? Did the saints come down to visit you? No, this is America. You pay for what you get. You work for what you're paid. And suddenly the feeling you have in your stomach's pit is fear. You are angry and you are scared and you are proud, not wanting to tangle with the law over the lamp of a rich lady. Not that rich lady. Not after all your hard work. No! So you will take it back. And you will say: "Hello, rich lady. Here is your lamp of beauty. My crazy girl gave you a dollar for it and that is wrong. Because I know this beauty and you know that I know. But my daughter is no thief and I am no thief—even for beauty. So I bring it back and we will have no trouble, and you can keep the dollar." That is what you will say, all right. To the rich old hermit lady. Yes, that is what you will say. And yet you still feel the tears welling up fine and high just by looking at it. And you cannot deny that the beauty is speaking once again to your stomach's pit. . . .

Mesmerized by the lamp, Juanita had pulled her truck up to the stop sign at Old Waco Road and wasn't moving, so full of her thoughts, so unable to take her eyes off the beauty. Finally, a car passed, jerking her back to the moment and on her way again. As she turned onto Old Waco Road, the truck hit a pothole. Reaching out to steady the beauty on her floorboard, Juanita's hand lingered. She quickly snatched it away, and what she saw when she looked down the street at the mansion almost made her run right onto the curb—the amazing sight of the rich lady's old fancy things spread across the big house's big lawn.

Juanita gasped. How could this be? Her rich lady treated her fancy things better than she did people! Treated them like they *were* people! Juanita had seen her talking to the lamps of beauty and even the big pictures of the people on the wall. No, no—everything had its place and everything was always in its place, thought Juanita. Yet they were not in their place. Everything was out in the dead grass as if it were nothing.

Was her rich lady dead? she wondered. Only a dead rich lady would think her fancy everything was nothing.

Juanita parked her worn little Ford truck, got out, and turned toward her daughter, who was defiantly standing in the truck bed with the Walmart lamp.

"You stay here, crazy girl!" she hissed. "You stay here with that ugly lamp. You will not embarrass me." Throwing her purse over her shoulder, Juanita took careful hold of the authentic Tiffany, kicked the truck door closed, and marched toward the lawn, recognizing the fine things that she knew in a way only someone who'd cleaned them could. Forcing her eyes away from everything scattered like so much garbage across the dead December grass, it was all she could do not to scurry around looking for coverings to protect them. Recognizing the old cleaning maid feeling, Juanita got angry. You are not a cleaning woman anymore, Juanita Lopez! she told herself. You are no one's maid! And these are not your things!

She forced her eyes onto the people, scanning for the rich hermit lady whom she had never seen outside the walls of the big house. And there she was—in a sun hat, talking to a skinny lady with a big straw purse. Ah, good, the lady is not dead, Juanita thought. But she's smoking. Her rich lady didn't smoke. Maybe this was not her rich lady. But yes, yes, it was. Juanita studied her, wondering what had happened to make her not care for the beautiful things anymore.

But wait. Her rich lady wasn't moving at all, Juanita realized, and she didn't move for so long that Juanita inched nearer, gripping the Tiffany ever closer to her breast. Was her rich old lady sick? The skinny lady with the big straw purse was talking, staring at her rich lady's hand that already had a big Band-Aid across its palm. The cigarette had burned her rich lady's knuckles. Juanita came close to look at her wound. And that's when Juanita realized something: why, her rich lady no longer recognized her! This made Juanita proud . . . *proud!*

Hugging the lamp of beauty, Juanita didn't know what to do now with her prepared speech. As the skinny customer applied green goo from a packet she pulled from her big straw purse, chattering about aloe vera and first aid, Juanita's mind was alive with new thoughts. Her rich lady could never sell everything as if it were nothing . . . her rich lady had changed.

Gazing down at the lamp of beauty cradled in her arms that her crazy girl bought for $1, Juanita wondered what it is that makes something more than nothing. Was it just money? If a rich lady no longer put a high price on a lamp of beauty, then wasn't its true value in the eyes of the beholder of its beauty?

Just then, however, Juanita's thoughts were interrupted by a very old, very loud fat lady in house slippers and a housedress as big as a tent, shuffling right by her to stand in front of her rich lady. It was the old neighbor lady from across the street; she never liked that old neighbor lady, especially now that she was shouting at her rich lady. "I can't believe it!" the fat old neighbor lady yelled, spit flying. "They're all gone! You've sold all your Tiffanys for pennies to the town's riffraff and you wouldn't sell one to me! Fifty years I've been your neighbor, Faith Darling, and I'm treated like this? Why, I've never been so insulted!"

Could it be true? Juanita wondered. Careful not to drop her lamp of beauty, she climbed the front porch steps. Then with a look back toward her rich lady, she cautiously went in the doors, through the familiar foyer, then to the left, the pit of her stomach stirring out of forgotten habit in anticipation of the big room so full of beauty, color, and light. But when Juanita pushed the room's door open with her free hand, she saw it was now no longer a room of anything but dust.

Juanita could not believe her eyes. All the beautiful lamps *were* gone. As she slowly traced the outline of the empty room with her gaze, she suddenly realized she would never give her speech. She had no reason now. And the pit of her stomach was telling her why, because with another squeeze of the lamp, she knew exactly what she should do! Hurrying back outside to her rich lady, she eased the lamp down to her feet, pulled her wallet from her shoulder purse, took out all the money in it, and left it on the table right in front of where the rich lady stood. And then with a defiant, chin-up smile at the flustered, fat old neighbor lady—now watching her every move—Juanita wrapped her loving arms cautiously around the lamp of beauty and headed for her truck. Because all she wanted in the world was to go home and shine, shine, shine the beauty that was now and forever rightfully hers.

On the walkway, though, between her and her truck was her disobedient daughter standing with her own chin up and the Walmart lamp in her arms. Juanita prepared a tongue-lashing for her crazy girl. But then came a shriek from behind her:

"No fair! No fair!"

It was the fat old neighbor lady who'd put two and two together seeing both Juanita and her daughter holding lamps and came up with too many.

The next thing Juanita knew she felt the tent housedress brush her arm, heard those house slippers shuffle by, and saw a fistful of money being waved by the loud neighbor lady—at her crazy girl. "I'll give you three hundred for that lamp!" she was calling out. "Cash!"

Juanita gasped, seeing what her crazy girl was about to do. She was holding out the Walmart lamp—and *Holy Mother Mary*—the neighbor lady was taking it!

Before Juanita could get there, the deal was done and the neighbor lady was making her getaway past the little Ford truck and across the street to her own big house.

Angelina, counting the neighbor lady's money, looked up to see her mother headed her way *muy pronto*. Instinctively, she hid the money behind her back, waiting for her *mamacita* to blow. Would she yell at her for disobeying? Would she grab the money from her hand? Would she make her give it back to the old senora stupido?

But Juanita did the last thing Angelina ever expected her mother to do. She laughed. Until the tears came to her eyes, she laughed and laughed. And when Juanita finally stopped long enough to catch a breath, she just smiled at her crazy girl, her Angelina: her American daughter.

PORTRAIT OF JESUS

Mass-produced dark-hued print of Jesus with blue eyes
that follow viewer from every angle · 24″ x 36″ ·
Imitation gold-leaf frame optional

Circa 1960   *Value: $10 (frame)*

---

*On the morning of July 1, 1960, upon becoming president of Bass State
Bank after the death of his father-in-law, James Tyler Bass III, young
Claude Angus Darling found a present waiting for him from the staunch
Baptist deacon and old-fashioned banker when he moved into the old
man's office: a large, kitschy picture of Jesus Christ with blue eyes. Thanks
to the old man's prim, longtime secretary—who was immune to Claude's
charm no matter how hard he tried—it was hanging on the wall to
greet him.*

    *First he was mad at the old fool, still preaching from the grave. Then,
as he realized the picture's eyes followed him around his new office, he
began to laugh, until finally he took it off the wall and turned it face-
down. At the end of the day, he would take it home to the mansion—his
mansion now, he corrected himself—and talk his spoiled, holier-than-
thou wife, Faith Ann, into hanging this last thoughtful gift from her*

father in her sewing room where she and Jesus could enjoy looking at each other all the damn day.

Then sitting back in the old man's swivel chair behind the massive oak desk, he put his feet on the desktop, lit up his first Lucky Strike of the morning, and savored this moment a long time coming.

At the curb in front of the Darling mansion, Father George Fallow got out of his old Toyota to stare slack-jawed at all the things strewn across the mansion's front lawn. As he wandered up the sidewalk, he all but bumped into Faith Bass Darling standing in her sun hat near the front brick steps.

George cleared his throat. "Mrs. Darling," he began as dignified as possible. "Hello."

She turned her head slowly around, the sun hat moving as if in an orbit all its own. "Well, hello yourself, George. How nice to see you. What are you doing here?"

George paused. "You, ah, left a message on my voice mail."

Faith's face didn't change.

"You don't remember?" the priest asked.

Faith seemed to be considering the question, then, instead, said: "It's been a while, hasn't it?"

"Yes, yes, it has," he managed. Faith stared at him long enough to make him fidget. When George found himself smoothing down what was left of his hair, he stopped himself. "You asked me to come. I mean, I'm rather sure it was you. . . ."

She walked over to a box and put her hand out to grasp what looked like a gold frame sticking up from it.

For the moment that it took Faith to reach for and grab the top of the frame, George felt his heart leap to his throat, certain that, after all this time, she was about to give him back the church's water lily oil painting. He could already see it—it would be small and square with its ornate gold frame and its beautiful paint globs of blues and yellows and whites so artfully stroked. His mind excitedly jumped ahead at the prospect, thinking of how good it would feel to put the painting back in its proper place, to have that strange, lingering burden off his conscience, finally free from the tiny well-intentioned impulse grown bigger than it should have ever been. Then maybe, maybe he could begin to understand the young man he was the last time his eyes had been filled with it. His heart was pounding. *Yes!* he thought. Thank *God*—this was why she called! This is why I've come!

"Here, Father, take this." Faith lifted a big gold-painted frame at least three times the size of the small water lily painting and held it out toward the priest, who now found himself staring at Jesus—a cheap print of a bearded enigmatic Jesus with piercing blue eyes that seemed to be staring right at him. "Can't imagine why I had it," Faith Darling was saying. "Not really my taste, this trick it does with the eyes. Must have been a holdover from my Baptist days. Perhaps you can put it to good use."

She continued holding out the big dusty thing until the stunned priest slowly raised an arm and took it.

"Would you like some tea?" Faith offered. "I was about to go inside and make some."

"No, no, thank you," George murmured.

"Now, why is it you're here, George?" she asked, resting her hands on her hips.

Father Fallow stared at the picture of Jesus with the Mona Lisa expression and the come-to-me look—the kind of kitschy mass-produced picture that he used to see when he was young (if nowhere near this big). And he kept staring at it for the time it took him to reel in all his happy thoughts and find his tongue again. Finally pulling his eyes away from the blue eyes looking back at him, he repeated, "Mrs. Darling, as I said, you called me."

Faith cocked her head, her sun hat taking a tilt toward him. "I don't recall doing that. Are you sure?"

"Perhaps it was something to do with this sale?" he said wearily, scanning the yard for another gold frame. "It's all rather sudden, isn't it?"

"God told me to do it," Faith answered. "I'd imagine that sort of thing is always sudden."

That brought the priest's eyes back to Faith. "Excuse me?"

Faith gave him a disgusted shake of her head. "I've never understood this about you people. You talk all day to God but if God talks back, you just can't believe it. I mean, that sounds pretty silly to me. Say what you want about holy-roller Pentecostals, at least they expect a response for all that praying."

"God told you to?" George repeated.

"Yes, George, God." Faith fumed, leveling her gaze at the priest. "That's what I said. It seemed rather prudent to obey. Because I know why. I obviously have to get my house in order before I die. And since that's happening by tomorrow, I best get back to it." She moved past him.

George just stood there for a beat, digesting Faith Darling's words. Then collecting himself, searching for the right thing to say, he followed her. "Perhaps you're having a bit of a crisis," he tried. "All of us now and then feel the need to do some internal housecleaning. And sometimes just getting older—"

She stopped in her tracks, empty of all pretense or patience. "Don't give me your usual 'old lady' song and dance! At least come up with something original, for heaven's sake! I have Alzheimer's, George," she said, pursing her lips as if the word itself tasted bitter. "And since today is the last day of my life, I don't have time for this," she went on, giving the whole matter a dismissive flip of the wrist. "Take anything you want." She pivoted as if to walk away, but instead looked back at him as if she hadn't just pitched a small hissy fit: "George?"

Once again, George felt a stammer coming on. ". . . Yes?"

"Doesn't the soul have a memory?" she asked, now pensive. And then she raised her chin and stared straight into him. "If not, what's all this living for?" With that, Faith turned and left.

Father Fallow collapsed into a nearby leather wingback chair. His eyes fell on what he was still clutching in one hand, letting Jesus look enigmatically up at him with those eyes that never looked away. And he sighed a sigh of sighs.

"Well, hello, Father Fallow!"

George sat up to attention. It was Faith again.

"So nice to see you. How's your lovely wife?" she asked.

Once again, before George could form a coherent thought, Faith drifted off to the other side of the lawn. He slumped even deeper into the old cushions of the dusty wingback.

"Father?"

George turned his head and saw Deputy Sheriff John Jasper Johnson, who'd just slammed the door to his patrol car parked at the curb, heading his way.

"John," Father Fallow acknowledged glumly.

"Glad to see you here." John Jasper paused, looking at the frame George was still gripping. "You bought something?"

"Hmm? Oh. No, a gift," he answered, both of them now looking at Jesus. Then he pulled himself together and up to his feet to discuss the matter of Faith Darling.

"You talked to her, then?" John Jasper asked.

"Indeed I did," the priest answered, as they both gazed toward Faith. "She just asked about my wife," George added.

"I didn't know you were married, Father."

"I'm not," George answered. "Not for twenty-five years."

The two men glanced at each other, and then back at Faith, who was now selling a candelabra to a woman wearing a Burger King uniform.

"How long has she been like this?" the priest asked.

"Don't know," John Jasper answered. "She tell you why she's doing it?"

"God told her to, it seems," the priest responded matter-of-factly.

At that, John Jasper rested his hands around his gun belt and began scanning the sale for Claudia. "You talk to CJ?"

"Who?"

"Mrs. Darling's daughter, she just showed up." He kept looking around. "So, can you help me out here, Father?" John Jasper asked. "I'd call the Baptist preacher, but they don't have one again."

George cut his eye toward the deputy sheriff, wondering if he'd forgotten who they were talking about. "What makes you think I can do anything? You're the law."

"You're a priest," the big man answered.

The priest heaved another sigh. "John, if you knew how many old ladies I've known who think they hear God, you'd be shocked. I have two right now who think they are conduits of the Creator and that it is their duty to inform me of each new understanding from Above, especially pertaining to budgetary matters." George paused to watch

Faith take a single piece of paper money for a six-foot-long buffet. "While I give Mrs. Darling credit for a unique twist, it's an old theme. Trust me."

John Jasper screwed up his face. "Then how about the 'dying today' part? She tell you that, too?"

"Yes." Father Fallow slowly nodded, touching a finger to his lips in thought. "You know, perhaps it's something to do with all this millennium talk. World's ending and such. There's historical precedence for millennium fear." He paused. "And maybe even for this kind of giveaway, which is essentially what she is doing." George felt himself relax a little as he moved into the comfort of intellect. "Yes, actually, I can see a correlation. At the first millennium, in 1000 A.D., people believed the same thing, you know. That the world was going to end, the apocalypse at hand. Farmers didn't plant the next year's crops, monks stopped copying text, the rich gave away their belongings, and peasants stormed their lords' castles. Imagine their chagrin."

John Jasper, in no mood for a history lesson, interrupted the priest. "Yeah, okay, but, about the God part—"

"Hmmm?" George looked around at the deputy sheriff and then smiled, giving the idea a slight brush-away wave. "Oh, I doubt very much this yard sale is an edict from God, John."

"But it's not *impossible*," John Jasper shot back, a hand flying off his gun belt, "right?"

George paused, not used to the deputy sounding so animated. "Excuse me?"

"It can happen, right? It's not like somebody has to be crazy, right?" John Jasper was now gesturing with both hands. "I mean 'God' can do—be—something hard to believe, right? Ain't that like the whole point?"

"Well," George began, eyeing the deputy, "I believe faith calls for us to be careful how we interpret—"

"*'Interpret'?*" John Jasper cut him off. "You mean 'explain away'— don't ya? What kind of a goddamn faith do you call tha–?" The deputy stopped himself, biting off the rest of his blurt.

Taken aback, George paused. "Son, is there something you'd like to tell me?"

John Jasper was wrestling with himself, working yet again to control the old blood-rushing rage and all the mortal questions he'd been stuffing along with it for twenty years. He wiped the sudden sweat from his brow with the back of his forearm and fought to stay calm as, through his mind, raced the words: *Engines off.*

Father Fallow studied John Jasper Johnson, concerned for this man everybody in town embraced during his high school glory years and still loved like a wronged son. "John," he tried, "is this about yours and the Darling boy's accident? That would make anyone ponder the big questions. You've handled it all so—"

"Father, you don't know your *ass* about it," John Jasper spat. With that, he looked down, away, anywhere but at the priest, knowing he should apologize yet not about to. "I don't want you calling me a saint. And that was where you were headed," he muttered. "I gotta go." And he strode off, favoring his knee for no reason but memory.

George watched the deputy limp away. He dropped his eyes to his Jesus picture, his ears still ringing with the deputy's words: *What kind of a goddamn faith?*

"Father Fallow? Is that you?"

He jumped, feeling a presence by his elbow. It was Faith Darling.

Faith smiled sweetly for an instant, her face impossibly young. "You know, I truly enjoyed our afternoon studying your church's antiques. Such a pleasant time. We should do it again. But not for a while. Appearances are important. You understand, of course."

George found himself stammering yet again. "Of course."

As she wandered away yet again, George felt inexplicably as if he were watching Faith Darling vanish a little before his eyes, and a wave of sadness washed over him. All the years she'd been living in this place on her own, she was at least living, if troubled, and, in his mind, she was still the Faith Bass Darling he'd admired. But now he saw she was not.

Gazing at Faith, her perfect posture and elegant air now ever so slightly compromised, the funeral words he'd soon be saying over big Belva Bowman came to mind . . . *ashes to ashes, dust to dust, in my Father's house are many mansions* . . . And he suddenly feared that Faith might be right and he'd be saying the old words over her very soon, because he *did* believe it possible to will oneself to let go and die, the soul perhaps having more weight in such matters than we know. He'd seen such things with old people—if usually much older than Faith Darling. Or maybe he'd just done too many funerals. God knows he'd said words over more bodies than he cared to count. That's what he always felt they were—bodies, not people, by that point. In fact, lately, the only number he'd been able to keep in his head when the subject came up was the number 21—21 grams—the weight a dead body loses at the moment of death. Or so it's said. He'd once been the kind of man who jumped at the chance to debate whether the famous missing grams were truly the weight of one's soul. But after standing over as many dead bodies of old friends as he had, he had begun to see it as less a topic for debate than an article of hope.

And now, here amid the old mansion's antiques strewn across the lawn, with all this tumbling through his mind, he could only gaze longingly, sorrowfully, wearily at Faith Bass Darling, at what had become of her, at what would become of her—and at what he feared she'd wanted from him with her phone call. Ashes to ashes, grams to grams, mansions to mansions.

The vroom of the police cruiser's engine roaring to life made George turn to watch John Jasper Johnson's leave-taking. As the patrol car shot away, George was suddenly irritated, just plain tired of it all:

What do they expect from me? What does everyone expect of me!

But he didn't have the energy for a sustained snit and his eyes fell on the framed print he was still holding. The priest moved it left, then right, watching the eyes watching him. And not knowing what else to do, he shuffled toward his car, Jesus in hand.

Inside Geraldine Hitt's little house, four blocks down from the Episcopal church, the water lily painting sat perched atop the upright piano. Geraldine stood staring at the globby little painting she'd found inside the rolltop, trying to decide what to do with it. If nothing else, she could always hang it in the guest room where only Hiram's mother would ever see it.

But then, garage sale instincts kicking in, Geraldine began to inspect it. She searched the canvas's corners for the artist's name, finding nothing. So she carefully opened the back of the ornate frame just as she had learned how to do watching her favorite TV show, *Antiques Roadshow*.

What she found there took her breath away—a signature that read:

J. Claud de Monet

"Lord have mercy . . ." She drum-patted her chest. "Lord-Have-*MERCY!* Isn't that the famous *painter*?" she yelped as the thrill of her garage-sale career rippled down Geraldine's bargain-hunter spine.

"Hiram!" she crowed. "We're going to be rich!"

Father George and John Jasper, having driven off in opposite directions from Faith Darling's sale, had far too much on their minds.

Veering right, Deputy Sheriff John Jasper Johnson had almost taken out a fire hydrant getting the hell off Old Waco Road, deep into beating himself up for what he'd almost let slip to the priest.

While an utterly deflated Father George, turning left, was contemplating the quandary of what a person of the cloth does with a picture of Jesus he doesn't want.

He pulled to a stop in the church parking lot and sat there a moment, just staring at the cheap Jesus print. Finally, wrestling the big picture from his old Toyota, George lugged it into his office, careful not to stumble on the crumbling step, and leaned Jesus against the nearest wall. Checking his watch, he sat down to get back to the business of coming up with the expected joke and blessing for his noon budget committee meeting to help it go smoothly. But he made the mistake of looking back at the painting, and now he couldn't take his eyes off Jesus, who wasn't taking his eyes off him.

Frowning, George sat back in his squeaky desk chair to wipe at his brow, feeling a little feverish after the warm, strange morning. He studied the enigmatic picture out of the corner of his eye, and, retreating into the comfort of intellect again, began thinking of Catholic icons, of statues and paintings and shrines and shrouds that inspire mystical manifestations of people's imagination: faces of Jesus in pancakes, saints appearing in tree bark, Mary statues crying tears of blood. And he must have been staring a bit too hard, because Jesus' piercing blue eyes now seemed to be welling up with . . . tears.

George froze. Blinked. Then, eyes wide, he leaned toward the picture. Now (*of course*) Jesus looked totally dry-eyed.

My Lord, tears? the priest thought, chuckling nervously. Settle down, George, ol' boy, he told himself as he eased back in his chair.

The old priest swiveled around to gaze at the Currier & Ives print above where he sat, hoping its snowy nineteenth-century New England Christmas scene would help cool down his obviously over-heated brain. Instead, it just reminded him of the little water lily painting and his stunning naïveté for expecting a bit of George-shaped grace at Faith Darling's sale to fix his small personal obsession. As if the Creator of the Universe pays any mind to such silly things as water lily paintings.

George folded his arms and swiveled back around, embarrassed at the thought, just wanting to forget the last hour. But the one thing he couldn't quite dismiss was John Jasper Johnson's outburst: *What kind of a goddamn faith?* He wasn't sure which bothered him the most about the deputy's words—that its insinuation might be true or that someone else had noticed.

Could he have once thought it infinitesimally possible that God was speaking to Faith Darling?

Retreating yet again into the comfort of intellect, the priest was suddenly contemplating the word "God," considering how it wasn't really a name at all but a capitalized noun: *The* God. The Supreme Being With No Name who told Moses to call him Yahweh, which just means: "I Am Who I Am." It was as if the Creator of the

Universe was making a riddle. But why? George cocked his head, working on the thought: Could the Creator have known the Created made in his own image would only try to possess anything named? That we just can't help making things over in my own image?

The old priest stiffened, instantly hearing the gaffe he'd just made: *my*.

And suddenly, with Faith Ann Darling before his eyes and the deputy's words in his ears, Father George Fallow dizzily felt the punch of a personal epiphany:

I'm a priest made over in *my* own image. . . .

Aren't I?

George sat up, swallowing hard, knowing the sound of truth when he heard it. All these years . . . was that the real problem? Had he become a priest not because he loved God, but because he didn't? At least not like he should. He should long for God like his father and grandfather. But he'd only longed to long for God, hadn't he? It was as if he thought that if he became the picture-perfect priest, doing the good work, saying the right words, acting the right part, that his father and grandfather's passionate longing for the un-explainable would just come—as if it were just a matter of finding it along the way.

And it had never happened.

Instead, he'd settled into a safe God of common sense, beautiful words, and plodding service, hadn't he? A nicely explainable God. And the only revelation he'd ever experienced was the kind he'd just had—that there would be no voice of God, no Jesus tears, no re-deemed water lily painting to save him from his burned-out logical soul: Did you hear the one about Episcopals being the first to enter heaven? The dead in Christ shall rise first. Maybe he should use that joke today. But he'd just be talking about himself.

The priest looked back at Jesus, who was still staring back at him.

No, George, old man, he told himself, it's time to accept who you are and what you are, and maybe to start planning for early retirement.

There was nothing more he could do for Faith Ann Darling. Or Deputy Johnson. Or even, it seemed, for himself. With that, he sighed the sigh of all sighs, perhaps of his entire mediocre career.

He checked his watch again. Now he had a budget meeting followed by a funeral. There was still some comfort and meaning in service. Plenty of time to prepare before the noon meeting if he just focused. God forbid he be late and not have a joke and a blessing ready for the committee members.

"And God knows I could use a blessing," he mumbled, pushing away the fear that he'd become the joke.

At the same moment, five miles out of town, Deputy John Jasper Johnson was still beating himself up. He was sitting in his cruiser at a crossroads, motor idling, staring down a weedy old river bridge road that led to an old oil lease and a concrete bridge forever in his nightmares.

He'd avoided this old road his entire adult life, despite driving all over the county as a deputy. He could always find a way to keep from going by Claude Darling's oil property and the scene of the accident—nothing on earth could make him take the goddamn road.

But John Jasper had sat at this crossroads more times than he could count. For years, when the blood-rushing red rage would come over him so bad it'd flat scare him, he'd find himself out here staring down the cracked pavement until calming all the way down. He hadn't come out here in so long he thought he was done with it.

But the way he blew up at the old priest had him sitting right here again, thinking about what he'd almost blurted out:

Engines off.

That was the image that had kept thundering through John Jasper's mind as the priest jabbered on, because that's what it felt like that goddamn day . . . soaring . . . silent . . . engines off. . . .

But you don't up and tell somebody something like that, John Jasper thought, watching the swaying of the roadside weeds in the breeze. Not even a priest. There's no way to make something like that sound right coming out of your mouth. Especially mine, he thought, since I ain't what anybody around here would call a religious man. "And I don't want anybody to start thinking of me as getting religion, either, that's for damn sure," he muttered. Something weird like that could be the last straw that could lose you friends or even a job—he knew that for a fact. Some words you just can't take back. But he couldn't help what he remembered, what those moments between living and dying and living again felt like:

All calm. Silent. Weightless. Wind wrapping him up like arms.

John Jasper had been seeing this in his head for going on twenty years, remembering the soft breeze on his skin, face, legs, like he'd cocked a window on the moment and flew right out of it.

He wasn't stupid. He knew a person's mind can play tricks. He'd heard all about people's near-death experiences, the out-of-body thing. And he'd tried real hard to believe it was something like that and let it go.

But I'm done, he told himself. Whether it was Something Bigger or not, don't matter at all when it gets right down to it. Because it wasn't meant for anybody else and wasn't meant to be told to anybody else. What it was . . . was fuel, he'd finally decided, for what happened the day I should've died along with Mike. So I could keep on going, living, moving on.

That's the way it felt, whether it made a bit of sense or not. The moment when all hell was breaking loose, grown men screaming, blood gushing, concrete crashing, tires leaving the bridge road, what it really felt like right before the worst was:

Quiet

Engines off

Flying.

Bobbie Blankenship stood in front of her old Sears oven, circa 1969, staring at her copper teapot, Claudia's old letters in hand. She was about to find out if the steaming trick she'd seen in movies really worked. When the teapot whistled, Bobbie opened the lid, held one of the letters over it, and, voilà, with a touch of a little Bobbie finesse at the edges, the letter seal opened.

Gingerly, she laid it on the genuine Formica top of her early 1950s chrome kitchen table, nudged the flap back, and pulled the letter free. The story she saw unfolding there on the Formica made her heart pound and ache at the same time, her eyes returning to the same passages, the same words:

> January 4, 1980: . . . *I didn't take the ring, Mother. It never left the house, just like you wanted. Go see for yourself . . . But I won't come back, not for a long time. Maybe not ever. . . . You're my mother. And I needed you. I always have . . . but not anymore. . . .*

Bobbie quickly steamed open the last four unopened envelopes and found that each one contained an unsigned marriage announcement, except for the last one, almost eight years old, which held only a new address:

June 28, 1984: Claudia Stephenson, 3721 Sand Aster Drive, Carlsbad, CA
March 6, 1988: Claudia Armstrong, 3 Shell Beach Street, Oceanside, CA
March 13, 1991: Claudia Kendrick, 232 Avenida Rorras, Solana Beach, CA
January 31, 1992: Claudia Darling, P.O. Box 183, San Diego, CA

Bobbie suddenly felt a little sick. And she knew why. She was sick
with regret. It was as if she finally grasped why it is called an "inva-
sion" of privacy. Possessing these letters, opening them one by one,
was like peeping in windows or watching a car wreck; it was impossible not to look, not to open, not to read, yet the longer she looked
the more she wished she hadn't. But there was something else, the
regret went deeper. It was also for herself, for the loss of a long-
nurtured little-girl dream of the Heaven of Being a Darling that had
remained intact all these years beyond all reason, despite all proof to
the contrary.

Bobbie sunk down in one of her shop's genuine antique repro-
duction rockers to sit, rock, and think for a while. To get used to the
change in her universe. To enter the world according to her childhood friend who'd written her young heart out to a mother who
refused to read anything at all. When she finally got up, Bobbie re-
sealed the old letters as carefully as she had unsealed them.

Then the phone rang.

"Ms. Blankenship? I tried you on your cell phone." It was Mr.
Delacroix, the curator from the Houston museum.

Bobbie began to blather. "Sorry, sorry, I seem to have misplaced
it. . . ."

"Ah, well, I have good news. This may be quite a find. But very
few of my colleagues are still in the office because of the New Year's
Eve holiday. And they need to see this. I assume you *are* the owner?"

Bobbie paused. Then she heard herself say:

"Yes. Yes, I am."

"Then with your permission, we'll pursue the authentication and we'll talk after New Year's."

Bobbie put down the phone, feeling euphoric, yet, at the same time, a little sick.

She stared at the phone a moment.

She glanced at the letters.

Then she went to find Claudia Jean Darling.

Back inside the piled-high mess of a kitchen, Claudia had finally come back down from her bedroom and was now maneuvering her way around everything, headed in the general direction of where the wall phone was the last time she'd seen it in 1979. And there it still was. She hadn't even had to worry about finding a phone directory. After all, there was a pile of them under the phone.

Claudia paused. With another glance around the room—its dusty clutter all but confirming her fears—she summoned her courage.

Picking up the directory on top, she thumbed quickly through the slim phone book to find the first number she needed, knowing full well it would still be the same. It was. She dialed.

"Bass State Bank, may I help you?"

"Hi . . ." It took Claudia a moment to figure out how to explain who she was to the young, lilting female voice who answered. "My name is Claudia Darling. I'm Faith Bass Darling's daughter . . . of the Bass family?"

"I'm sorry," the voice answered. "There's no one here by that name."

"No, no, you don't understand," Claudia said, hating the sound of it all. "My father, Claude Darling, was the president of the bank—"

"No, that's not the name of our president," the voice said. "Who did you say you were again?"

But Claudia couldn't go another round. "Could I speak to someone who's worked there a really long time?"

"Well, okay," the voice said, rather reluctantly, "but most of the older employees like to take an early lunch. Please hold."

Soon, though, Claudia was talking to a career teller, a Miss Hazel Ledbetter, who liked her lunch at noon and who did remember her family. "Helloooo, Ms. Darling, so nice to talk with you! We sure miss your daddy and granddaddy around here," she crooned. And after a bit of awkward "I remember when's," Claudia was soon connected to the current bank president, a stranger.

"It's an honor to talk to a family member of the founders of the bank and our nice little town," he began. After more awkward "howdyadoo's," Claudia stated her reason for calling, was put on hold a moment, and then she heard something she could hardly believe.

"Mrs. Bass—excuse me, Mrs. Darling—has not had an account here in decades," he explained. "It seems that when your family sold the bank to our corporation right after your father's passing, your mother closed out all her accounts along with her safe-deposit box."

Claudia gave her head a quick shake, trying to get her mind around the news: She took out all her money when she sold the bank? But why would Mother do that? "And where did she put—?" Claudia caught herself, realizing she had just said the last part out loud and the new president of her family's old bank was still listening.

"Is everything all right?" the man's voice asked.

She thanked him and hung up before having to field the familiar small-town nosy mixture of concern and curiosity. Her hand, though, lingered on the phone; she felt more than a bit blindsided.

Needing a moment to find her balance, she gazed out the kitchen window toward the sycamore, watching her mother arranging and rearranging items on a bookcase.

Finally, she picked up the phone book again and thumbed through the small list of doctors in town until she found one named Peabody, the closest one to her mother's "Pea-something" memory blip. This time, with a single mention of her mother, she was put right through to Dr. Gerald Peabody. Soon she was listening and listening hard, nervously wrapping and unwrapping the long stretched-out cord around her fingers.

"A deck of cards," she repeated.

"A shuffling deck," Dr. Peabody was saying. "Your mother thinks you're not real because of a phenomenon called 'sundowning,' which scrambles, shuffles, and sorts memories, often playing them out in some real or imagined fashion before a patient's vision. It's a side effect of the plaques and tangles of protein accumulating around her brain's nerve cells, slowly causing them to die. And they can be vivid in late-stage Alzheimer's like your mother's."

"Plaques and tangles," Claudia murmured.

"It's a relief to finally talk to a family member," Dr. Peabody went on. "Your mother has been adamant to the extreme about her privacy, so it's rather providential you've arrived. She'd begun to miss appointments and I'd feared the worse. Then two days ago, she appeared for a checkup on her own, surprised at my surprise. And now this sudden sale of hers—she must be miraculously focused between her episodes, totally contradictory to the disease's usual cognitive discord. Quite remarkable . . ."

As the doctor continued to talk, the facts mounting up, Claudia leaned back against the wall for support. Finally, she interrupted: "How long?"

"Excuse me?"

"How long has my mother had this?"

She could almost hear the doctor shrug. "She's classically pro-
gressed for the decade I've known her, but early-onset Alzheimer's
such as hers can play out over twenty years."

"I'm sorry. . . ." Claudia paused. "Did you say twenty years?"

"It's possible."

Claudia slowly slid to the floor. The doctor was still talking.
Something about their long-term care center, about her mother bolt-
ing on her visit there, refusing to be some patient she recognized.
Claudia, though, was no longer listening, stunned at the import of
plaques and tangles on unopened letters and long, painful silences.
She felt queasy, all her memories in rewind, everything up for grabs.

Then she heard the doctor's voice from a long way away: "You do
understand how serious this is, what your mother is facing?"

"I'm trying," Claudia answered.

Dr. Peabody paused before going on: "Then forgive my indelicacy
in telling you this: your mother has always been very neat and proper
with her appearance, always immaculately dressed, as you know.
When she was last in my office I noticed urine stains on her dress.
That often is the moment a patient begins to deeply deteriorate—a
loss of bladder and bowel control and the embarrassing public moments created by them."

Claudia winced.

"Your mother's mind's retreating—that's her reality and future.
The center's really the only safe option. And soon. Before something
serious happens."

Leaning her head all the way back against the wall, Claudia lowered the phone receiver to her lap and closed her eyes for a moment.
Plaques and tangles.

"Ms. Darling, are you there?"

She raised the phone back to her ear. "Doctor," she began, "did you know Buddhism teaches that what exists in the mind *is* reality?"

The doctor hesitated before answering: "I know this is a shock. We'll talk it through, I promise. Right after New Year's."

Getting to her feet, Claudia hung up the phone in slow motion. A breeze blew through the sycamore's branches outside the kitchen, the calming sway of the branches in the tall windows catching her eye. Then the kitchen's old air-conditioning unit rattled back on, its finicky thermostat bringing it whomping back to life loud enough to make anyone else jump, but it was an old familiar sound for Claudia. She turned her face toward it, its cold air another kind of familiar—the feel of a California beach morning—then sank back to the floor trod by all her Bass generations to let the doctor's words and her mother's new reality settle in.

Her mother had Alzheimer's . . . her mother would soon be and not be . . . her mother had become a Zen riddle.

Claudia began rubbing her temples, trying to rid herself of the thought. She didn't need riddles, she needed concrete thinking, answers to what she had just heard if there were any.

Yet despite herself, a Zen riddle popped into her head:

What is the answer?

And then, of course, the frustrating, inexplicable Zen punch line:

What is the question?

Claudia gave up, dropping her hands. Because the truth was, for the last twenty years she'd been pretty much a Zen riddle, too, hadn't she?

What is the meaning of everything? Yes.

What is the way? Go!

She hadn't allowed herself to think much about it since the day her Texas plain-speaking soul finally got tired of all the Zen double talk and gave up on Buddhism. Just rolled up her mat and ran away. Like she always did. Like she'd done her entire adult life. Yet so much of Buddhism still made sense to her. She still couldn't step on an ant. She still thought twice before she swatted a fly, still believed in karma and the idea that everything was connected. Buddhist philosophy was certainly better for the kind of life lived beyond mansions. When everything you have is taken and you are left with nothing but your ommmms, it works so much better than the alternatives. A real Buddhist would say: "My things are only things. They don't possess me," she thought. "What's mine is yours. My mansion, your mansion. My antiques, your antiques."

Isn't that better?

Claudia pulled herself to her feet. *Isn't it?*

She gazed through the tall windows of the mansion's big kitchen toward the yard sale. Just a few feet away, a lumpy woman in flip-flops was opening and closing the drawers of a tallboy chest that had been in her father's room and her grandfather's room and probably her great-grandfather's room, while nearby, still and lifeless as a piece of furniture herself, stood her mother. She knew what answer her generations of Bass relatives would give her: their true-believer Faith was call-the-cops-crazy-sick and had to be stopped.

But what do I think? Claudia wondered, suddenly realizing she was seeing her mother through her own reflection. She knew full well she wasn't strong enough to be a real Buddhist, and she had no idea what she truly was. But Claudia did know that the best part of herself still did not want to be a Bass or a Darling. She needed things to be just things and houses to be just houses. To be nothing more, she thought as she stared at her mother, nothing more that could make her anything less.

Claudia began rubbing her temples again:

So what—now—*is* the question?

Fighting to calm down, she closed her eyes and tried a few yoga breaths—in, out, hair to toenails, inhaling, exhaling, deeply, desperately—futilely—because this time it didn't work. All she felt was light-headed from all the damn breathing. And when she grabbed for the kitchen counter to steady herself, she knocked over the stack of her mother's unopened mail instead.

After a few seconds of cathartic cursing, feeling better than she had in hours, Claudia bent down and began picking them up. That's when her eyes were caught by several letters with the same two words in red ink stamped across the envelopes:

FINAL NOTICE

Quickly shuffling through the mail scattered around her, she found even more—gas, electric, utilities—all with the same warning in red on the envelope. But the most ominous bore the Official State Seal of Texas. That one, she ripped open and began to read:

This letter is to inform you that a lien has been placed on your
property at 101 Old Waco Road, plat 0001 of record for Bass
County, Texas, for failure to respond to all official inquiries
concerning unpaid property taxes now in arrears for the years
1992–1999 plus fees in the amount of $122,001.02. If you feel any
of the facts in this decision are incorrect, or if you no longer own this
property, or you are currently filing for personal bankruptcy, you
have the right to appeal this decision to the governing body of the
Central Texas Tax District by appearing in person before the County
Tax District's court on or before Jan. 2, 2000.

For a wobbly moment, Claudia gaped at the words. She raised her eyes to gaze out at her mother, who was now depositing what looked like a quarter in her cash box as four men picked up the massive mahogany dining table that had been in their family for five generations and carried it away.

Bobbie Blankenship sat in her minivan near the Darling mansion, searching—the hundredth time—for her cell phone. She got out, slammed the van's door, and turned to gaze down Old Waco Road. "Boy, word sure has spread fast," she groused, weaving through the cars parked willy-nilly.

Up on the lawn, she saw Claudia Jean's mother talking with a bunch of high school boys—what looked like half the starting lineup of the high school football team—who were moving more things from the mansion. Bobbie's antique-store-owner soul slowed, her fingers lingering on each thing she passed, and she had to whip it into submission to keep focused on finding Claudia Jean.

Not seeing her, Bobbie hesitantly made her way past Mrs. Darling and the boys to scurry up to the mansion's broad porch and through the carved front doors. "Claudia Jean?" she called to no answer. So she headed up the grand staircase to the same place she'd been that morning—her childhood friend's bedroom.

There she found Claudia Darling standing with her arms folded, vacantly staring at something across the room. Bobbie paused, unsure how to act considering the way Claudia Jean had hopped out of her van an hour before. She followed Claudia's gaze across the room, to the fireplace mantel—the empty mantel—and Bobbie cringed. A minute passed. When she couldn't stand it any longer, she asked: "Uhm. What are you looking at?"

"An elephant," Claudia answered, hardly loud enough for Bobbie to hear.

But Bobbie heard, all right. "Claudia Jean," Bobbie began, "I meant to tell you something earlier—"

"You believe in ghosts?" Claudia interrupted, not looking around.

Bobbie frowned. "What?"

"This place always felt loaded with ghosts," Claudia said. "I'd forgotten just how much." She paused. "But if you've really forgotten something, I don't suppose you know you've forgotten it, do you?"

Bobbie recognized an inner dialogue when she heard it, so she just waited, moving her weight from one shoe to the other.

Claudia kept staring at the empty mantel. "All the years I was gone, I didn't recall anything very clearly about growing up here, probably on purpose. I've blocked out most of what happened on the days my own brother and father died. Yet that elephant clock I never forgot; I couldn't live without it as a child—its trunk moved." She absently wiggled a finger and sighed. "Guess it's already gone, too."

Bobbie started up again. "No, listen—"

"Even the antiques are ghosts," Claudia went on, gesturing weakly at the mantel. "No wonder she thinks I'm not real. Maybe nothing's real."

Bobbie opened her mouth to start yet again, but then Claudia said something that made Bobbie momentarily forget everything else:

"Mother has Alzheimer's."

Bobbie gasped. "Whoa, that explains a lot."

"And she has no money left in the bank," Claudia went on. "She took it all out years ago."

"Whoa!" Bobbie gasped again. But how can that be? The Darlings are rich. Or are they? The question was making Bobbie a little ill and she wasn't even related to them. Then, her eyes darting around her, she suddenly thought: Could the money be here?

"I just wanted one thing out of all these things, you know?" Claudia was saying. "And I only wanted that because I thought it was my chance to get the fifty thousand dollars for a real future of my own. But nothing now feels real. That big magic number—fifty thousand—doesn't even feel real. Or even big. Not anymore."

Bobbie was feeling more confused by the second. "Claudia Jean, what are you talking about?"

From her jeans pocket, Claudia pulled the lien letter she'd found in the kitchen and handed it to Bobbie.

The weight of what Bobbie Ann Blankenship was now reading, plopped on top of everything else, sank Bobbie right down onto Claudia's old canopy bed. "What are you going to do?" she asked breathlessly.

Watching Claudia closely, arms folded, still staring at the empty mantel, she read her friend's mind. And that propelled Bobbie right back onto her feet to head off any such nonsense: "Hold on now, Claudia Jean Darling! I know what you're thinking. You're thinking you have no right to interfere with this ridiculous sale because you ran away." Bobbie waved the lien letter at her. "But this changes everything. If the things at the sale are all she has left, all *you* have left—and she owes all this on the mansion—" Bobbie's cheeks flushed red. She stomped her foot. "You've got to stop the sale right now!"

Claudia only sighed, pulling her arms even tighter around herself.

All the way over to the sale, Bobbie had been preparing a speech she had to say before she weakened again. She knew her antique-dealer soul—she knew the longer she kept any of the Darling antiques, the more she'd long to keep them, the more she'd rationalize a way. Especially the elephant clock. Yet she also knew that if she kept them, it would always feel wrong. That went double now that the Darling mansion was in trouble.

So Bobbie straightened her shoulders, summoned all she had, and launched in: "Claudia Jean, I have something to say: I bought as much as your mother would let me. The best stuff—like your Spode Gloucester china and your Gorham Imperial Chrysanthemum sterling silverware. And the rarest Tiffany—"

Claudia, though, was only half listening, missing the point entirely. "You should keep whatever you bought, Bobbie Ann," she said over her shoulder. "I know how much it means to you. It's okay."

Hearing that, Bobbie pretty much swallowed her tongue, doing yet another moral backflip. "*NO,* it is *not* okay!" she blurted, putting so much into it that a clump of her red hair fell into her face. Smoothing it back, she made herself settle down. "No, it's not okay," she repeated, softly, evenly. "You have to take them back."

But Claudia, still lost in thought, hadn't heard a word.

Frustrated now, Bobbie plopped her hands on her ample hips and got down to business. "Look, you're still in shock or something, that's what it is. But even Buddhists have to eat and pay for sick mothers and save family mansions. So we need to focus, Claudia Jean. I've been thinking about this, and if we stop this sale immediately, everything could still be all right. I can sell the antiques for you on commission, and then—"

But just as Bobbie hit her stride, Claudia Jean turned and wandered out of the room.

Bobbie stared after her for a long, cranky second. Then, realizing she was still holding the lien letter on the Darling mansion, she slipped it into her jacket pocket and followed. She found Claudia standing at the bottom of the grand staircase turning in a slow circle, taking in the entire foyer, until her eyes landed and stayed on the foyer's heavy drapes.

"Now you're spooking me—" Bobbie called, stamping down the stairs. "You're staring at curtains!"

Claudia looked back her way as Bobbie huffed to a stop by her side. "Bobbie, have you ever heard of people draping clocks?"

"You mean after a death in the family? Yeah, it's some old custom. Why?"

Claudia stared past Bobbie for a beat; then, for no reason she could explain, she drifted back up to the top of the stairs and turned slowly around to face the foyer below. She took a good solid hold on the banister as a memory began to trickle back. And then another and another.

This is where I sat, so I could see and hear everything from up here all day . . . she realized. Except for the emptiness of the foyer below, right now, this very moment, could be the day Mike died and she could be the fifteen-year-old Claudia Jean who has come out of her room at the sound of the ringing telephone, to stare down at the day that changes everything, happening at the bottom of the stairs.

She sees her mother, through the door leading to the kitchen, answering the phone. Claudia sees her knees buckle, sees her rushing out to be gone for hours without telling her daughter where she'd gone. Then she sees them both return, her father and her mother, together but alone, her father's arm in a sling, his face bruised and swollen. She stares at the glaze over her parents' eyes as they move past her, up toward their rooms, as if she did not exist. As they pass, she sees blood, a glimpse of it on his clothes, a spatter of it on her mother's sundress hem. And behind them comes Dr. Friddell, who has brought them home and who has to be the one to tell her.

Then the memories of the rest of the day's images blur, fast, fast forward to the sound of the ticks of the grandfather clock echoing through the foyer. Claudia sees all the covered dishes that friends and neighbors have brought. She sees the banquet laid out along the big kitchen buffet and overflowing into the family dining room amid the Tiffany lamps, like some pagan burnt offering. She hears all the coming and going through the front doorway, the rattling of the kitchen air conditioner going off and on. She hears the kitchen's screen door slapping, and feels the sensation of each slap as if it were across her face. She feels the press of people below like a river moving by, their whispers floating up to her up here in this place at the top of the stairs where she stays and stays and stays so she won't have to mind her manners with the church people discussing "God's will." Or talk to anyone—anyone, at all. She doesn't see her parents again for hours and when she does, she sees that they cannot look at each other. And worst of all, she sees they are both working hard not to look at her.

Claudia feels herself sink to the top step of the dusty landing, her hand still holding on to the banister. She gazes through the railing's spokes, and in her mind's eye she watches, feels, her fifteen-year-old self standing, sitting, waiting in the dark, being shuffled here, there, long gaps of time with no sound, not even the grandfather clock's ticking. She hears only whispering. She feels out of place, in any place, wrong in just being alive . . . in not being the one who died. And she remembers how her teenage self wanted to scream that in-nate understanding over the whispers—the clear kind of awful truth a kid knows, just knows, no matter what a sister survivor might be told.

She stops herself from seeing the funeral home viewing time. She cannot conjure her brother in the casket; she is willing herself not to. All she sees are his hands, those football hands, crossed, sickeningly still. And she remembers nothing else until she is back sitting here at the top of the stairs again after the service, seeing everyone leave as the day turns to night. From up here, she sees her mother place a black cloth drape of some kind over the grandfather clock and she sees her father march into the foyer and yank the drape off. Then she sees her mother, without any words exchanged, move back to the foyer, pick up the drape, and place it carefully over the grandfather clock again, smoothing it out, gently, caressingly. To stay.

And from up here on the stairs' landing, covered with cobwebs and dust, Claudia could now see the hole in the space of them all, a hole where Mike should be, a pinprick at first, then growing steadily, daily, into the huge yawning gap of Mike. She recalled her teenage self working hard to cope, repeating to herself over and over: *I can't think about this now. I'll think about it tomorrow, when I'll know what to think.* But tomorrow never came and the feeling became frozen, and with it, some part of herself. By the time she was doing it all again in just a matter of days when her father died, she had nothing left to tell herself at all.

But it was always there, right where I stored it, she now realized, her mind still working on that tomorrow that never came.

Claudia closed her eyes to let those lost days and their impact mesh with all the lost runaway days that had followed:

For the first few months, camping on California beaches or sleeping in cheap motels with her motorcycle prince, Claudia had sometimes allowed herself to daydream. What if the accident hadn't happened? What if Mike hadn't died and I hadn't left? What if my family hadn't vanished before my eyes? she'd wondered. But while she sometimes imagined her parents in her "what if's," more often than not her daydreams roamed the possibilities of a life with an older brother in it. She imagined them both in the same college, close, maybe even dating each other's friends. Or anything-but-close, dating each other's worst nightmares. She imagined them handling their parents as a tag team. Or she imagined them fighting over something and not speaking for years. She even imagined them ignoring each other completely, living their own lives. Growing old, growing bald, growing fat, growing wrinkled. But being there, always being there. Like normal siblings, normal families. Her daydreams roamed here, there, everywhere, because they could, because there would never be a Mike, ever again.

Only one daydream ever lingered long enough to invade her real dreams. But it wasn't like her elephant dream. It was the kind of forgotten dream that she'd wake up trying to go back to sleep to finish yet never quite recall why. It was the kind that was always out of reach of her conscious mind, the kind that went unacknowledged for years, long after her motorcycle prince was gone and she'd settled into a restless life along the Southern California coast.

Then one day a therapist had asked: "Do you ever dream of your brother?"

Suddenly the dream was as big and "there" as any elephant: she'd see Mike in a crowd, at a gym, on a beach, along a trail in a redwood forest, along a muddy riverbank. And she'd run toward him, to the miracle of him, but he'd never see her, he'd look right through her as if she weren't there, as if she were the ghost, the one dead yet not gone. And even though she "saw" the entire recurring dream the instant the therapist asked, she'd lied.

"No," she had told the counselor. "Never."

But then the therapist had asked: "Do you ever dream of your father?"

Claudia remembered not hearing the question at first, off somewhere hearing only her own lie. When the words sank in, she'd said—as if she had forgotten the meaning of the word: "My father?" And when Claudia heard herself saying "no" again, she recalled feeling a sigh of relief that if she were to be haunted, it was not her father who would be the ghost of her life.

But now, once again sitting on the mansion's upstairs landing after all these years, it occurred to Claudia that maybe what she'd really been haunted by were a handful of hours, minutes, and seconds of a single day: the one long-suppressed ghost of a day watched from above. Claudia stood up, fueled by the sensation of all the stored memories finally sinking into place. It was the day all the rest of my days have boomeranged away from, she realized, all the befores and all the afters. And she knew the same was horribly true for her mother as well.

Staring down now at her mother's clock-less foyer, empty of everything but drapes and woodwork and the family's portrait parade of the dead, she suddenly understood the draping of the clocks, too.

Time stopped, even as it continued on.

It can—it did—do both.

"Claudia *Jean!*"

"Claudia *JEAN!*"

Claudia snapped back to herself to see Bobbie below, standing spread-eagle in the middle of the wide-open front doors, gesturing for her to come outside.

"John Jasper just drove up! He'll be a big help," Bobbie called up to her. "And your mother's about to sell your Cable Nelson player piano—come *down!*"

John Jasper was already heading their way up the mansion's brick walk by the time she'd come out on the porch. Seeing him after all she'd just remembered upstairs, Claudia kept wanting to shake herself, her reaction twenty years too young and too raw.

John Jasper was now within earshot and Bobbie began babbling, filling John Jasper's ear about this, that, and the other. So for another relieved moment, Claudia didn't have to say anything. Thankfully, Bobbie kept on talking for a nice long while, giving her time to settle into the reality of him. A deputy. Standing in front of her. On her mother's porch. And she kept having the same thought: Why would John Jasper Johnson help my mother after all our family did to him? He was acting as if there were nothing unusual about his being there at all.

"John Jasper was one of the first over here, like me," Bobbie was saying, glancing over her shoulder. "Tell her, John Jasper. I'll be right back. Your mother's going to sell the player piano for pennies, I just *know* it. That piece restored could be worth five grand easy!"

They both watched Bobbie scurry away, then turned back to each other.

John Jasper smiled. "How's it going?"

"She did all this just this morning?" Claudia began.

He nodded. "Started up crack of dawn pulling everything out."

"But why?" Claudia asked. "She give you any reason?"

"She says this is the last day of her life," he answered.

Claudia paused. "She told you that, too."

For a beat, both of them glanced toward Faith, who was now drifting into the mansion, Bobbie trailing behind.

"You think it might be possible?" Claudia finally posed.

John Jasper paused. "You talk to Dr. Peabody yet?"

Claudia sighed. "Yes."

"She's sick," John Jasper said, knowing now it was a fact.

Claudia nodded. "Alzheimer's."

John Jasper's face dropped. "Ah, damn," he cursed softly. "I was afraid of something like that." He sighed. "Well, she's been her sassy self all day. I got my doubts about any buckets being kicked before tomorrow, but it's hard to tell for sure since she pretty much never leaves the house."

Claudia took this in for a moment. "Never?"

John Jasper shook his head slightly. "She's been getting people to deliver things to the house for years. After a while, stuff I started hearing made me ask around a bit. Learned she quit going out at all except to the doctor and the hairdresser. Then she made the hairdresser start coming to her, things like that. But the times I stopped by, she'd seem fine."

Claudia looked at him oddly. "You've been stopping by?"

He shrugged off the question. "Now and then."

Claudia kept studying him. "Has she ever done anything like this before?"

"Maybe, now that I think about it." He frowned. "A few years back, her yard and her flowers started looking pretty bad. That sure didn't seem right. You know how neat and particular she always was. When I came over, she didn't give me the time of day, acted like she couldn't understand a thing I said, then just shut the door on me. I won't lie; that surprised me. Next day she seemed back to normal, but I started checking on her after that. Nothing seemed all that out-of-line from what I was able to see. Till today."

Claudia found herself at a loss for words, taking all this in. "John Jasper . . ." she finally murmured, "why have you been so good to her?"

Just then, Bobbie came bounding down the mansion's front steps to where Claudia and John Jasper still stood awkwardly, inches apart. "Do you know where your mother is now? Back upstairs! Standing like a statue in front of that closed-off bedroom at the end of the hall," Bobbie explained. "I bet those antiques are coming down next."

Claudia took in a breath; she knew whose room that was.

The three of them looked at each other and then around at the sale. The lawn was beginning to clear of sale items if not sale customers, and they knew it was about to be cluttered again with a whole new round of antiques.

"You've got to stop this, Claudia Jean," Bobbie pleaded.

"What do you think I can do?" Claudia asked.

"You're her daughter!" Bobbie howled. "You could get a lawyer. Surely her doctor would do some sort of vouching, wouldn't he?"

"Not in time," John Jasper pointed out. "She'd have to be declared mentally incompetent, that sort of thing. And she's not breaking any laws I can figure."

"Did you tell him about the lien letter?" Bobbie said, whipping out the property tax lien final notice from her pocket and thrusting it at John Jasper. "Look at this!"

Claudia sighed, watching John Jasper begin to read, feeling an odd sense of embarrassment.

He looked up at her and said nothing for a beat. Then: "We can fix this."

"Yeah, by *stopping* the sale!" Bobbie exclaimed, nostrils flaring. "For crying out loud, why won't your mother just let me take the rest, like I've been saying all day?" At that, Bobbie cocked her head, placing a finger to her lips in thought. "You know . . . I could do it anyway. . . ."

John Jasper and Claudia both cut an eye toward her.

"I'm just saying—" Bobbie threw her hands up. "I mean, what would happen if we just yelled 'STOP'? Why are we always so afraid of one old woman?"

Faith found herself standing in front of the master bedroom's closed door. But this time she didn't run away, because she was beginning to grasp why. She listened to the silence. And she wondered if she was alone.

In this room, Claude Angus Darling had taught her all about the silence between a man and a woman, a husband and a wife, the kind that makes the intimate act of physical love something with loneliness at its core. Something that crushes any storybook hopes of Song of Solomon love into the silent fumbling acts of procreation she came to hate. Until finally she'd ended them by moving down the hall, leaving this one room of her family's mansion to him, beginning their separate lives in separate ends of the mansion . . . beginning their separate peace.

Faith paused at those words, fighting the urge to plead with God to spare her this. But that was a whole other Silence, wasn't it? She glanced quickly upward. "Is this what you want?" she demanded, edgy, defensive.

With that feisty sideways prayer, Faith Darling felt the full force of the void of all those years of not speaking to God—an emptiness so sharp and visceral that her wobbly old hand had automatically gone to her heart. Faith steadied herself against the doorframe.

She was so tired. She was trying hard to do whatever she was supposed to do to get her final ultimate blessing before day's end—to "go" before she was gone, determined to have it whatever she had to endure. But she was rusty in this communicating with the Creator of the Universe, as if she'd once known a foreign language but lost it by refusing to speak it. After the fluent wonder of her midnight message, she wasn't quite sure whether feeling this Silence again might not be worse than feeling the one on the other side of the door.

It had begun with her son's death. All her Bible-reading gave her no peace. All her praying got nothing but Silence. And all her churchgoing turned only to noise full of the horrible Silence that comes with the loss of a true believer's fine certainty about the way things have always been and always will be. Faith longed to yell, *Speak up!* but couldn't talk that way to her Heavenly Father, still her late deacon daddy's daughter. And when the Silence went on, she'd closed the mansion doors behind her, deciding to just be silent, too.

Her hands began to tremble. She pulled them to her chest to still them, her cut, burned hand sharply stinging, and breathed in. It used to be so natural talking to God, as natural as breathing, Faith recalled. As natural as waking and sleeping and going to church on Sundays. Praying was part of the day, part of life, of every waking moment. For a motherless child living in a mansion, it was like being introduced to the most Real Kind of imaginary friend. And the blessing that came from it—the "peace that passes all understanding"— that feeling had been just as natural, hadn't it? Faith sighed quietly at the tender memory of such amazingly blessed peace. Even now she couldn't deny that the sudden loss of that peace, in the face of all her other losses, had felt like the disappearance of a part of herself. And she missed it. She missed her life before the pain, before she matched her silence with God's. Before she began to blame the Almighty for everything, because the Almighty was easy to blame. After all, if God was the one "from Whom all blessings flow," as claimed in the Sunday doxology she'd sung her entire life, then wasn't God the one Who turns off the blessing faucet as well?

And yet.

She missed it so . . .

Leaning against the doorjamb, she allowed herself to do something she had denied herself for two long decades: she thought about life before everything went bad. Back when the blessings came like a steady river and no one questioned its beginning or end. Faith felt herself breathe easier and softer. She felt the old comfort of the world in which she once had daily talks with God, when everyone she *knew* had daily talks with God. Not talking to God would have seemed odd back then, she remembered. Of course, God talking back happened so rarely no one thought it much of a problem this side of burning bushes. No, it was the nudge, the inspiration, the conscience, the "still, small voice"—that was how God talked back. Or so her Sunday school teachers had told her, along with how very blessed she was to be the daughter of her saint of a father.

Blessed.

Blessed beyond blessed.

Faith placed a still-trembling hand on her dead husband's bedroom door.

And when you are that blessed, coming from a long line of the blessed, you have no expectations of anything but more blessing, do you? she pondered, momentarily closing her tired old eyes at the thought. Claude had seemed like just another blessing, hadn't he?

With that, Faith Bass Darling saw the one important person she had not seen yet—*herself*—as the innocent face of her twenty-seven-

year-old blessed-bride self, Miss Faith Ann Bass, floated to the front
of Faith's mind.

And the sight forced another sigh right out of her.

A sigh of what? Faith wondered even before she finished sighing.
Regret? Chagrin? Too big a bag of hindsight? But she couldn't help
mellowing as she drank in her younger peaceful face hovering before
her mind's eye. She had been so in love with the idea of Claude
Angus Darling that she had failed to notice that he didn't quite care
for her as much as he did her blessings.

But being blessed poses this type of problem, doesn't it? mused
the now older/wiser Faith. If you feel blessed, if every person you see
treats you as blessed, if you are heir apparent to generations of such
blessing made manifest in an earthly mansion full to busting with
material blessings, you may fail to notice that being blessed might
have little to do with God or with yourself or even with the man
who decides to marry you. You may not even notice that you weren't
blessed with the physical beauty of the other women in your family
tree no matter how you comport yourself. And you may have no
clue, most unthinkable of all, that being blessed just might come
with an expiration date.

Faith winced, wishing away the vision of her young unlined face,
so naïve, so achingly unaware of what her future with Claude Angus
Darling would hold. But it had seemed so preordained, hadn't it? she
thought, resting her gray head against the closed bedroom door.
After all, she'd met him at church. Claude and his mother were
front-row Baptists, sitting in pass-the-plate distance from her and
her father. Yes, Claude was only twenty-two to her twenty-seven, but
that didn't matter. Yes, he was new in town, but that didn't matter.
Yes, he was poor, but that didn't matter. And oh, how he could talk
a bird down from a tree! Faith had forgotten that, forgotten it the

same way she'd forgotten the last time Claude Darling had set foot inside a church door.

Back then, she hadn't even minded how other women continued to look longingly at him—as well they should since Claude was now hers—or so Faith recalled her young blessed-bride self thinking so very proudly. Had he carried on with all those women? Faith wondered. Perhaps, perhaps not. Perhaps it was always the money he loved most. But Faith knew far too well that Faith Ann would have suspected nothing unseemly as adultery even if he had. What blessed child thinks of such things? No, no. A handsome, charming, smart-as-a-whip man was marrying her and taking over the family business. It was meant to be. It was Miss Faith Ann Bass's birthright. If her being "blessed" helped such a perfect man up to the altar, what of it? Wouldn't that be just as much God's will as everything else that seemed predestined for her family? Oh yes, Faith thought, that would have been my response. So what if her young blessed self never quite saw that Claude Angus Darling didn't look at her the way she imagined? So what if she never quite understood why his charm turned a touch melancholy as the wedding drew near? After all, wasn't he the perfect husband their first seven years, living with her father in the mansion? Oh, her bridal bliss had been quite blinding. Until, of course, the moment she began to suspect her husband might not love her.

Such knowledge comes slowly when you see only blessings. And hers had come so very slowly. Her father's death, Faith knew, had begun her education. She closed her eyes at the memory of her hallowed father's death and what followed afterward—her first argument with Claude. After she lost the seed pearls from her great-grandmother Belle's heirloom ring. After they repaired it with new seed pearls just to lock it away in a safe-deposit box. After he lost his temper. After he began to seem like another man, Faith thought, absently touching her cheek. Yes, that was when she saw Claude. And saw how Claude saw her . . .

Stopping, Faith rolled her eyes at herself. Oh, this is *ridiculous,* she fumed, crossing her arms. What did it matter now? "It's all because of you, Claude Angus Darling! Haunting me today of all days!" she yelled toward the door and any ghosts beyond it. But she knew she was talking to the other Claude Darling, the man who had begun to haunt her long before he died.

Uncrossing her arms and setting her jaw, Faith focused hard on the door right in front of her. "Today—" she reminded herself, "you have to make today happen today."

So, once more, she commanded herself to reach out and grab the doorknob.

But it was no use. Before she could open this door, there was still something else to be reckoned with, because not all the silences were from Claude or God. There was also the special silence of her own creation, the one she had relied on to save her so long ago, starting with this closed bedroom door, the stone-cold solid silence that held all the other silences together. *That* was why she was here, she feared, and it scared her more than anything else. *If it broke, would she?*

For a soft moment, Faith listened to the mansion's intimate quiet, letting it envelop her and calm her again as it had done for so many years, as it had done even that very day. Living so long within it, she had begun to know, hear, even feel the different kinds of silence: the characteristics, the textures, the quality of the air and the space around it, its quality in different parts of the day, month, year.

There was the kind that came with the hum and the rattle of her kitchen window air-conditioner unit during the long, hot Texas summer. There was the high, continuing hiss of the space heaters in the rooms she occupied in cold, drafty Decembers. There was the

silence shimmering with the slightest rustling of the draping sycamore and oak leaves over the house, larger each spring as the big
trees' limbs grew slowly lower and lower over the mansion in what
she'd fancied as a silent embrace. And late in August, there was the
cicadas' buzz rising and falling that had begun to feel like the sound
track to her shrill, silent soul.

In fact, hers became a life so intimately silent she even began to
see her silences by certain hues: grief's silence was blindingly white,
the humming air conditioner's silence a clear blue, the space heaters'
silence was yellow, the sycamore and oak's green, the cicadas' buzz
brown, and the shadow's silence was black—all of them layered like
sediment, harder each year to disturb. She's created a world where
silence is not just an answer but a world in which you live and breathe
and have your being, and you forget there are other worlds. And it
had been so for twenty years. Until the day she began losing even
those silences, slipping in and out of a growing abyss of a new silence
where there was no light, no layers, nothing but coming sundowns.

Until last night, Faith reminded herself. At midnight, she'd heard
Something suggesting she could change things before it was too late.
There was still time. Even now, twenty years into her self-made
sealed silence . . .

Faith still had a choice. *That* was her true revelation.

So now she stood hovering at her dead husband's door, because
as with all choices there was a catch. And Faith knew this was hers:

She had to break *this* silence—and she could do that only by giving up the world of silence she'd created to save herself from it.

Faith took in a long, slow breath. Reaching out again, she let her
hand rest on the doorknob's cold brass until it turned warm. Then
she pushed. And with a soft, hesitant step forward, Faith moved
back into the noise.

ᥬ PROVENANCES

$10,000 BILL

Legal tender/U.S. currency • Circulation discontinued
1969 • Front: Salmon P. Chase, Secretary of the Treasury
1861–1864 • Back: Embarkation of the Pilgrims • Only
336 still known to exist • Highly sought collector's item

Series 1918   *Value: $200,000 (mint condition)*

FAMILY BIBLE

Deluxe Oversized Wedding Edition • King James
Red-Letter Version • Velva gold edges • White leather
cover • Family record insert with family tree • Keepsake
pocket

Circa 1955   *Value: sentimental*

*On the occasion of her son Claude Angus Darling's wedding on June 8,
1955, Mrs. Beulah Pirtle Darling took the jar of coins she'd been saving
for years from her cupboard and bought Sears & Roebuck catalog's biggest bright-white, gold-trimmed Deluxe Family Bible, the likes of which
not even the fancy Basses with all their fine things had ever seen. The*

baby boy she raised on her own after her wastrel husband, Angus, saw fit to up and leave them poor as dirt clods was now marrying into the richest family in the county, just like she'd planned.

Her handsome boy, who learned the hard way that a man ain't a man without money, could have had any pretty girl in town. But pretty don't last; plain with a bank and a mansion does. And he knew she'd slap him silly if he ever forgot. Like the Good Book says, "Spare the rod; spoil the child."

So, dreaming of how her wedding gift would be a Darling heirloom for generations to come, and how soon they'd all be living in that fine mansion, Beulah sat down and wrote the entry of their marriage—Miss Faith Ann Bass taken in holy matrimony by Mister Claude Angus Darling—*on the gilded parchment-paged family record section in her spidery cursive.*

God willing, Beulah planned to live to see the day the name Darling would be the important one in town.

Before the wedding bouquets wilted, however, God willed that Beulah Pirtle Darling meet her Maker, after which the enormous white Bible was stuffed unceremoniously in a back corner of her son's master bedroom bookcase.

And there it stayed untouched until her son, Claude, hell-bent to be a man with his own money, began to wheel and deal. Stashing cash away from prying eyes at the bank, which was and always would be Faith's, he found a practical use for his mother's garish Good Book. He slipped a plastic-sleeved, extremely valuable piece of paper money inside its pages to await the right collector at the right price, then carefully returned the big Bible to his bedroom bookcase's farthest back corner.

It was high noon at Faith Darling's garage sale. Word had continued to spread and the lawn was packed with new shoppers accustomed to suburban ranch-house garage sales of broken bicycles and baby clothes, now gawking at the strange and wonderful old things, waiting to see what else would come from inside that legend of a mansion.

A couple of teenage boys came down the front steps carrying a smoky-stink chesterfield leather sofa fresh from Claude Darling's old room, dropped it, and headed back into the house. Bobbie, Claudia, and John Jasper turned to stare after them before continuing the great debate on how to handle Faith, who was still upstairs.

Somebody cleared his throat. At John Jasper's elbow stood a stumpy little middle-aged man in a stained Texaco shirt and cap pulled down low over his face, a stack of paperback books under one arm. Seeing Mrs. Darling nowhere in sight, he shoved coins into the lawman's palm and then scooted away.

"Moon? That you?" John Jasper called after him to no response.

Mr. Moon Devine—longtime local Texaco gas station attendant with grease under his fingernails, electrical tape holding his thick black glasses together, and a face so white and round it gave him his nickname—wasn't all that excited about chatting with a deputy sheriff at that exact moment, however. He had just spent the last few minutes innocently perusing the western paperback collection of the late Mr. Claude Angus Darling—a man Moon had idolized back in the day. As he'd started shopping, he was feeling all nostalgic-like.

Jeezus, I've sure missed that man all these years, he was thinking. And looky-here, Mr. Darling liked westerns; I like westerns! A coincidence? Moon thought not. He'd smiled at a matronly woman minding her own business at the other end of the bookcase.

"Mr. Claude Angus Darling lived here," he'd said her way. "A great man. Me and him were tight." The woman cut her eyes at the odd little stranger and instinctively inched the other way.

Moon, however, had already cocked his jaw skyward and launched into his well-worn Claude Angus Darling anecdote:

"You may not know this, but back at the start of my career at the Texaco, I was tapped to wash Mr. Darling's fancy Dodge truck every Saturday morning. I'd wash 'er right up while he sat and had himself a Dr Pepper. He used to be real smooth in his young buck days, I hear tell, a way with words and the ladies and such—but not so much by my truck-washing era. Like a colored fella I know used to say, 'Mr. Claude Darling ain't prejudiced; he don't like nobody!'" Moon sniggered. "But he liked me, even before I told him we might be cousins once removed. I say, 'Hey, Mr. Darling, you from Texarkana? My mama's cousin married a Darling from there who was kin to an Angus Darling that everybody lost track of.'" Moon paused. "Well, that perked up his ears. He sez:

"'Texarkana . . . ?'

"So I say: 'That your daddy? Bet he's mighty proud of you. Never knew my own, he up and left when I was a little-bitty baby.'" Moon nodded. "Well. I could see he'd taken a shine to me, the way he pushed back his Stetson and all, so I decided it was the right time to ask for advice on making my fortune. 'To help me catch a woman (wink, wink),' I say to him, man-to-man." Moon chuckled. "Know what he sez back? He sez:

"'You want advice? Steer clear of women.'

"So I say: 'Even women with money?'"

Moon gave his round head a shake. "Mr. Darling cut his eyes at me so sharp they coulda cut me in two! Guess he figured I was makin' a crack about him and the Bass family, but I swear I wasn't. That's when he goes snake-eyed and drops his voice all low and serious." Moon demonstrated, going slit-eyed and basso. "And he sez:

"'Make your own money—a man ain't a man without money.'

"Then he flips me a *silver dollar*!" Moon crowed. "And every Saturday till the day he died, he flipped me *another* one!" He sighed wistfully. "I'd like to say I still had those silver dollars. I'd like to say I married one of them girls I gave 'em to, too."

Moon glanced back at his audience for the expected oohs and aahs from his impressive Claude Darling anecdote, but the woman had vanished. Used to such disappearances, he'd just turned back to Mr. Darling's western paperbacks. With visions of silver dollars still dancing in his head, that's when he'd picked out a paperback from a shelf, put a thumb to its pages, and out floated a $100 bill.

Some people might call Moon slow, but there was nothing slow about the way he scooped up that $100 bill and slid it back in the book. Glancing this way and that, he'd adjusted his glasses and cautiously reopened the book . . . and jumping Jeezus—it *was* a C-note.

Moon yelped. With guilty pleasure galloping through his heart, he surveyed the perimeter. When he surmised the coast was still clear, he closed his fingers around the bill to slip it straight into his Texaco shirt pocket. But then he'd had what he considered a better idea. He eased the $100 bill back into the paperback western and placed the book securely onto his "buy" pile. After all, if he paid good money for the book and happened upon something in it after the purchase—say, while reading it one night in the safety of his own domicile—it was his fair and square, right?

Moon gazed up at the row of bookshelves stretching out before him, and an absolute fountain of hope gushed up inside his little hapless heart. All his life, he'd looked on the bright side of life waiting for his big break, for his ship to come in, for his pay dirt to hit, for a way to finally make that fortune he and Mr. Claude Angus Darling discussed. By the time he'd gone down a single shelf full of westerns and found paper money in each one, he was sure that day had come.

Yet no sooner had Moon Devine paid the deputy sheriff for his first big "buy" pile and rushed back to claim the rest of his future fortune than he felt a nudge. Moon whirled around thinking the woman who'd missed his great Claude Angus Darling story was back. But instead, he looked down.

There, hovering around his knees, stood a little-bitty kid—a raggedy, towheaded, white-trash girl in red shit-kickers. Not more than six years old if a damn day! And the kid was pulling books one at a time from the shelf and turning them upside down. Hell's bells, Moon thought, did the kid even read?

That's when the awful truth finally rumbled to the front of Moon's brain:

The kid knows.

Moon cussed.

The little kid rolled an eye his way; their gazes met. Then they both saw—stuffed on the bottom row exactly halfway between them—the most promising book of all for mighty-fine cash-stashing:

An enormous, gold-trimmed, bright-white Family Bible.

They both lunged.

The kid got there first, faked to the left, went right, and was gone, leaving Moon tripping over his own greasy work boots.

Moon gave a good rolling cuss to the whole episode and spat on the ground. Then with a wipe of a forearm across his mouth, he took up his position again with visions of much more than just silver dollars now break-dancing in his head.

Moon was now a man with a mission.

Mr. Claude Angus Darling's last great Texaco tip lay waiting before him.

From his perch on the porch, John Jasper Johnson was picking up a change in the way the customers were acting, or he thought he was. Something seemed off, but he couldn't quite put his finger on it and it was making him nervous. Like, for instance, there sure seemed like a lot of people looking at books all of a sudden.

He studied the crowd a bit longer. Then, with a glance back down at Bobbie and Claudia, he pivoted on a boot heel and strode inside the mansion.

A few seconds later, John Jasper reappeared heaving a tall, slender glazed floor vase full of pennies down the front steps to rest on the uneven brick walk, his bum knee needing a moment. He'd just hauled it down the entire flight of stairs, completely unable to say no to Faith Darling. The only reason he'd gone up there was to try talking sense to her again, and instead he wound up hauling this goddamn thing down. He leaned on Claude Darling's penny-pinching penny pot to catch his breath, felt it teeter, and was working to steady it by pushing it onto the grass just as a teased-haired lady in a polka-dot dress came over to inspect it.

"Oh, my," she said, bending over and sticking her nose over it. "Now isn't that lovely. But what is all this inside?"

At that exact moment, a glazed-eyed Faith Darling stepped onto her broad front porch, froze, and then screamed:

"HELP! *POLICE!!!!!*"

For a beat, Faith gawked at the hordes on her lawn and the hordes gawked back as everyone whirled around to face the hysteric old lady on the porch, including Deputy John Jasper Johnson standing only a few feet away.

Then Faith began flailing her arms: "GET OFF MY LAWN! STOP STEALING MY ANTIQUES! *HELP!*"

John Jasper couldn't believe his eyes, despite knowing Faith Darling was sick. His dignified Mrs. Darling was frantic, crazed, unaware of her own sale—and he was so shocked he lost a firm grip on the teetering penny pot. At that instant, the startled polka-dot lady grabbed at the vase to steady herself and knocked it free of John Jasper's grasp.

It wobbled a moment. Then obeying the laws of gravity and penny-weight, the vase tipped over, bounced off the grass, and began to roll down the sloping Darling lawn, bobbing, bouncing, and spewing forth pennies for all the crowd to see, slowed only by a side-swipe of several of the remaining antiques.

Moon Devine, the first to grasp the happenstance's true potential, gave an audible cry as he thrust himself into the rolling fray with a dozen other book browsers following suit, the vase finally brought to a full halt before hitting the street by the sheer force of that many hands grabbing at it.

As John Jasper was attempting to restore order by loudly pointing out that the contents were just pennies, the first paper money was spotted.

"I'll give you fifty dollars for the whole thing right now!" screamed one book browser. But too late. At that point, someone of either great strength or great adrenaline picked up the vase and emptied the whole thing onto the grass. And there, among the gobs of pennies were not just dozens of crumpled bills displaying a nice denominational collection of ex-presidents, but also individually wrapped gold, silver, and copper coins—small ones of antique U.S. mint with visages of double eagles and Indian chiefs, and large gold ones of a foreign coin that any discerning eye would recognize as South African Krugerrands, once a solid investment item for the conscienceless rich, a group for which Claude Angus Darling had certainly qualified.

There was a pause of a worshipful nature. The money mound sparkled in the setting sun, copper, silver, gold, and green, like pirate's booty on dry land.

Then the melee ensued.

Even the lady in the polka-dot dress was outgrabbing poor Moon Devine, who had somehow gotten sat upon by another customer before scooping even one good handful, which was at least his right as first among thieves.

The resulting mass of legs and arms, growls and yelps, torn pockets and shrieks of delight was an inspired one, fueled more by the power of legend and geography—Claude Angus Darling's legend plus the pioneer spirit that lies within the genes of any Texan—than the truth of what actually lay on this patch of yellow-dead grass lawn. But it was a thing to behold. Which is exactly what even Deputy John Jasper Johnson did, gaping at the spectacle for a full fifteen seconds before attempting an authoritative deputy scream that no one heard. So he resorted to a sound every person attached to each of the flailing extremities before him would hear and obey: he raised his gun to the sky. And fired.

A crow in the nearby sycamore at which John Jasper's gun was inadvertently aimed dropped with a plop to the ground, now as unmoving as everybody else on the lawn.

"Okay! *Up!*" John Jasper ordered the mess of humanity in the grass. "Shame on you! Now empty your pockets and haul your greedy selves on home! This sale is closed as of right damn now!"

Everyone obeyed, a few red-faced, others furtive, still others grumbling. Within a few seconds, the whole group was back on its feet, in full slink, moving off the Darling lawn's sale and back to their cars, all with more than a few pennies in their pockets, some, the more slippery, with bills of various denominations; and one, fittingly Moon Devine, with a gold coin he would always treasure, at least until he decided to rebuild the motor of that old Chevy pickup of his.

Finally, when the last of the parked cars had slowly rolled out of sight, John Jasper took a deep breath and holstered his fire piece.

Claudia, who had watched the entire episode from the brick walkway, suddenly remembered her mother, who was still standing on the porch frozen with a look on her face that Claudia had never seen before, a look of confusion and . . . fear. But she wasn't screaming anymore. Claudia ran up the front steps toward her. Faith, though, didn't budge.

"Mother . . ." she tried.

Faith still didn't respond.

Claudia reached out and gently grasped her arm, wanting to lead her from the railing to a chair on the porch. But all her efforts to get her mother to move failed. Faith would not acknowledge her, much less sit down.

So Claudia slowly returned to the lawn where Jasper and Bobbie were still beholding what Claude Angus Darling had wrought, glancing back to her frozen mother at the rail whose gaze was now frozen on them.

A few minutes later, as Claudia and Bobbie began picking up the money, John Jasper raised the butt of his gun and came down hard on the homemade sign he'd just created, the stick going sturdily into the ground.

He stood back to inspect his work:

GARAGE SALE

<u>CLOSED</u>

MONEY HAS ALL BEEN FOUND!

Sign or no, people were still driving by to gawk surreptitiously at the lawn. To John Jasper they might as well have been mosquitoes for their irritation factor. He raised his gun butt and gave the sign another lick, whether it needed it or not.

Directly in front of the two big money piles, Claudia, Bobbie, and John Jasper leaned wearily back in the grass. After counting all the penny pot's money spilled across the dead St. Augustine grass, they were finally still. Final count: 433 hundred-dollar bills, 82 fifty-dollar bills, 113 twenty-dollar bills, 32 ten-dollar bills, 20 five-dollar bills, 16 U.S. gold double eagles, 51 Mercury head dimes, 34 Buffalo nickels, 16 Standing Liberty quarters, 44 Seated Liberty half-dollars, 66 Morgan silver dollars, 32 gold Krugerrands—all in protective sleeves—and God-knows-how-many pennies.

All the pennies were piled into one pile, all the silver coins and paper money in another, and the gold coins in yet another.

Claudia was gazing at the penny pile. She was suddenly remembering a moment when as a kid she'd crawled up on the furniture in her father's forbidden bedroom to plunge her little hands into the tall penny pot. But she'd only come up with pennies, at least as far down as the length of her preschooler's arm.

John Jasper and Bobbie, though, only had eyes for the gold. Sitting up on his haunches, John Jasper was fingering one of the Krugerrands, while Bobbie plunged her hands into the pile of gold coins just for the cheap thrill. "Wow," Bobbie said, reverently. "All of this, just stuck inside a penny pot. Talk about not taking it with you."

"Crazy SOB," John Jasper muttered. He chucked the Krugerrand back on the pile with the other gold coins. "That crazy SOB," he repeated under his breath. Then he glanced back at the mansion. "And if the SOB was crazy enough to hide that kind of money in a penny pot in plain view, I wouldn't be surprised if he did some real hiding inside that big house."

Claudia felt the color drain from her face. For the next few moments, the three of them sat in front of the piles, wondering—John Jasper wondering how much the crowd had stolen in the melee, Bobbie wondering how many monetary surprises were in store for today's buyers, and Claudia wondering what the devil was going to happen next.

"Do you think Mrs. Darling knew about all this?" Bobbie asked.

John Jasper looked up at Faith Darling on the porch. She was gazing down at them with the same blank expression she'd had since the money was found. She hadn't seemed to move one bit. "I'd say no," he answered, "but she could have forgotten."

Bobbie gave the idea a quiet little appreciative whistle. "Money could have been all over the place." And then her eyes went wider still: "Claudia Jean . . . didn't you say your mother closed her bank accounts?"

Claudia squeezed her eyes shut against the thought.

Still studying Faith, John Jasper felt a chill. He pulled himself up on his bad knee for a better look. And he felt the chill all over again. Faith Darling was there . . . but she wasn't. Whatever spark fills a person's eyes that shows the life within just wasn't there. And he didn't much like his next thought: Would it be coming back? He suppressed the urge to wave his arms at her, maybe even fire his gun again. Finally, he said: "She still hasn't moved."

Bobbie turned to look. But Claudia just couldn't. Instead, she stood up, too nervous, too confused, too infuriated to sit still. Then she strode over and grabbed one of the old-fashioned canvas Bass Bank bags someone had found in one of the attic boxes, got back down on her knees, and began furiously stuffing everything but the pile of pennies into it. And as Claudia grew more manic, John Jasper slowly moved near to help her. Then so did Bobbie.

When the bag was full, John Jasper cinched it with a hard yank, mumbling under his breath once more: "Crazy SOB."

For a moment, Bobbie and John Jasper sat back on the grass to rest. But Claudia didn't seem able to. Pushing her hair back out of her face, she picked up another old canvas bank bag and now began shoving handfuls of pennies into it so hard that Bobbie and John Jasper exchanged worried glances before pitching in to help again.

When they finally finished, every last coin and bill stuffed in one bag or the other, they all plopped back once again onto the grass to stare at the two full-to-busting canvas bags with the faded Bass Bank labels.

Finally, John Jasper pulled himself up, slow and stiff. Then he planted his big hands around his belt and glanced back at the mansion. "Guess we better check the house."

"So you really think there's more?" Bobbie asked.

"I think everybody who was just here is sure as hell gonna think so," he answered.

Claudia cut her eyes up at John Jasper.

John Jasper held her gaze for a moment. "Guess we better get on it," he said softly to her, checking his watch. "I've got overtime plus a charter tonight. So we gotta get this done by sundown. Your mama might be having knuckleheads sneaking back after dark, no matter what we do. If it wasn't New Year's Eve with everything else going on, I'd be goddamn sure of it." He leaned to pick up the bags and then glanced back at Claudia. "You should take this, CJ."

Claudia shook her head, answering quietly, "No, it's Mother's money, John Jasper."

Glancing up at Faith Darling, still standing frozen on the porch, he reached into one of the bags, grabbed a handful of hundreds, and gingerly placed them into Claudia's silk blouse pocket. "Well, she's giving some to ya." Before Claudia could disagree, he picked up the money bag stuffed with the paper money and old coins and moved toward Faith.

Although Faith Darling still hadn't moved, when John Jasper stepped onto the porch, he noticed something in her eyes that told him she had come back to herself a little, at least enough to be approached. He paused. "Mrs. Darling?" He placed the bag at her feet and launched into it: "We gotta do something about all this before dark. Then you need to lock up tight tonight. I'm calling this in to see about leaving a cruiser out here. But I doubt if we can spare it, being New Year's Eve and all. I'd get you to hire a guard if I knew anybody not already working tonight."

"That won't be necessary," Faith answered, barely above a whisper, her gaze still on the lawn.

"Mrs. Darling, you need to hear me: it's just not safe. I don't even feel right leaving you here tonight." He pointed at the bag. "There's fifty thousand dollars in here easy, not even counting the old coins. I'm calling the bank president right now and escorting you and your money down to the bank. Then after New Year's, I'll take you to help stop that lien on your house with it."

"No bank," she said, refusing to look his way as if he were some stranger. Then she abruptly picked up the canvas money bag with both hands.

"But . . ." John Jasper didn't get any further, because Faith Darling had already turned her back on him, money bag in tow, and gone back inside. And all he could do was watch the big carved wooden front doors close behind her.

At Bass Public Cemetery, Father George Fallow was standing at the gravesite of the dearly departed seventy-eight-year-old, 350-pound Belva Bowman saying the words he'd said hundreds of times before.

He had already passed "gathered here in the sight of God," moved through "ashes to ashes, dust to dust," and "I am the resurrection and the life" and was well into "In my Father's house are many mansions" . . .

. . . when he lost his place.

No one noticed for a moment, since it was a funeral and everyone was full of their own mortal thoughts. But then, one by one, each head raised to stare at the unmoving, suddenly mute priest.

The truth was Father George hadn't had his mind on the words, any words, at all. After his strange morning, he'd been thinking instead about numbers—a certain number, actually. Not ashes and mansions and resurrections, but grams: 21 grams. He was still hearing Faith Darling, her eyes so strangely lit from another place, asking about souls and memories and dying. And his mind had wandered to those grams—the possible weight of the soul and the poetry of such a thought. Standing over big Belva Bowman in her top-of-the-line, heavy-weight maple-and-titanium coffin, he'd been dutifully repeating the funeral words, his mouth on autopilot. But what he was really thinking about was whether her big soul had gone and what it had weighed. And his imagination had gotten the better of him: he had been picturing 350-pound Belva Bowman, at least the possible 21 grams' shape of her, levitating right above the huge coffin. For the oddest out-of-body instant, he was certain it was happening: big Belva lifting off, up, up, and away.

That's the moment he'd stopped talking. When the priest showed no sign of starting back up, one of the funeral home directors leaned over and whispered, "Father?"

At that, George came back to himself, big Belva having gone wherever she was going. But he couldn't move, still completely unable to get his mouth or mind in normal gear. And worse, he had no idea where he was in the service.

So the funeral director inched near his ear. "'In my Father's house are many mansions,'" the mortician whispered. "And I go to prepare a place for you . . ."

". . . If it were not so . . ." George said, finally jumping back in, back into the familiar words of comfort. ". . . If it were not so, I would have told you."

If it were not so.

At the mansion, Claudia, John Jasper, and Bobbie spent the rest of the afternoon searching everything, inside and out—trunks, cabinets, closets, beds, books—looking through all the mansion's remaining contents and all the house's nooks and crannies for any more stashed Darling cash. They'd found nothing but cobwebs and dust.

So while Bobbie and Claudia finished up, John Jasper took a break to check up and down the street for knuckleheads. He stood on the brick walkway, hands on hips, surveying the still-cluttered lawn.

He hadn't spoken much since he'd closed the sale, thinking troubling thoughts about this old white woman who had been as much a part of his life as any relative of his own, truth be told. If he had to put into words what had happened when she came out on the porch and set the money pot rolling to discovery, he'd have said the "sassy" had gone out of her, right in front of his eyes—and it had yet to come back. Somehow that scared him more than anything. Plus, he was now fearing for her safety more than ever. Bad enough he was about to deal with the normal knuckleheads of any New Year's Eve, but he knew word was already spreading about the penny-pot money. Even in a small town like Bass, all these old mansions on Old Waco Road were like sitting ducks for lazy thieving knuckleheads, full as they usually were with old ladies and valuable things, and the Darling mansion had always been the biggest sitting duck of all. While he'd done his damnedest to keep Mrs. Darling and her place knucklehead-free all these years, now he couldn't help but worry how this was going to end, considering her state of mind. Too many times, he'd seen how such a mess can become a police matter before it rights itself and how often it never quite rights itself at all. But this mess wasn't going to.

Not if I've got a thing to say about it, John Jasper thought, striding to his patrol car and grabbing up his police radio.

Three other deputies soon arrived, and within a matter of minutes the lawn was empty, every remaining antique shoved back in the front doors—the foyer and the formal dining room now stuffed wall-to-wall. Then John Jasper went one better by stretching some yellow police tape across the big front doors.

Meanwhile, Faith Darling had been upstairs in her room, seemingly oblivious to what was happening to her sale. About two o'clock, a few minutes into the house search, Claudia had decided to check on her mother. She had opened the bedroom door to find Faith standing and staring out the window toward the front lawn, her sun hat lying on the floor of the empty room near the canvas money bag. So Claudia had retrieved a pink vanity chair from her own still-untouched bedroom down the hall and set it down right behind her unmoving mother. Then she'd left, shutting the door behind her.

Now, three hours later, Claudia opened it again. What she found was her mother still standing in the exact same place—the scene unchanged.

Claudia shuddered slightly at the sight. She began to speak to her mother, but something about the scene, the silence of the room, stopped her. So she closed the door again and stood there for a long time not quite knowing what to do about it, about any of it.

Unable to shake a growing sense of dread, Claudia came back down the stairs to stand in the foyer among the yard sale's clutter pushed in for the night. She fought a feeling of melancholy at the bunched-up state of her little girl's wonderland of antiques. Without her mother hovering near to take all her attention, she was really looking at the furniture for the first time, and she couldn't deny being a little unsettled at the sight of the remaining antiques stacked up like so much kindling—her father's chesterfield sofa lying on its side, the dining room chairs her brother always straddled backward stacked this way and that, the grandfather clock her mother had draped pushed against the staircase banister, the cedar hope chest from the hallway, the love seat from the parlor . . .

You hate these things, she reminded herself.

But you also loved them, another part of her responded.

She turned in a slow circle, taking in the foyer that now looked very different to her—and not just because of the clutter. It seemed weary, as weary as she was, as weary as her mother surely was, a century-long bucket-load of weary.

I need some fresh air, she thought.

Ducking under John Jasper's yellow tape, she stumbled onto the walkway to gaze back at her childhood's mansion, and her eyes landed on her mother's unmoving shadow filling one of the upstairs windows.

"I'm not her," Claudia heard herself say.

Just then, the setting sun broke through a cloud bank and set the windows across the front of the house on fire with the reflection. It made the mansion seem alive in a sort of looming, all-consuming way she could literally feel somewhere sharp right behind her heart, the broken place that long ago had pushed her out its doors.

And this is *not* me, she thought, setting her jaw, even as her eyes strayed toward the giant sycamore whose rustling leaves might as well have been a soundtrack for all her childhood's nights.

Claudia took a step back. Something crunched under her running shoes. It was a glass shard—a piece of her great-great-grandmother Belle's Venetian crystal, the broken glass that her mother must have cut herself on earlier. Gingerly, she picked it up. But instead of checking around for the other shards before she was bleeding, too, Claudia paused, surprised by a sense of loss over the jagged swirl of exquisite old-world filigree, aware of all the Bass-grandmother fingerprints that had touched it as if it were the same as touching them. And with her Bass grandmothers' portrait-faces suddenly bobbing before her mind's eye, she had the bizarre sensation that it was their grief she was feeling, that all her grandmothers were right here with her, mourning this glass.

Then her grandmothers' faces vanished and in their place appeared the one thing they would mourn far above filigreed glass: her great-great-grandmother Belle's lost filigreed wedding ring.

Claudia tried to blink it away, but it was no use. After stuffing her own feelings for hours, something was making her finally face her own grief over the antique ring. It was a horrible feeling. Flooded with guilt, Claudia fought the crazy urge to apologize to her grandmothers, one and all.

It's this *place*! she told herself, staring at the sunset reflecting like fire off the windows. The mansion really *was* alive. It was alive with all the living that created everything here from brick to glass to antiques . . . to flesh and blood, she realized with a start . . . including her *own*.

"Oh dear God, it *is* me," Claudia murmured.

She looked down at the broken piece of the past in her palm. Bobbie was right. No one really leaves the past behind. Everything she knew in her bones was not good for her to ever want was still here, amazingly right here—and now even *she* was here again. She stared back up at the mansion. *Things and places do possess you.* Claudia took in a quick breath. How could a bunch of brick and mortar have such a hold on a living human being? It was insane. But as the heat rose up her neck, she began to understand that, whether she liked it or not, the mansion would be forever alive right here, always playing out all the dramas of all their stories, as long as *she* was alive and had a shred of memory.

Claudia's head jerked back to the upstairs window. And for the most macabre of moments, she envied her mother.

She felt her breath catch. Short of the mansion blowing to high heaven, her mother's sale was probably as close as she'd ever get to being free of this place, and oh how she wished her mother had finished the job, because what was she supposed to do now? What am I supposed to do with the mansion? she thought. And with her eyes still on the upstairs window, Claudia let herself ask the rest:

What am I supposed to do with *her*?

Wincing, Claudia dropped the glass shard, surprised to see blood dripping from her fingertip. "Breathe," she commanded herself. Something big—big as a house—was sitting on her chest. *Breathe*.

"I just came back for the ring," she gasped out, to the mansion, to her mother, to the Universe, to Somebody, as every nerve in her body told her to turn and run.

Bobbie was coming down the steps toward her, talking. "Well, we've checked pretty much everything." Then she stopped to stare. "Claudia Jean, you're white as a ghost. And is your finger bleeding?"

Without warning, Claudia began walking away in long strides down to the street as if her life depended on it, every step pumping life back into her lungs.

Bobbie hurried after Claudia, walking at top speed, which was not a thing she found possible to maintain given her plumpness. "Hey, wait! Where are you going?" Bobbie called. Just to keep up with Claudia's brisk strides, she began to jog in her business wedges. "C'mon, stop, will you?" Bobbie yelled. "Jeez, these shoes. I'm going to turn an ankle."

Claudia broke into a jog in the practiced, graceful strides of a long-distance runner. When she hit the corner, her jogging turned into a run, breeze rippling through her silk shirt, blowing her shirt-tail behind her.

That was it for Bobbie, left now in the dust. She gasped, leaning over her knees and watching her friend's shirttail rising and falling with her strides, until finally she caught enough breath to yell: "Claudia Jean, are you coming back?"

Claudia kept running.

"Hey! *Stop!*" she tried again. "Stop or I'll *SHOOT!*"

At the crazy sound of that, Claudia paused in mid-stride to roll an eye back at Bobbie Ann Blankenship, who was now hunched over in the middle of the street, half a block behind her.

"Where-do-you-think-you're-*going*?" Bobbie wheezed.

"I just came back for the ring—" Claudia called back breathlessly. "I can't stay—I can't do this—"

"But you can't run away," Bobbie managed. "Not this time!"

"Just leave me *alone*—" Claudia yelled.

"*Make* me!" Bobbie yelled back.

Claudia began walking in circles as if worn out from a personal marathon she'd never quite been able to finish. "W-what if I gave it to you?" she stuttered back to Bobbie.

"What are you talking about?" Bobbie threw up her hands. "Give me what?"

"The mansion—" Claudia called. "You've always wanted it. You can pay the property tax lien; I can sign something. Take it. *Please.*"

Bobbie stared stupidly up the street at Claudia Jean. It wasn't every day that someone offers you your childhood's dream.

She paused too long: Claudia was already striding away.

Bobbie lowered herself onto the curb, down the block from the mansion of her dreams, to let Claudia's offer simmer a glorious minute. Just trying the idea on for size, she told herself. Nothing wrong with that. But then her eyes fell on something by her shoe. There, only inches from her now scuffed brown business wedges, lay a hundred-dollar bill. Bobbie turned her eyes ever so slightly sky-ward. "This *is* a test," she muttered. "Isn't it?"

Just then, the police cruiser rolled up to her, John Jasper at the wheel. Bobbie climbed in. In a second, they'd caught up with Claudia, cruising along beside her.

From the passenger side of the car, Bobbie leaned over John Jasper and softly called to her: "Hey—"

Then John Jasper, reaching a hand out his window, near enough to touch her, repeated it, even softer: "Hey . . ."

Claudia turned to look at the two faces staring back at her, these two old worried friends she could never see running from anything. She slowed and inhaled.

Then, exhaling, she squeezed her eyes shut and stopped running.

Claudia and Bobbie sat quietly perspiring on the mansion's porch steps, not having said a word in the fifteen minutes since sitting down.

The sun was finally going down, the day beginning to cool off, but not fast enough. Bobbie inspected the sweat rings on her cotton business jacket now lying on her lap, and then wiggled her blouse to catch a bit of the cooler breeze, trying to dry off the last of her sweat. Holding her hair off her neck with one hand and fanning with the other, Bobbie stole another of a dozen glances toward her friend. Claudia's hair was a mess and her blouse was just as sweaty, but somehow she still looked gorgeous, which made Bobbie just shake her head at the wonder of being Claudia Jean Darling.

Eyeing the drops of dried blood on the front of Claudia's white blouse, Bobbie quietly asked, "Is your finger still bleeding? I could get you a Band-Aid."

Gingerly touching her finger's stinging cut from the Venetian glass shard, Claudia shook her head.

"Listen," Bobbie began quietly, kindly, "about the mansion."

"Bobbie Ann—" Claudia tried to wave away the whole subject.

But Bobbie pressed on. "Even if it was mine, it could never really be mine. You know that. It'd still and always be yours. That's how the past works." Bobbie paused. The look on Claudia Jean's face said she knew far too well that what Bobbie was saying was true. And since this seemed the time for truth, Bobbie had one other thing to say right this very minute. There's something else that's yours and could never be mine, Bobbie thought, as she took a deep breath and finally said it:

"I took the elephant clock, Claudia Jean."

Claudia sat up. "What?"

"I tricked your mother, took it, and I should have told you. Your mother wouldn't sell it!" Bobbie exclaimed, throwing up her hands. "Out of all the things here, she said it wasn't for sale, but I just *knew* it wouldn't stay that way, what with her memory, and, Claudia Jean, that clock could be a French relic—a museum piece! I got so excited when I saw it, I called a Houston museum curator I know, and he got so excited he actually drove out here to take it back for authentication!" Bobbie paused to catch a breath. "So I don't have it, but I promise I know where it is." She looked down. "I just had to save it . . . but now I think we need to save it from me."

Claudia stared at Bobbie for a beat. "She wouldn't sell it?"

"Nope," Bobbie answered, "before she forgot and sold it to me." Claudia was about to speak, but Bobbie raised a hand, not quite finished with her speech.

"I know what you're going to say, Claudia Jean," she went on. "You're going to say you don't want it or that you can't want it or something crazy. But you know what I think? I think it means more than you'll admit. I think it may be the one piece you may need more than any ol' museum. And when you realize I'm right, you'll tell me." With that, Bobbie heaved a big sigh and sat back, all this true confession having flat tuckered her out.

For a moment, neither of them moved. Then Claudia leaned her head back against the porch railing and let the thought settle in: *Mother wouldn't sell the elephant clock.*

Bobbie watched Claudia Jean for another moment, and then she decided to let her friend be. She patted Claudia Jean Darling on the knee, got a sad smile in return, and then pulled herself up to go. In all the hubbub, she'd almost forgotten what day it was. She had a big New Year's Eve date with a chunky hottie from Texas City she'd met at Weight Watchers, for the town's midnight fireworks display. So, with one last look at her friend and the mansion of her little-girl dreams, Bobbie Blankenship headed for her minivan. The mansion isn't going anywhere, she reminded herself. It would be right here when she returned. Always right here, Bobbie thought, smiling to herself as she drove away.

As the Yesteryear Antiques minivan's taillights disappeared down the street, Claudia sat alone on the porch, gently pressing the cut on her finger to silence its sting. Then she wrapped her arms around her knees and tried being completely still, not thinking of anything at all.

After a few quiet minutes, she heard the sound of John Jasper's boots scuffing across the floorboards of the porch. Feeling his big presence settle in beside her, Claudia looked around, seeing, savoring, some of the beautiful young athlete still alive in his face and his movements.

"Here." He was holding two glasses of ice water, one outstretched toward her.

She took it.

"Your mama's still up there in her bedroom," he reported, wiping his forehead with the frosty ice-cold glass then taking a sip. Then he turned to stare at her with his deputy sheriff gaze until she finally took a long drink from hers as well.

"Could we not talk about this for a little longer?" she asked, setting down the glass to touch her stinging cut finger again. "I know we have to. But not right this minute, okay?"

John Jasper, having noticed the blood on Claudia's blouse and the way she kept touching her fingertip, had grabbed a Band-Aid while inside. Pulling it from his shirt pocket, he opened it, and then stilled Claudia's hand to slowly wrap the Band-Aid around the dried cut. His sudden touch was embarrassingly intimate, but as it continued she felt herself soften. When the Band-Aid was firmly in place, he dropped his hand from hers, and she let her eyes linger on those once legendary hands as they settled peacefully on his knees. When she raised her eyes, he was looking at her, smiling slightly. She smiled back, fingering the new Band-Aid. Then they both turned toward the view off the porch.

For a little while they listened to the day turning into night, to the December sounds of an everyday South Texas dusk, like normal people, as if there weren't two decades and two deaths and two sides of a long-ago railroad track between them. The crickets were warming up nicely and she could hear the backyard live oak leaves rustling in the tiny, hot breeze. It was a sound that made Claudia feel a little better. It sounded like a long time ago, through a window; safe, young, and sweetly untouched, devoid of all drama and all history. And it calmed her almost all the way back down.

Absently, she turned her head his way. "Did I hear you say you had a 'charter'?"

He nodded. "Flying a family around for New Year's Eve fireworks."

Claudia turned all the way around on that. "John Jasper, you're a pilot?"

He smiled. "Got a four-seater prop; do some charters now and then. Mostly to pay for plane upkeep. So I can fly. When I need to."

"When you need to," she repeated.

"Yeah."

"You fly," Claudia said, wistfully. She let the thought simmer a little between them, letting the years settle in, letting who they were begin to turn into who they had become. Then in a timbre of voice she barely recognized, one she hadn't used since her football hero–worship days, she said: "John Jasper Johnson flies."

As if in response, John Jasper leaned back on his elbows against the top step and turned his gaze to the sky. Claudia's gaze followed. But her eyes wandered back to him—the last person on earth she would ever have imagined sitting with her on her family's porch, this man who had every right to hate her and her whole family. And she abruptly asked: "John Jasper, why are you here?"

John Jasper sat up.

"Please don't get me wrong," Claudia quickly went on. "I'm not sure what I'd have done if you weren't. But I don't understand why you've been so good to my mother."

John Jasper paused long enough to make both of them uncomfortable, as if straining to find the words, and then finally said: "She was good to me."

Good? Just as Claudia opened her mouth to question that concept, they both heard a noise and jerked toward the mansion, but it was just a car sound drifting on the evening air from one of the dirt streets. When the quiet returned, they relaxed.

"How did your daddy die?" John Jasper suddenly asked.

Claudia frowned. "A heart attack. Why?"

John Jasper paused. "She says she killed him."

Claudia studied John Jasper's face to make sure he wasn't making some sort of crass joke. He was serious. "What would possess her to say such a thing?"

He paused again. "She tell you about God ordering up the sale?"

And that was one revelation too far. Claudia began rubbing her temples, a headache coming on strong. "My mother's murdering people already dead, thinks she's going to die today, and now she's getting messages from God. What's next?"

"You believe in God?" he asked.

Claudia dropped her hands to gape at him. John Jasper's gaze didn't waver. "Bobbie said you said you're a Buddhist."

"That was a long time ago," she replied, hoping he'd let it go, which he didn't.

He cocked his head toward her. "How'd you get into that?"

Claudia bristled slightly.

"Just asking," he added, noticing.

Claudia still didn't want to answer and she wondered why. She studied this man sitting there in his deputy sheriff's uniform, so big and tall and upright, still so charismatic in a beat-up way, and so obviously used to asking a question and getting an answer. Was that why? But no, it had nothing to do with authoritative questions or even hero-worship memories: she realized she cared what he thought. And she was too tired to deal with how to answer such a question, explain such a thing so wrapped up in all her years gone from this place. At least not if she cared what he thought . . . which she did . . . which she hated that she did. So she gave him a casual flip of her hand, hoping he'd drop it this time. But he just kept studying her. Waiting.

"You won't understand," she finally answered.

"Try me."

Claudia fidgeted, and then tried getting away with the short answer: "Buddhism says life is suffering. It helped. At least until it didn't."

"Why didn't it?" came his quick response.

"I suppose you have *your* shit together?" she blurted.

John Jasper now was the one bristling—until he burst out laughing. "Man!" he exclaimed. "For a minute there, you looked just like Mike."

That took the wind right out of Claudia's sudden snit, because she realized, for a minute there, John Jasper had sounded just like Mike—her big brother with all the answers, who always had his shit together. She could almost hear him and see him in John Jasper. She really could. It startled her, this abrupt, clear vision of Mike outside her foggy dreams. And then it was gone.

So as a cautious quiet again settled between them, Claudia pushed her hair back from her face, performing her usual nervous tic. But slower now as she hazarded a worthy explanation, choosing her words, her truth, thinking of husbands and Harleys, of all her mistakes stretching back along the road behind her. "It didn't help anymore," she quietly began, "because it's supposed to teach enlightenment and life's sacredness." She paused. "But I felt nothing. I didn't feel bad or good or enlightened or sacred or anything a person who really wanted to should have. All I ever felt was what I'd always felt. Numb." She struggled with the last thought. "So finally I did what I always do," she added, her voice trailing away.

I ran, she finished to, for, herself.

As John Jasper took this in, working it around, trying to make sense of it, they both fell still again, the dusk filling the quiet space between them. Claudia's hushed voice broke the silence. "John Jasper . . ." she said, "I am so, so sorry for what my family did to you."

Some words, however long you've waited to hear someone say, however much they need to be said, are hard to hear. For a very long moment, John Jasper did not move. Finally he hunched over his knees, steadying himself to say something important. "My plane," he began and paused. "That's what I got with what she handed me."

"What who handed you?" she asked.

John Jasper's head snapped around. "You don't remember me coming to the door that night?"

Claudia stiffened. She remembered what she'd screamed at him and she could not bear to admit it. So she lied.

"No."

"And you don't know what your mama did?"

That Claudia didn't know. But John Jasper looked suddenly so off-balance that she had to resist the urge to put out her arm to steady him. Instead she said: "John Jasper, it doesn't matter. Please. Don't talk about it if you don't want to."

John Jasper was now sweating. "No, no . . ." he fumbled. ". . . I *can't*." He suddenly felt as if he were going to burst, the word like sandpaper on his tongue: *can't*. He was tired to death of the goddamn word, of the jammed-up feeling of the thing. He knew he needed to talk—more than anything—but all he ever seemed to be able to do was swallow it back down, the habit of stuffing it too old. And that made him madder. He should get it out right the hell now, bite the bullet, tell this one person in all the goddamn world who might understand.

Fidgeting, he wiped at his forehead with the back of a hand. Maybe, he told himself, maybe if I went at it like talking reason to somebody making no sense at all. Work my way into it. Work it like a good deputy sheriff—slow, steady—unlooping twenty years of thinking about why things are the way they are whether they made sense or not . . . like, like . . . that everything that happens, the forces of nature and such, are set into motion with each choice you make, touching everything and everybody you touch and everything everybody else touches. And each thing that happens to you from all that multiplying is just one of a million things that could have happened to you . . . and that maybe the entire point of being alive is to keep afloat in what's left after the one-in-a-million thing that could happen to you happens to you . . . and the only thing you got an inch of control over is whether you keep holding on so you won't get washed clean away. . . .

John Jasper took a mental breath, stilling his dizzying thoughts, because the real thing he needed to say was how tired he was, how so goddamn tired he was, of holding on.

Just then another car passed, the muffler rumbling loud and long down the street, jolting John Jasper back to the mansion steps where he still sat. The two of them were now sitting a little too close for the sudden intimacy of the deepening dark. The streetlights flickered on. And he noticed that Claudia had been watching him the whole time he'd been working so hard saying nothing. He glanced away, dropping his eyes.

But Claudia kept watching him. She gazed at him now as if he weren't real, as if she had conjured him somehow by coming back, as if he were the one thing she didn't know she needed most in order to handle her homecoming. For the slightest of moments, she imagined herself leaning toward, even leaning on, this man, tempted by the small calming comfort of their spontaneous hug at the first sight of him. As she had watched him struggling with what he just couldn't make himself say, her arms ached to be around him again, as if that could make up for all the things both of them had lost. But she caught herself. Instead she said in a voice so paper-thin that she wasn't even sure he'd hear it: "I wonder what Mike would think of us now?"

John Jasper's head snapped back around again as if she'd been reading his mind. The big sycamore tree began to disappear into streetlight shadow with the last rays of the sunlight until the sound of the leaves' slight movement in the air was the only sound at all. And with nothing moving between them in the dark but their own swirling thoughts, he suddenly saw Mike's kid sister exactly as he had the last time he saw her twenty years before—opening the big carved front doors right behind them. On that day. Saying what she did as she ran past him, what he had never forgotten either.

And the words he just couldn't make himself say out loud began rolling around and around in his head wanting so damn desperately to come out.

I missed his funeral . . . John Jasper thought, stealing shadowed glances at Claudia, knowing that was the first thing he'd tell her if he just the hell could. I didn't even know there was a funeral, he was thinking. Nobody told me Mike didn't make it. I was flat on my back over in Austin and I was gonna be right there for a long time, but I should've been told.

But no. That shouldn't be the first thing he told her. The first thing should be what happened—what he'd never told a soul. What he'd kept inside all these years: start with the job her father gave him and Mike working on his oil rigs every afternoon until dark-thirty. Start with the first day, John Jasper thought, stealing another glance at Claudia. How pumped he was when Mike and her daddy came barreling up in that fancy truck, thinking about the good money he'd be making with his buddy and his rich father. Start with how he'd opened the door of the truck's cab to scoot in as Mike pushed over in the middle. Start with how her daddy's first words to him were "What do you think you're doing?" which had frozen him on the spot, having no idea what the man was talking about.

"Getting in the truck," John Jasper remembered answering.

But her daddy, sitting behind the wheel in his big straw Stetson, just jerked a thumb toward the truck bed behind the cab. John Jasper had just stood there staring at Mike, who, frozen between the middle and the window, was staring back at his daddy. Finally, he'd closed the passenger door and crawled in the back. And just as the man gunned the truck forward, he was slamming on the brakes, jerking them all back to a halt again, because Mike was halfway out the passenger door with the truck in motion, vaulting into the back with him.

And that was how it was gonna be, John Jasper remembered. Every day that whole week—when the truck pulled up to his house, Mike jumped out of the front and into the back from the get-go.

Like it was fun, like there was nothing to it, John Jasper was thinking. If he'd had a lick of sense, he'd have taken that for a sign and jumped right the hell back out and told ClaudeDamnDarling what he could do with his summer job.

But he didn't. He should've, but he needed that money. And from there, it just got worse with nobody but the three of them out there all afternoon long. John Jasper had figured they'd be working with at least one oil field roughneck out there, somebody who knew what the hell he was doing. No way two teenage boys should've been doing that work without a lick of experience. But they were saving the SOB money. John Jasper got that quick. So all they had was ClaudeDamnDarling pointing and yelling and spitting orders at them. Every single hour, there was a hundred chances to get hurt bad, trying to keep all that machinery cranking, looking for oil and getting nothing but dirt. And that meant a hundred chances for ClaudeDamnDarling to yell his ass off and, worse, push Mike around. He'd yell at Mike to do a thing, and if he didn't do it fast enough, the man would be grabbing him by the arm and jerking him around like he was a kid or a goddamn puppet: "Get over here! Grab this handle! You're letting it slip. Watch yourself, boy! You hear me?"

"Yessir," Mike'd always answer.

Even then, even when Mike did every little thing exactly the way he ordered and giving a son's "yessir" back every damn time, his daddy would still be starting up all that stuff about making a man out of him, about Mike being a spoiled mama's boy, about knocking the girlie Bass right out of him.

And saying it all in front of me like I wasn't standing right there, like I didn't exist, John Jasper remembered. Like the whole world was him and Mike and whatever burr he had up his butt about the Basses—like both their lives depended on it or some crazy ClaudeDamnDarling shit. John Jasper watched Mike getting more and more pissed. Saw it clear as day by the third afternoon, but Mike just kept sucking it back in, as his daddy kept right on.

So John Jasper knew what was coming. The very next morning, Claude Darling tried doing him the same way, grabbing at his arm to jerk him around. And when he'd flung the old man's hand off his forearm, he'd come within an inch of knocking the old guy flat.

"Don't touch me, man," he'd snapped, looking down on the guy's sorry old ass. That made him stop for damn straight, but he wasn't gonna let me have the last word, John Jasper thought.

Popping his hands on his scrawny hips, ClaudeDamnDarling had said:

"Aren't you working for me, boy?"

"Don't call me boy—" John Jasper spat back.

And the SOB laughed. "What are ya getting your panties in a bunch over? I just called Michael a boy, didn't I? Stud, you are a boy," he said, cocking his hat back, and it was all John Jasper could do not to knock that Stetson clean off. "Both of ya!" he was now snapping at Mike. "And don't either of ya start thinking any different just yet. You two don't know a lick about life—about what it takes to be your own man! So, let me ask ya again: You working for me?"

boy

He didn't say it but it was hanging in the air, all right, John Jasper remembered, still hearing the silent sound of it.

"Well, are ya?" ClaudeDamnDarling had repeated.

"Yeah," John Jasper'd muttered.

"You work for me, you do what I say," the man started up again. "Now, get over here on this side of the rig! And grab that bar while Mike works that handle."

So he did. But he didn't like it and he didn't plan on taking it much longer. And that's what he'd told Mike the first break they got out of earshot, leaning against the truck bed drinking water from the truck's orange thermos.

"Why do you take his shit?" he'd said to Mike.

"He's my father," Mike answered, pouring water over his head and down his shirt to cool off. "Keep out of it."

"If the man shoved me, he'd be sucking through a straw," John Jasper'd gone on.

Mike just took a big swig from his cup, then said, all low, like he was talking to himself: "It's just another year."

Then Mike started up his usual fooling around, pouring another cup over his head and shaking off like a dog, flicking water at him. But John Jasper just ignored it, mopping off the spray, not through talking: "And the SOB better not call me a nigger—I don't care if he is your daddy, I'll break his goddamn jaw."

"He ain't gonna call you that," Mike said. "Nobody's gonna call you that—not *you*! Not the famous John Jasper Johnson, Triple

J–Triple Threat! '*Number eighteen in your programs / Number one in our hearts!*'" Then flashing that shit-eating grin of his, he picked up his work gloves and whapped John Jasper on the arm, starting back into his joking thing that worked on everybody pretty much all the time. But not this time.

"I ain't lying, Mike!" John Jasper had said, walking off. "He touches me again, I'm gonna break his jaw."

"Hey, c'mon." Mike grabbed for his arm, but he was still thinking how he wanted to lay Mike's old man in the dirt. So he'd whirled around, fists up—ready to go—

"Whoa!" Mike stumbled back, throwing out his hands. "Don't you get it? Don't let him win!"

But John Jasper wasn't listening. "In fact, he touches *you* again, I'm gonna break his jaw!"

That's when Mike lost it. First time I ever saw him mad enough to do anything about anything, John Jasper remembered, and he was aiming it right in my face.

"Leave it *alone*, JJ—you hear?" Mike yelled. "It's not about you!"

So I backed off, but in my mind it *was* about me and nobody was gonna tell me different, John Jasper realized.

He'd met men like ClaudeDamnDarling since. Men who hate anybody halfway young and mighty because they ain't anymore their own selves. Men who've got to drag everybody else down so they can feel big—even their own sons, much less a black boy lighting up Friday nights for the whole county. He'd come to understand that men like that ain't bigots as much as junkyard dogs, hating life itself and spreading the joy, and not even knowing why they're doing it.

But to his seventeen-year-old proud self who wasn't used to being disrespected to his face, Claude Darling was just a goddamn-to-living-hell bigot. And he knew Mike was flat wrong. . . . His daddy *was* going to call him a nigger.

It was coming, John Jasper thought. Like he now had a burr up his butt about his son's black buddy, too, and was going to see how long he'd get away with it. Like he'd been ClaudeDamnDarling, Town Big Shot, a little too long for good sense, because what other old white fool would keep pushing somebody a head taller who could pick up his scrawny ass and drop-kick it into the river a hundred yards away?

Yet that was also the moment John Jasper had realized, even at seventeen, that it meant something more to him, too, something way beyond hanging on for the money. Now it was about all the tired black-white shit running straight through every blasted thing in their lives that even he couldn't outrun.

Looking back, John Jasper wanted to think once he'd gone on home that night and calmed down, he'd have wised up enough not to get in the back of the SOB's pickup the next day—not with that golden football future of his waiting, making more money than any Small-Town Big Shot would ever see poking holes in the dirt. He was going to be flying down lush green miles of turf, leaving the old man crying on the sidelines, wasn't he? Then who'd have won any dirt-spitting throw-back bigot games?

But he'd never know, because that was the day he'd spotted something in the dirt, something poking up from a dry backwash off the river—something that looked like a gun handle. Grabbing a shovel, he'd started digging, and in a second he had it full out of the dirt. It was a rusty long-barreled six-shooter that looked like something straight out of a cowboy movie.

Wiping off the crud, he could see it was busted. Its cylinder was jammed; wouldn't budge even when he put all his strength behind it. If there were bullets in it, there was no way he was going to see them, but there was no way they were going to fire from a busted cylinder, either, so he didn't much worry about it. Even the trigger was stuck, gritted up, wasn't moving at all. So after eyeballing it good and careful, John Jasper remembered how he started enjoying it, clutching it, testing the heft of it, wondering how the hell cowboys lugged the thing around on a hip. Mike noticed and started coming over. Then ClaudeDamnDarling noticed from fifty yards away and was striding his way fast, kicking up dust, almost running, all of a sudden hooting:

"God damn. God diggety damn! That's a Dance Dragoon!"

John Jasper had never seen the man look so happy. He was clean out of his head with excitement. Still a dozen yards off, he was already barking orders to watch it, give it over, quit horsing around.

And I know he ain't worried about my health, John Jasper thought. He just didn't want me touching it, didn't want me getting any ideas about finders-keepers and such, since he sure thought it was worth hooting about.

So John Jasper held on to the heavy thing a little longer just to make the SOB's face turn redder. And he was about to give it to the man, was already moving the thing his way . . .

. . . when ClaudeDamnDarling said it:

"Give me the Dragoon, now, you stupid *nigger*!"

"Dad!" Mike yelled.

That's when I pointed the gun, John Jasper remembered. I pointed it at that word and at the goddamn bigot who didn't have the sense not to use it anymore, and I swear to God Almighty if that trigger could've moved, the bastard would've been dead in the dirt.

Mike, who knew damn well what I was thinking, moved up close: "*Stop* it, JJ."

But I wasn't about to stop, John Jasper thought. In fact, I raised that long barrel eye-level and aimed it right at ClaudeDamnDarling's mouth that said the goddamn word, loving the hitch in his step, the pause on his arrogant face, the tiny little question I was putting in the SOB's mind, because he didn't know the thing was busted, didn't know he couldn't be killed dead on the spot.

Then the SOB had enough.

"Stop horsing around!" he blustered, barking orders again. "*Give it to me!*"

And Mike had enough. "*Shut up,* Dad!" he yelled, the tiny little question now in his eyes, too, because he didn't know the gun couldn't hurt a thing but his daddy's pride.

Then it happened so fast . . . John Jasper thought. Mike's jumping between me and his daddy, and he's grabbing for the pistol barrel because he knows I'll let him but his daddy's suddenly there grabbing, too, and before I can get my hands clear of the goddamn*goddamn* thing—something happens with all the hands on the jammed gun, some backfire sound, a thud, the cylinder black, barrel smoking— and Mike's looking at us, panic pulling at the edges of his shocked shit-eating grin, because his thigh's turned into a gusher of red.

And the only thought in the world is: *artery.*

And the only thing moving in the world is a leather belt his daddy's flopping around a leg bleeding more than any slapdash tourniquet can stop.

And the only words in the world are: *Start the truck!*

And John Jasper's sprinting to the truck, slamming it into gear, and backing up to Mike. And ClaudeDamnDarling, covered in blood, is yanking him out of the driver's seat ordering him in the truck bed where Mike was now lying, bleeding out, bleeding everywhere: *Keep your hand on the artery. Keep your hand on the artery.* And he hesitates, because his buddy's already looking halfway to dead, his shocked shit-grin gone, his eyes glazing over like fish eyes, his fingers slack on his daddy's belt. Then John Jasper plunges his hand onto the red . . . the warm, wet, thick gaping bloody hole in his buddy's jeans. And Mike is suddenly grasping John Jasper's hand like he could help stop his own blood's gush, his grip so weak on John Jasper's fingers to make John Jasper's own blood freeze, and the only sound filling the space between them is the sound of the truck's tires spinning and spinning . . .

Until they are lunging *forward* . . .

Fast, faster forward—racing for the dirt road . . . lurching through gates . . . bouncing onto river road asphalt . . . screeching off the left shoulder . . . careening back right . . . veering toward the river bridge sliding, swerving, spinning out and out and out and out until they are missing the curve, slamming into the guardrail—metal screaming on metal, gravel spraying-peppering glass paint wood skin— then going . . .

airborne as the rig rolls throwing them   up   down Out.

And John Jasper isn't in the truck anymore and he doesn't have blood on him and he isn't watching his buddy turn dead and he isn't himself as good as dead.

He's alone.

Light. Warm. Calm. Flying.

A blink of an eternal eye.

An eon between here and there.

Before he hits.

. . .

John Jasper stiffened. He felt Claudia's eyes on him. But he could not look at her. What he was now thinking was so dark he could not even stand to be sitting there at all, sitting anywhere at all, being still alive at all, and he closed his eyes momentarily against it, fighting the red, blood-rushing rage. He forced a breath through his lungs and slowly, reluctantly, breathed it out.

And he let himself feel the rest:

The nothing. After he hit. After they all hit.

When he woke up, coming out of that nothing, he'd wished to God he hadn't. White-uniformed people going in and out of his room while he went in and out of consciousness. Nobody talking to him straight. Nobody telling him what was happening. Nobody looking him in the eye. Nobody seeming even to know him, his grandparents who raised him too old and too poor to come. And nobody telling him about Mike.

A full week passed before he came back to the world . . . a cast around his spine, his leg up in the air.

John Jasper swallowed hard at the memory of that next moment. He'd flipped out. He thought he was paralyzed. He screamed-screamed-*screamed* like he never knew he could scream—before he lost consciousness again. It was a whole other week before he found out he was in Austin. And a whole other week after that before some of his football buddies drove all the way over for a visit that he found out about Mike.

After six surgeries, he'd missed the whole football season and pretty much his whole senior year. It took him seven months to walk again—with a limp—about the time everybody else was graduating. It was clear to everybody but him that he'd never play ball again. No college was going to take a chance on him. Not a cripple, he'd slowly understood, no matter how good you might've been before you weren't.

He hadn't gone back to school. What the hell was the use? He just hung out around town, doing nothing all day but feeling sorry for his sorry ass and doing nothing all night but drinking and busting anybody's face stupid enough to come near enough for him to bust. He kept seeing ClaudeDamnDarling's face everywhere, kept trying to break his goddamn jaw by smashing whatever jaw was handy— even after finding out the SOB was already dead, God getting to him first. He could've fucked up his life a dozen times, just like that, but the county deputy sheriffs kept cutting him slack, pulling him off whoever was the unlucky chump of the night and driving him home. They were pulling him out of fights every night of the week.

On one of those nights, maybe because he just couldn't find anybody to fight or buy him drinks, he drove his grandmama's beat-up car to Old Waco Road. To right there, John Jasper thought, gazing down to the street. Smack-dab in front of the mansion. Then he'd gone around the block, around and around and around, in some sort of drunk loop de loop, until finally landing the car half up on Maude Quattlebaum's curb, where it died. So he got out, limped to the curb, and sat down to stare across the street at the mansion.

The next night he did it again. And the night after that. He kept doing the same thing—circling the block until parking the car in front of Maude Quattlebaum's house, sometimes more successfully than others, to get out and sit on the curb and stare across at the Darling mansion, awash with feelings he couldn't control, couldn't even name.

Five nights in a row he'd done it before finally getting up the drunken nerve to limp across the street, up the front steps, and bang on the door. He didn't know why. All he knew was that he was finally here. Then John Jasper cut an eye toward Claudia, remembering what happened next.

There I was with my fist up in the air, all set to start pounding, John Jasper thought, when the door opens and there you are, Mike's little sister. And what do you do? You take one look at me, bust out crying, say what you said, and race off leaving me in front of those big, open doors, drunk as a *skunk*. . . .

Five nights in a row must have been Maude Quattlebaum's limit for having a drunk black man sitting on her front curb—or maybe that night he'd just stayed long enough to still be there after her nightly 911 call—because the deputies arrived in time to see him standing wobbly on the Darling front porch with Claudia Jean running down the steps and away. They were the same deputies who'd been saving his sorry ass for a month. But since Maude Quattlebaum was watching from across the street, this time they arrested him, and as they hauled him off the porch, he remembered how he kept looking back.

Looking for what? John Jasper pondered, eyeing the doors behind them. I still the hell don't know, like maybe I was waiting for Mike or ClaudeDamnDarling to show up, despite being dead.

He'd slept it off with the other drunks in the "tank," retching and wishing for more alcohol to retch some more. Then the next morning, he was taken up to the front where the sheriff himself was waiting.

"John Jasper, you're free to go—go back over to see Mrs. Darling, that is," the sheriff told him. "Seems she got Maude Quattlebaum to hush up about filing trespass charges and didn't file any herself." Then he leaned right in John Jasper's face. "But damn straight we'll slap some drunk-driving ones on you if you ever get behind the wheel of a car shit-faced again, ya hear?" Fuming big, he leaned back on his boot heels and went on. "So like I was saying, Mrs. Darling wants you to stop by. So clean yourself up and get over there."

John Jasper—now far too sober—didn't want to do any such thing. And he must have set his jaw in a way that said so, because the sheriff was shaking his head.

"Who do you think paid your hospital bills?" the sheriff asked. "Don't you know, son? You think state services cared a lick about you? You think the Great State of Texas could give a rat's ass about getting you on your feet again, offering you surgery after surgery till they got it as good as it got? You probably wouldn't even be walking if it weren't for her. Now go see what the woman wants. She's been through hell, too."

So he'd come back over here, come right up the steps he was now sitting on. And there stood Mrs. Darling swinging open those big doors for me, John Jasper remembered, like we did it every day of our lives.

"John Jasper," she'd said, nodding, that chin of hers high.

"Mrs. Darling," he'd said back, his chin wanting to go just as high and not getting there, focusing every ounce of energy on not looking away.

"Are you hungry?" she asked.

"No, ma'am," John Jasper had answered a little too quick. No way he could go into that kitchen, sit there like he'd done with Mike, and eat her food. All he remembered thinking was: What does she want from me?

Did she want him to thank her? No way he'd be able to do that, not yet convinced he even wanted the miserable life he got back. Did she want him to tell her what happened? Talk about Mike or her SOB of a husband? Sit down and bawl like a couple of old ladies? Because there was no way he was able to do that, either—even if he'd wanted to. No way he ever had, ever could, not for all these twenty years.

But I was the one showing up here last night . . . what the hell do I want from her? John Jasper recalled wondering.

Suddenly, standing in that fancy doorway with his dead best friend's mother before him, all the anger and sadness and grief and guilt and loss—the entire burden he would carry to this very day— had come pouring over him and he felt himself wobble, so light-headed and dizzy he was about to fall out right in *front* of the woman. Damned if he was going to let that happen, he started grasping for the doorframe to steady himself. But then Mrs. Darling reached out for his arm, grabbing it in the same place ClaudeDamnDarling had done that goddamn day. When he went to jerk it back, her touch turned soft, gentle, just guiding him inside.

And I let her, John Jasper thought.

The moment they'd cleared the door and he got his balance, she had dropped her hand from him, quick. Like she'd maybe crossed some proper line of her own, he'd always thought, remembering how her eyes had filled up with tears to the point she had to look away but how that chin of hers never dropped an inch.

That's when Faith Darling had blown him away. She went behind those big stairs and came back lugging three long canvas bags—the SOB's entire antique gun collection. John Jasper could still hear all the metal clunking, banging together as she lugged it across that nice wood floor and dropped the whole thing at his feet.

"John Jasper," she began, all calm, proper, polite, "would you please do me the kindness of taking these out of my sight and my life? They are rather valuable or I'd have thrown them in the trash. Maybe you could find a use for their value and help me in the process."

So he had.

He took them back to his grandmama's lean-to garage behind their shotgun shack, throwing a tarp over the canvas bags to keep out the dirt and raccoons, and just left them there. Because he'd never had nothing and didn't know what to do with having something, and he wasn't ready to do anything but keep on giving in to his nightly fury.

When he cracked open the town wise-ass Lucky Hinton's head for looking at him funny, almost killing the guy, the deputies let him go again, talking Lucky out of pressing charges. But John Jasper could tell things were different. He could see it in their eyes. He finally got it. He knew one day—and it'd only take one—they'd decide his sorry ass wasn't worth saving anymore. That time was coming soon.

So he started rehabbing his leg himself out at the school weight room, and when he got it back as good as it ever was going to be and saw what everybody else already knew, that it wasn't ever going to be good enough, he got shit-faced one more time.

Then he got his GED and a job, any job they'd give him down at the county sheriff's department, filing, answering phones, cleaning up shit, and started working toward being a deputy. Then he got a second job out at the county airport, working for nothing, talking his way into the air, and working his slow way up to lessons and hours and finally a license. Then he threw that tarp off all those old guns and bought a used plane with what he got for them. Because the last second of his other life, the second after he and Mike went sailing out of that truck bed—a second that should've been nothing but hellfire itself—felt instead like Flying Full of Everything Good and God. And he had to keep that feeling near enough to grab onto when he needed to grab onto something.

I got a job, a plane, and a life—that's what Faith Darling gave back to me, he realized. Even though I'm the one that killed Mike. It was *me*, John Jasper wanted to shout. Even if the goddamn bigot was Mike's daddy, even if I was already a better man than he'd ever be—even if I knew not to do what you want to do when somebody named ClaudeDamnDarling calls you "nigger" when the whole world knows not to do that anymore—I just wanted to feel what it'd be like to point a gun right at him. Because I knew I could. It was jammed; it wasn't gonna hurt anybody. But it did.

So I did it.

I killed Mike.

I killed us both.

John Jasper realized he was staring at Mike Darling's kid sister. Who was staring at him, placing her slim fingers lightly on top of his big hand. Her eyes were filling with tears exactly like Faith Darling's had, just like the ones he felt surfacing in his own. And he heard himself begin to tell her the whole goddamn thing.

Upstairs in the front bedroom, as John Jasper's voice drifted through the open window, the setting sun's rays were streaming through the sycamore and dancing on the walls of Faith Bass Darling's bedroom much as they had all her life.

Faith was sitting in a pink chair, in her starched white sundress, peacefully watching the familiar shadows so much like sheltering arms, and she felt herself going down to the river. . . .

". . . In obedience to the command of our Lord and Savior Jesus Christ and upon the profession of your faith in him . . ."

Twelve-year-old Faith Ann is standing waist-high in the Brazos River with nothing on but her pink cotton underwear and a starched white baptismal robe which is floating up, up, up, as the preacher holds a handkerchief over her nose and says:

". . . I baptize you my sister in Christ, Faith Ann Bass, in the name of the Father and the Son and the Holy Ghost. Amen."

As she goes under, kicking and splashing, the handkerchief bobs off her face and she gulps down the muddy Brazos River to the sound of the congregation chuckling and the red-robed choir belting out "Washed in the Blood of the Lamb." Then she feels herself being grabbed up from the water. It's her daddy in his Sunday-best suit, wading in to wrap his arms around her and hug her hard enough to pop.

"Aren't you the lucky one?" her daddy whispers. "You just went 'down to the river.' Baptized in the 'Brazos de Dios'—the 'Arms of God'—like every Bass since the first James Tyler Bass beat back the devil on the Brazos River to stay!"

They stand dripping on the shore, hand in hand, to the sound of the choir's screeching joyful noise. She feels her fingers swimming in the warmth of his big fist against the gold wedding band he still wears even though her mama is already with Jesus.

> *The Lord Bless You and Keep You*
> *The Lord Make His countenance to shine upon you*
> *And give you peace*
> *And give you peace . . .*

As the choir finishes the benediction, her daddy is again whispering:

"I have a surprise, my darling girl! Something your blessed mother and all your Texas grandmothers wore: a *ring* to wear on your next big church day, your wedding day. And I'm going to tell you its wonderful story, all about your great-grandfather James Tyler Bass and his only and eternal love, Belle."

✍ PROVENANCE

LOVE LETTER

Circa 1879   *Value: ephemera*

On the 13th of May 1879, in the growing little railroad town of Bass, Texas, a thirty-five-year-old banker named James Tyler Bass stared out his office window, waiting for the sunrise on his wedding day.

As the light began filtering into the room, he turned out his oil lamp and ever so hesitantly opened a sliding niche compartment in his rolltop's middle drawer that had not been disturbed for nine long years.

From it, he took out a black velvet ring box and opened it.

For a quiet moment, he gazed sadly at the filigreed pearl-encrusted diamond engagement ring inside, before returning it to the sliding compartment to stay.

Then he took out a sheet of letterhead stationery, dipped his pen point into the ink bottle, and began to write in perfect cursive:

My dearest, my only and eternal love Pearl . . .

Hiram Hitt was hunched over the garage sale rolltop desk, rushing to finish cleaning the darn smelly old thing so Geraldine would let him get back to his Y2K preparedness. He was almost done checking all the nooks and crannies for dust bunnies, dead spiders, bent paper clips, and the like—griping all the while to himself about Geraldine's lack of understanding of the gravity of Y2K—when he suddenly jumped back.

"What the *heck*?" he blurted.

He'd accidentally pushed a cubbyhole drawer knob that was meant for pulling, and out had popped a little lever. So he pulled it. And the pencil holder dropped down, revealing what looked like a secret compartment—a horizontal slot about as tall as a dollar bill and as wide as a couple of his fingers. It occurred to Hiram that something might be in that slot. So he poked in a pinkie finger until he felt something and snatched his finger out. Grumbling at himself for being such a scaredy-cat, he opened the blade of his pocketknife and inserted it into the slot, coaxing out a yellowed envelope.

"Well, wouldya look at this," he mumbled. The envelope was sealed but had no name, address, or postage. As carefully as his beefy hands would allow, Hiram laid it on the rolltop's cracked leather writing surface in order to take a good gander at it.

The envelope flap was already half open from age, so Hiram edged a fingernail under the rest of the flap and nudged it open all the way, uncovering a single folded piece of writing paper. He eased out the sheet, unfolded it, and half of it immediately crumbled in his hand.

Hiram picked up the pieces he could salvage and carefully laid them out. Below the old-fashioned curlicue letterhead—*Bass Bank, 1 Main Street, Bass, Texas*—he was only able to make out a few words in the faded, scratchy handwriting:

May 13, 1879

My dearest, my only and eternal love Pearl,

I know I will never mail this, but I cannot help myself . . . I wish you had kept the ring, broken betrothal be damned. I continue to be possessed by it as surely as I was of you the day I was Texas-bound. Today I am to marry, because life goes on, just as you said. But this ring, your ring, can never be hers.
I thought I could not forgive you.
I know I cannot forget you . . .

Then ham-handed Hiram made the mistake of trying one last time to smooth the remaining pieces and the rest crumbled into bits under his hand. At that, he rolled his eyes and gave up. He didn't have time for this—Y2K was only six hours away. Besides, he didn't want to get Geraldine going on some silly letter about somebody deader than a doornail, what with the immediate apocalypse at hand!

So he wiped the whole mess into his palm, dumped it into the trash, and went back to finish his desk cleaning, lickety-split.

ɷ LOST PROVENANCE

Heirloom wedding ring

3-carat pear-shaped diamond ring • Seed accent pearls •
White gold filigreed setting • Custom-designed by
L. Francois of New Orleans • Inscription: *Love Eternal*

Circa 1870–1999   *Value: $135,000*

In the spring of 1870, twenty-six-year-old James Tyler Bass, having made good in Texas, sent for his long-betrothed sweetheart, Pearl, back home in Kentucky, by shipping her, via Railway Express Mail, a train ticket and an extravagant pearl-encrusted engagement ring bearing the inscription "Love Eternal," proving his prosperity and his devotion.

Instead of the train delivering his delicate cultured Pearl, however, it returned the ring. And a letter. The last he would ever receive from his first and only love:

"I cannot bear to finally write this," Pearl's letter began. "I have married and am bearing his child . . . Forgive me, please forgive me . . . I am weak and life goes on. . . ."

The young banker locked the ring inside his rolltop, too heartbroken to part with it. And there it stays even after he marries a loyal, pretty woman named Belle, who will die in childbirth and whom he will follow in death twenty-five years later.

James Tyler Bass, Jr., while emptying his deceased father's bank desk, will discover the ring. Reading its inscription—aware of neither the old love letter nor the secret slot compartment in which it still hides—he will mistake the dazzling ring for his long-dead mother Belle's and offer it to his new bride along with the sad story of how his beloved mother had died giving him the gift of life.

And his bride will proudly wear it until her own son's marriage, when the ring with the "Love Eternal" inscription will be passed down with the pioneer love story to the new generation's bride.

And that bride will one day do the same for the next generation . . .

. . . a great-granddaughter bride named Faith Ann, who will revel in the Bass family legend of the heirloom wedding ring and its sad and beautiful and completely untrue Love Eternal Story, forever passing it on.

Up on the second floor of the mansion, the sycamore tree's shadows were no longer dancing on the walls of Faith's bedroom, the day's dark growing deeper as the murmur of Claudia and John Jasper's voices continued to waft through the open window from below.

Just back from her baptism's river, Faith swallowed, coughed, and looked around. She didn't recognize the chair she sat on.

Then suddenly she did.

"Oh yes," she said, running her fingers along it. Little Claudia Jean's pink cane chair. The fact that it was in her bedroom didn't seem a bit odd. Nor did the fact that there was nothing in her bedroom but the chair.

It just was what it was.

Minutes passed as she sat waiting. To remember.

Her hand was throbbing, and she was surprised to see a Band-Aid across her palm and red burn marks on her knuckles. She could feel the memories stuck in the back of her mind, and it was as if she were coaxing them to come back within reach, like the chair, so she could get a grasp of the moment. As she waited, she sat in the silence of the empty room remembering only a single odd notion about the mansion—that she'd all but emptied it at the request of God (whom she was almost certain she hadn't spoken to in quite some time).

How very strange, she thought, her head cocked as the notion turned into a real memory. Such a fuss, such a strange request, in such a familiar place. What could ever have happened that she'd find herself in such an unusual mess? she wondered.

Her mental deck of cards began a new shuffle.

And her answer came. . . .

She's twelve again, still wet behind the ears from her baptism, looking at a big sparkly ring. Her daddy is holding it as he tells her the story of all the happy Bass brides who have worn it, especially her mother, for whom he had bought an entire room of beautiful Tiffany stained-glass light.

Then her father lets her try it on her too-small ring finger. . . .

. . . And her finger is no longer too small. She is *twenty-seven* and the man slipping the ring on her full-grown finger is Claude Angus Darling, heart-melting handsome in his wedding tuxedo, holding her hand and vowing before the ring and before God and before everyone in attendance to love and honor her till death do they part. She believes the legacy of the ring will be theirs in an unbroken circle of love. This wiry, charming man will love her like her father loved her mother, loving her enough to light up rooms. She will look at her ring every day of her life, remembering all the great eternal loves of the Bass generations, straight to her own love with a man perfectly named Darling, as if that were her lineage and her birthright. And their life in her family's mansion will go on, just as their Heavenly Father has seen fit to bless it all these years. . . .

. . . Then, suddenly she is *thirty-two*, pregnant, and hysterical.

Her heirloom wedding ring is missing half the seed pearls from its diamond setting. She is upset—and she cannot be upset. Only a few weeks have passed since her father's funeral, so Dr. Friddell has come for fear she'll miscarry.

"Stay in bed, honey, and try to be calm," Dr. Friddell is saying.

But she cannot stay calm because she has lost her family heirloom ring's pearls, and her toddler son, Michael, won't stop crying in his nursery because he can hear her crying.

Then Dr. Friddell vanishes. In his place stands her husband, Claude Angus, smiling. "I have something for you." He opens a green velvet ring box in his hands. She sees it is a brand-new diamond solitaire engagement ring and wedding band. And she doesn't understand . . . she wears her great-grandmother's ring.

Then her husband starts sweet-talking. "I want you to wear this one, Faith Ann. I picked it out myself," he says. "Your antique ring is far too valuable to wear every day and now you're losing its stones. Let's put it in a safe-deposit box. You can visit it anytime."

But Faith pushes the new ring box away. Who cares about her ring's value? What does it matter to him? It's not his. And they have lots of money. Then she sees something change in her handsome husband's eyes, a dark glint. He is talking again, but not sweet: "Don't be childish, Faith Ann. Give me the ring before something else happens to it."

She moves out of bed and down the stairs, calling back that she will not talk about it anymore, ever.

The next day, though, he tries again.

She still doesn't understand. In the seven years they'd been married and living in the mansion with her father, her husband has never demanded a thing, never even raised his voice. "I can't be upset," she gasps. "I can't lose this baby, Claude. I can't miscarry again!"

"Then give me the ring, sweetheart, and don't be upset," he says evenly, setting the new ring box in her lap. "I'm the man of the house now, and you're my wife. So do what I say—it's the best thing."

She refuses. Again.

"Give me the ring, Faith Ann—" he repeats.

"NO!" she screams.

With that, her husband suddenly loses his temper, something she's never seen before. His handsome face is distorted ugly, red, and he's using dirty, blasphemous language that she's never heard in her house nor in her presence. "If m-my father were here—"

Claude cuts her off, gesturing wildly. "Well, he's not! He's dead, Faith Ann! And he spoiled you fuckin' rotten like some shit-ass royal princess! I can't stand it anymore—I'm sick to death of your whole fuckin' high-and-mighty Bass family! Jesus Christ Almighty—grow up and give me the goddamn *ring*!"

Choking back shocked tears, she throws the bedspread back to leave again, knocking the new ring box to the floor.

And he slaps her with the back of his hand.

It's the first time he has ever done such a thing. And it will not happen again for a very, very long time. But she doesn't know that, once being more than enough. Holding her cheek, she reels back on the bed and stares at the sudden stranger who is her husband.

Who is now *apologizing*.

He'd squeezed his eyes shut and sighed. It was as if he'd sucked his temper back in, stuffed it somewhere deep again, like performing a magic trick he'd learned to do and do well.

"I am so sorry, Faith Ann," he's now saying, looking so very contrite, his eyes so very believable. "Honest to God, I don't know what came over me. I didn't mean a bit of what I said. I'm just trying to do right for you and the family. Protecting the things you love. That's all, sweetheart. You okay?"

He reaches out to touch her face. She jerks back, staring at him now as if she has been slapped into another world. And perhaps that is exactly what has happened, her rosy-colored life instantly turning black and white. Because she clearly sees something now she's never seen before—her husband doesn't mean a thing he's saying.

"Forgive me?" he asks, those eyes so very remorseful.

And she wonders how long he's held in that temper, how long he's been lying, and how much he hasn't meant for the last seven years. With a resolve she didn't know she had in her, she hears herself ask:

"Do you love me?"

He cocks his head. "C'mon, how can you ask that?"

"Did you ever love me?" she goes on.

With that, they both notice a pause as pregnant as she is. Then he is talking, fast, and she senses something of desperation curdling his charm: "Of course I love you—of course! Sweetheart, please stop it now. I said I was sorry. I've upset you, I know, and you're not thinking clearly. So you rest now and we'll talk about the ring tomorrow. But you know it's the right thing to do."

The next day, when he asks again, she still does not give up the ring. Not then.

Nor the next time. Or even the next.

But the time after that—the time immediately after the birth of their daughter, Claudia Jean—she does.

Then she moves out of the master bedroom, back to her old bedroom down the hall.

And their separate worlds begin. . . .

Momentarily returning to herself, Faith grips her daughter's pink chair, feeling a wave of nausea as her mind shuffles one more time. . . .

. . . Now *forty-nine*, she is standing in the office of the bank's vice president, Ernest Allen Hull, a man hired by her father out of high school who now has a comb-over. He has jumped to his feet. It's the day after Claude's funeral, and she has just informed him she's there to close the safe-deposit box and take home her great-grandmother Belle's ring for good.

He begins wringing his soft plump hands. "I'm sorry, ma'am, but you can't. It's collateral."

She gives him a brush-away flick of her wrist. "Nonsense. Give me my great-grandmother's ring."

Ernest Allen, as pink-faced a man as she'd ever seen, is suddenly beet red. "Oh dear, oh dear." And he begins smoothing down the comb-over. "You best sit down."

"Not until you tell me what the problem is."

He swallows hard, going back to hand-wringing.

"Spit it out, Ernest Allen!" she commands.

He drops his hands and obeys: "It was Mr. Darling's oil-speculating, ma'am. He kept taking out bigger and bigger loans, using your family's antique ring for the revolving collateral, done it for years. But he always paid it back. Until last year. Instead, he put up his interest in the bank as more collateral, and then put up yours—showed me your signature! I knew I should have checked with you, ma'am—but he would have fired me on the spot!" Ernest Allen stopped to take a breath, reclaiming his professional demeanor. "With his sudden passing, the debt is yours. So the bank owns the ring, ma'am, and that's just a portion of the debt you now owe."

"I *owe*? But the bank is *mine*," she reminds him.

Ernest's face has now gone white as milk. "Yes, ma'am. But, no, ma'am."

Faith feels her knees go a bit weak; she finally sinks into a chair.

Ernest Allen melts back into his own. "I wish we could continue carrying the debt, but the bank's in peril, the economy's so bad. The vultures are circling, ma'am, the big bank chains are waiting to take us over." Faith barely hears the rest, until the bank officer dares to offer a solution: "Perhaps if you're willing to sell some of your most valuable antiques, that might save your mansion and keep the bank in your hands."

"What? No!" Faith cuts him off, horrified. "How could my family's things go to strangers?"

"But, Mrs. Darling—"

Faith, though, has stopped listening, alone with thoughts of rings and lies, replaying memories she now understands far too well. Finally, chin out, she asks what she has no other choice but to ask: "If we sell the bank, will that allow me to keep my ring, my antiques, and my home?"

"Yes, ma'am, but—" Ernest Allen Hull falls silent.

Faith feels herself slowly get to her feet. She hears herself say what she has no choice but to say: "Sell the bank, then." She breathes in. "Now, if you'll kindly give me my great-grandmother's ring."

She takes home the ring to the mansion that will now always be hers, where she believes it will be safe among her family's antiques that will now always be hers. Until the day the ring disappears along with her daughter.

Her daughter whose pink chair she is sitting on . . .

Faith blinked, conscious of being back in her empty bedroom, feeling the leftover dizziness from the burning, churning memories. Closing her eyes, she clenched the arms of the chair to steady herself, waiting for everything to quiet down. But then Faith jerked, suddenly opening her eyes and searching. For what? *A ring. A bed-room dresser.* But when she saw the emptiness of the room, whatever thoughts she was trying to hold on to slipped away.

The window was open. She felt a breeze brush against her cheek from the front lawn. Warm for December. Is it still December? she wondered. She noticed the sun hat and the money bag lying nearby. Lord, it's certainly warm for December. Is it still December? she repeated, forgetting, as she dabbed at the sweat on her upper lip.

And it all came rushing back. From one instant to the next, she was once again fully Faith Bass Darling.

Unclenching her grip on the pink chair as the memory flood flowed on, she was vividly remembering:

That she had once loved sundown.

That she married a man who loved one thing and it was not her.

That she once had a beautiful boy.

That she once sold a bank to keep possession of a house, antiques, and a ring.

A ring she no longer possessed.

A ring that cost her all the family she had left.

And all the hope of any family future.

Faith groaned under the weight of her life. She'd always heard that people's lives flash in front of their eyes before dying. What would that be like for me? she pondered.

Just then, something flew past the window, her eye chasing it reflexively. And a new, scarier thought occurred to her: What will be the last thing I'll see?

Would it be a shadow moving past her? Something flying by? The ceiling of her bedroom? Someone's face? And how would she know if what she saw was real?

I won't, she realized with a start. *Dear God help me—I won't.*

And her mind went straight to what she did not want—could not allow—that last thing to be:

Claude Angus Darling.

That's when Faith heard the sound. She knew where it came from and she knew what it was as if she'd conjured it herself. Slowly she rose from the pink chair and found herself returning down the hall, stepping through the open door of what was once the master bedroom with its widow's-walk balcony overlooking the backyard. The shadows were deep. Yet she was able to make out a faint figure she'd know anywhere, hardly more than a lanky outline of him, roaming the empty room, searching for something methodically in furniture that was no longer there and closets with nothing in them, around and around the room, stuck in its loop. The sight slipped in and out of her vision, seemingly unaware of her, as if she were the unreal presence. Faith held her fear at bay, telling herself that as real as it seemed, it was just the sundowning. If he didn't speak to her, then she could think herself through this moment until the fading saved her again.

"It's the money; that's why I'm seeing this," she heard herself say, and she understood. The elephant clock is Claudia. The football is Mike. The money is Claude. But knowing didn't matter, because it was all real no matter what she told herself. She knew everything had meaning on this important day, whether she liked it or not.

So she knew what was coming. She braced herself, waiting for the deck to shuffle again and deal her the one memory she could no longer dodge.

And just like that, she moved inside the long-denied memory. She looked down at her *hands* . . . they're no longer an old lady's hands . . . they are middle-aged and they are trembling.

It has been days since her son's funeral, yet she can't get them to completely stop trembling. The silence through the mansion is hanging as heavy and cold as ice, the three of them, the "surviving" family, going through the motions of what everyone else calls a day, a week, a month, going on breathing in place of living. She still cannot bear to be in the same room as her husband, who survived the accident with barely a scratch, which somehow makes her blame him all the more. And then, like a contagion, she is unable to be near her remaining child, her teenage daughter. Faith no longer wants to be anyone's mother or anyone's wife or anyone's anything at all, unable to hazard any more pain. She cannot stop the trembling when they are around. And because she cannot send Claude away, she sends Claudia Jean. Her daughter is staying with friends for now. Or perhaps it is her daughter's idea. Faith doesn't know anymore; she only knows she's relieved.

That is how she is feeling—this shuffled day—the day the trembling has taken over again, the day she catches her husband hiding something she even now can hardly allow herself to *see*. . . .

. . . Dusk is sifting through the trees at the mansion.

Upstairs, Faith hears a truck pull up to the side of the house. Not recognizing the sound of the loaner truck Claude has been driving since the accident, she looks out. She sees a silhouette through the borrowed truck's back window and watches the shadowed shape turn into her husband as he opens the truck door and the cab light illuminates the truck's interior.

She is not much more than the walking, talking dead since her son's funeral, so she begins to turn away. But then she notices her husband reach for something on the seat beside him and hide it under his seat. And the cab's bright-white light against the dark night has given her too good a look at it, because it looked like . . .

oh, Dear Lord God no

. . . a long-barreled *pistol*?

She knows of only one such gun he would hide. Something she hoped to be spared ever seeing. Something she cannot imagine even Claude Angus Darling would ever want to lay eyes on again.

She finds herself rushing down the stairs and through the kitchen door outside before he can even close the truck door. Hearing her, he whirls around. She shoves her hand under the seat and pulls out a burnt-black, rust-encrusted antique revolver. Even though it is what she expected, a part of her is shocked that she's now holding the thing that has killed her son. She wants to drop it, but she cannot let go; she can only stand squeezing it in a death grip, swallowing down her bile and gaping back at Claude, who has finally found his tongue:

"It's not what you think, Faith Ann! You have to believe me, I tried to leave it. God help me, I did!"

Then her husband breaks down and begins to weep. Faith stares at his tears, wanting to trust them, wanting them to turn him into the man she thought she married. Wanting them to hold something that would help her let go of the gun and the hatred and finally forgive him for this, for everything. He is talking again, wiping at his eyes, gasping out words, and she waits. Hopes. But they are the wrong words.

"You don't understand, I'm trying to save us, Faith Ann! That's a Dance Dragoon—worth thousands even in this busted shape. I've already made the deal. I couldn't leave it out there when we could lose everything!" He is saying things she cannot believe: The family bank is in trouble . . . he's liquidating everything, his coins, guns, oil equipment, in order to save everything else. . . .

"I can fix this, Faith! You've got to let me fix it!" he keeps repeating, growing more and more manic. "I'm doing it for you—for the family—try to understand!"

Yet Faith won't understand until she is in front of Ernest Allen Hull at the bank, hearing it all later, too late. Standing in the truck cab's glow, half deaf with shock, she finds her husband's statements incomprehensible. How could her family's fortune need saving? Her family's bank was the one thing she'd entrusted to Claude. Her broken heart has no more pieces to break. He *must* be lying, she tells herself, gaping at the gun in her grip that now seems to have a death grip on her.

Then the father of her dead son says what she cannot forgive nor bear: "*Mike* would understand—"

And Faith realizes she is no longer clutching the antique gun. She has flung it into the backyard shadows, into the deep, endless dark surrounding the night that has become their lives.

For a beat, the two stand silent in the truck cab's light, eyes locked, their shocked hard gazes saying all the unspoken things of the years spent in their separate peace—all the compromises, the disillusionment, all the deceit, the blame, the lies—intimately understood by both in an instant. Then it is all too much for them both. Claude loses his temper, his face distorting blood-red in a way she hasn't seen in years, since the day he made her give up the heirloom ring. And for the second time in their long marriage, he slaps Faith with the back of his hand.

Faith's jaw quivers from the blow. Then her jaw stops its quivering and sets. And she does the one thing Claude Angus Darling never expected:

Faith Bass Darling slaps him back.

The world momentarily stops. When it begins again, it is to the sound of Claude cursing her to her face as everything begins to move slow, dream-like. She watches her husband rush into the backyard darkness, hears his thrashing in the holly bushes for the flung Dragoon, sees him reappear to search the truck for a flashlight, listens to him damn the loaner truck for not having one, feels his violent shove as he marches toward the kitchen to get one, yelling blasphemies back her way, damning God and calling on God to damn her, as he vanishes inside.

Until it stops in mid-roar. Mid-curse.

Midair.

Yet even the sound of the sudden silence doesn't shake her out of her nightmare numbness, and Faith moves through the kitchen door as if wading through molasses. There she finds Claude crumpled on the tile, clutching his chest with clawed hands, the bulging veins in his neck, temple, jaw throbbing crimson, gasping with the same mouth that cursed her and God to summon ambulances and paramedics like she's done so many times before.

Out of reflex, she moves toward the wall phone, her hand already reaching for the receiver. Then Faith Bass Darling does the second thing neither of them thought she could ever do:

Nothing.

Her hand has stalled on the cradled receiver and she closes her eyes against the sound of her husband's frantic breaths behind her, unable to follow through to help save his life again, to do what a good God-fearing woman would always do. Because it is no longer God she fears but what God might choose to do—again.

And so she stands doing nothing, her own heart seizing up, her own tears blinding her, as the sound of her husband's death rattle goes on and on and on. And on.

Until finally she hears *nothing*.

Faith came back to herself to find that she was no longer in the master bedroom but standing dangerously near the edge of the stair landing. She grabbed for the banister, Claude's last curse still echoing in her ears. And her first clear thought was:

Did God damn me?

The thought lingered. Faith raised her trembling chin and looked defiantly up.

Did *You* damn me? she thought. Because damned is what I've felt.

With that, sagging under the weight of all her furious shuffled remembering, she set her jaw. And her spine.

"Do You want me to say it?" she asked. And the words, half prayer and half wail, tumbled out:

"I *confess* I didn't do my Christian duty—I *confess* I let Claude squeeze his own chest until that weak heart of his finally stopped—

"And I *confess* I hated myself—because life was my duty. Death was *Your* duty!" She jabbed a shaky finger at the air. "*You* were the One in charge of who lived and who died, but look who You picked to live and who to die! And I have *hated* You for it all these years!" The horrid sound of those long-suppressed words echoing back from the foyer below choked Faith momentarily silent. She gripped the railing to steady herself.

Then from old dear habit, she was suddenly quoting scripture, her quivering voice rising with each once loved passage: "Where is the God who promised to keep me in '*perfect peace*'? Who is '*my shepherd*'? Who walks me '*through the valley of the shadow of death*'? Who prepares a place for me in His house of '*many mansions*'?" Faith closed her old eyes, her thoughts racing faster than she could speak them, and, for a moment, she stood clutching her heart with both hands before she could go on.

"All my life I did everything I was supposed to—" Her breath caught, she squeezed her heart harder. "I honored my father and mother; I loved You with my whole heart and soul and mind; I kept the commandments, I honored my marriage vows despite everything. I tried to live right and good and then it went so terribly wrong and bad and there was no perfect peace, no abiding souls, no shepherds, no You. . . ." Faith ended, voice trailing away.

She took a deep breath. "But then last night I finally heard You—I *know* I did—the still, small voice just like I was taught, and I did everything You asked. I did! So why is it all coming back? Why is everybody coming back but *You*?" she pleaded.

"God!" Faith gasped. The word bounced off the thick walls and big carved doors, echoing around the foyer emptily back to her. "How *dare* You disappear on me again! Tell me what to do—*please*— what are You always, always waiting for?"

Our-Father-who-art-in-heaven . . . hallowed-be-thy-name . . . Dear *God! . . .* God damn damn *DAMN You . . .*

Her old knees buckled. And, with a great groan, Faith sank to the landing.

Where are You?

Father George Fallow, once again, had driven his beat-up Toyota sedan to the Darling mansion. But this time he'd pulled around to the dirt alleyway alongside the Darlings' large property, doing just as he was told.

It was still the late sundown time of day once called "gloaming," when nothing is quite what it seems or is seen for quite what it is, the change from light to dark a visceral, semi-blinding thing. So he hadn't seen the pair still sitting on the mansion's front steps, just as John Jasper and Claudia hadn't thought anything of the car they saw turn and drive down the alley to the streets beyond. By the back hedge, though, George had gotten out of his car and followed the sounds around the fence and into the mansion's backyard. As he came close, he saw a woman, manic, hysteric, searching for something under the sticky holly bushes in the deep silhouette of the big oak tree, the light from a bedroom window behind them the only illumination of the eerie scene before his eyes. To his horror, he saw it was Faith Darling, a world away from the dignified Faith Ann Darling he'd revered. Dirt-smeared. Scratched. Wild-eyed. Hair a mess. So very, very old. And she looked as if she'd been crying.

"Mrs. Darling?"

She acted as if she hadn't heard him. So he slipped close and tenderly placed both hands on her shoulders to still her. She froze at his touch, collapsing slowly down onto the dead grass by the bushes, exhausted.

He let go of her shoulders and spoke quietly. "Mrs. Darling. You just called me again. To come around to the backyard hedges. Do you remember?"

"Yes," she said, gratefully. "And you came."

"Have you lost something?" he gently asked.

"Oh yes." Faith sighed, still not looking up. "So much I wouldn't know where to begin." She pulled her eyes away from the bushes. "A deal is a deal, George."

"A deal?"

"A deal is a deal. I'm supposed to die tonight, but things aren't finished and I have to finish, and how am I going to finish now?" she went on, slowly looking around. At the sight of the priest, she began to calm down, as if relocating a bit of her dignity and posture in his presence. Then she patted the grass beside her, expecting him to sit.

George didn't much want to sit down in the dead, sticky grass, especially in the dark, having on his good pair of wool-blend JCPenney slacks. But he finally gave up and slowly eased down beside her. "I don't know why I'm here," he said, landing with a grunt. "I don't know how I can help you."

Faith looked at him. "God started this. And I seem to have, shall we say, lost the signal, George."

"I don't quite understand."

Her gaze was now pleading. "I thought maybe He might talk to you."

"Oh, Mrs. Darling." George shook his head, shoulders slumping. "I have a confession to make. I haven't thought that in the longest time." He heaved a sigh. "And the truth is, sometimes, I'm not even sure . . ." He stopped himself, unable to put the rest into words, feeling a bit queasy.

But she didn't notice.

"George, you know those people in the portraits lining the foyer?"

"Yes?"

"I don't know which is which. I can't place their names."

"I'll help you with your portraits," he said. "We'll figure them out."

"That would be lovely, but my memories are dancing so wildly now, I'm not sure I'd remember." She looked up at the early-evening sky and the moon already shining bright. "You know, I try to imagine myself dying, but I always come back to the moment after, and I'm always breathing again."

"That's only natural," responded the priest.

"R.I.P.," she said under her breath.

"What?" asked George.

"R.I.P.—Rest in Peace," she answered quietly. "Always annoyed me, those letters on tombstones. Seemed lazy not to just spell it out. Where did that saying come from, George?" Faith rambled, hardly above a whisper. "Never much liked it. How much rest and peace did my son Michael need, answer me that? Didn't make a lick of sense." And her voice trailed off to nothing. "But now, I'm so very tired."

A bit of moonlight played off Faith's disheveled hair. George squelched an urge to smooth it back into place.

For a long moment, she stared at the evening sky filtering through the oak tree limbs. "Did you know I used to be scared of the dark?" she went on. "I seem to remember that suddenly. My mother brought an elephant clock into my room to help me sleep through the night. I'd never heard such a soothing sound as that old thing's tick-tock. And its trunk moved so cleverly." She wiggled a finger. "It's all coming and going so fast, you know, the things I remember. It is hard to believe that they just vanish."

"Yes. I imagine."

She turned her head back to the holly bush and let another moment go by without a sound. As George waited for the next thing to come from her lips, he realized that she was just a little too still. And he grasped that she was not deep in thought but without thought, gone. He felt a chill, glancing back at the house, wondering if he might need to call for some help. But as he sat there watching, waiting for her to come back, he caught a glimmer of the woman who had admired the water lily painting with him that afternoon so long ago. George wondered what it was she was going through, where it was she went, and what it was she truly heard and saw there, if anything. But he wondered, most of all, what it must sound like to think one hears the Voice of God.

Delusional, of course, he reminded himself, they're all delusional, but so, they say, were the saints. Hearing such a Voice could make even a sane person lose one's mind and certainly be branded as such, yet he was quite certain many would gladly choose to hear it anyway. But would I? the priest wondered.

Faith began to rouse herself, snapping George out of his latest philosophical flight of fancy. She suddenly noticed him sitting beside her as if it were the most natural thing in the world, and she smiled at him. It was such a genuine, young smile, so much like that first afternoon visit years before, it grabbed his heart.

"Hello, Faith Ann," he softly said, finally calling her the name she'd requested long ago.

"Hello yourself, George," she said softly back. "I'm so tired."

"I know."

Then she frowned in sudden concern. "Do you believe in ghosts, George?"

"Not really," he answered.

"Not even the Holy Ghost?"

George paused. "Well, that's different."

"Yes, it always is, isn't it? Can't see why."

"Uhm, well," George tried, "because the Holy Ghost is really the Holy Spirit, I suppose."

"Isn't the Holy Spirit God?"

"Well, yes . . ."

"So doesn't that make God a ghost?"

George got clumsily to his feet to avoid a no-win theological discussion on the Trinity. As he was wiping the grass off his pants, he finally saw the bandage on her hand. "You're hurt. Perhaps I should help you up and inside."

Faith studied him. "You don't believe God told me to do all this today, do you? Tell me the truth."

"No," George said, then quietly added: "But I'd like to."

A moment passed, George standing over Faith, waiting to help her up as Faith looked away. Then she looked straight up at the priest. "What if none of this is true, George? What if I don't really die tonight? What if it's only my mind that will be dying?" She looked stricken. "What if I do have to be dead before I die? What kind of 'Rest in Peace' is that? I can't stand it—I just . . ." She paused, staring at him for another beat as if she'd lost her train of thought, and then abruptly turned her head back toward the holly bush, scanning again.

"What are you looking for in the bushes?" George gently asked. "I'm rather confident I can help you with that."

She made a small move that looked as if she wanted to get to her feet. "Here, let me help you." He touched her elbow, but she didn't budge.

"Why?" she said, under her breath.

"Why . . . what?" he asked, dropping his hand.

"I want to know why," she said again.

George tried to think of something to say. "I don't quite—"

She pursed her lips, back to her feisty self. "I need an answer. The right words, George. And don't give me any of that Job nonsense. Never understood that story one bit."

George sighed. "What do you want me to say?" The words sounded dead even as they came off his tongue.

"I need you to say something profound, George," she said, eyes still straight ahead. "And if you use that 'God works in mysterious ways' line, I'm going to scream. I need profound and I need it right now."

Shifting his weight from one foot to the other as he hovered over Faith, George opened his mouth and then closed it, opened it and closed it, feeling like some oxygen-starved guppy. Why couldn't he come up with anything? How useless was he? Just say something, George, he berated himself. *Anything*, for God's sake.

The priest began to sweat. Why couldn't he do this for her? He had a wealth of Sunday sermons and decades of biblical study; he'd counseled hundreds, giving advice of dubious quality perhaps, but still advice. Just because it was Mrs. Darling, just because this seemed so much like last time, just because he was old and tired himself— that was no excuse! Be a man, George, pull it together! he thought. The woman wants to know why. But he had to wonder—with more than a touch of despair—which "why" did she mean? After all, there were so, so many with so few responses worth the breath to say them. Hadn't she just emptied a mansion after not finding out "why"?

Why? George grumbled at himself: God only knows why, that's why. But may God strike me down if I can't say something for her and say it now.

So Father George Fallow focused hard, directing all he had on her unusual sale and the entire day's happenings here at her mansion. Then he cleared his mind and waited for the right words from all the ones he'd mouthed for decades—for Faith Bass Darling. Kneeling down, he said the first thing that came into his mind: "The rich young ruler."

Faith swiveled her head his way. "The Bible story? What about it?"

"Do you remember it?"

"Of course, chapter and verse," Faith said. "The rich young ruler—the pompous young man who asked how he could get into heaven and Jesus told him to sell everything he owned."

"Which was the one thing he thought he couldn't do," George finished.

"And your point?" Faith snapped. "Considering that is exactly what I've been doing?"

"The problem isn't 'things,'" George answered. "It's *the* thing. Everybody has one big, blinding thing that's in the way."

For a beat, they both went silent, George holding her gaze as Faith knit her brows in thought. Finally, she sat up straighter and said: "That was rather good."

George was somewhat surprised himself. He got back to his feet, feeling his shoulders straighten and an actual smile beginning to form.

"Yes," Faith mused as he helped her to her feet, straightening up once more to her famous posture. "Yes, that was more than good. That was perfect. Of course! That's how I'm to finish. I need to finish cleaning house . . . of *Claude*. That is my one thing."

George froze. "Oh, no, no, that wasn't what I—"

"Oh yes, yes," Faith cut him off, eyes shining with purpose. "It's Claude. And you!"

"Me?"

George saw the bag in the shadows for the first time. It was a heavy canvas money bag that banks once used for sorting and collecting, the kind he hadn't seen in years. Faith was now picking it up with both hands and holding it out toward him.

And George immediately felt an overwhelming sense of doom. Something bad was about to happen, he just *knew* it.

"Take it. For the church," Faith was saying, dropping it at his feet. "If you'll do one more thing for me. I have to rid my family's house of Claude, do you understand?"

"No, I honestly don't!" George exclaimed.

"I have to get him unstuck to get *me* unstuck, George," Faith went on, turning to look back at the mansion.

George shook his head. "But why?"

"I killed him," Faith said.

Before George could find his tongue, Faith waved his question away. "Don't start talking about sin and forgiveness and the like," she said as George gaped. "I'm past that and time is short. It's about getting unstuck to finish the deal—and now I know how!" Faith brightened, turning back to the priest. "You did it, George. God talked through you."

"Oh, Mrs. Darling, I don't think so," George moaned, taking a step back.

"Well, I do." She glanced down at the money bag. "I'm going to trust you to do this one last thing."

"Please don't do that," George begged, feeling the worst still coming.

"George," Faith said, "I need you to do an exorcism."

George laughed, a nervous cackle of a laugh, and then stopped: "You're joking."

Faith leveled her gaze. "Do you see me laughing?"

"Episcopals don't do exorcisms!" George exclaimed.

"Don't know why not. Catholics do," Faith said, logically.

"Maybe in the movies, but this is real life!" George answered.

"Your English Episcopals—what do you call them, Anglicans—they do or used to. Your African Episcopals do, for certain. I've read about such things." Faith frowned. "Besides, seems to me you might as well be Baptist if you don't believe something like that."

"But . . . but . . ." George couldn't stop stammering.

Faith cocked her head. "Don't make me wish I'd called a real priest, George."

Ouch. "That was uncalled for, Mrs. Darling," he muttered.

"Don't get your feelings hurt, George. Just do it."

George took another step back, attempting some authority. "If you think God is now wanting you to do an exorcism of your dead husband from this house, well, I just have to say—"

"Don't," Faith said.

"What?"

"Don't say whatever it is you were about to say," she went on. "This is my one thing—you were exactly right."

George groaned. "Oh, please, Mrs. Darling, don't listen to me."

She pointed to the bag. "There's at least fifty thousand dollars in there, so I'm told."

Hearing that, George had to swallow hard, having just experienced the pain of another church budget meeting. "But this won't solve your real problem, even if I find an 'exorcism' rite of some kind! You can't expect magic. Don't you understand? Even if I find it, it'll all just be words. They won't make a bit of difference!" And he surprised himself that he had said that out loud.

Faith shook her head. "I don't know if I agree with you about words, George. After all, do you think it's a coincidence that 'possessed' and 'possessions' are the same word?"

"Yes, yes I do!" George exclaimed, waving his hands. "Your dead husband isn't haunting your house or your things, I promise you. There are no such things as ghosts—stuck or unstuck! It's all in your mind. This won't help. You'll be giving me all your money for nothing. I'll feel bad about it, but I'll take it, because the church needs it. And there'll be nothing blessed about it. I'm just being honest with you! They'll just be *words*."

"Then why do you care?" Faith nudged the bag his way. "Take the money with my blessing. And in case I don't remember by the time you do it, you have to have it done by midnight. It has to be done today, this last day—a deal is a deal. I'm going to trust you. Because I do trust you. I always have."

When the priest still didn't move, Faith leaned her head his way, her eyes softening. "George, take the money. Please," she said quietly. "Do this for me."

In the backyard, where the limbs of the old oak stretched low and long, Faith Bass Darling stood alone. She was standing very still where she'd just stepped—into the stream of light coming from the mansion's bedroom window.

The priest had gone, lugging the money bag, leaving by the dirt streets behind the mansion. But not before making Faith promise to go inside. So Faith, a woman of her word, had been on her way to do just that, heading toward the kitchen side door, when she'd found herself momentarily blinded by the sudden light. Pausing, she put up her hand to shield her eyes and squinted at something caught in the tree limbs. Something in the busted metal shape of an old, deadly thing she faintly recalled she'd been looking for in the nearby bushes . . . something, in another moment, she didn't recall at all.

Now lit by the glow of mansion light, Faith Bass Darling had last things on her mind. With Claude on his way to being exorcised, the deafening noise of him had begun to fade away enough for her to finally hear something else that had been trying to be heard for a very long time. The mother in her was now hearing the elephant clock—hearing its *tick* but oddly not its *tock*—and she instantly knew why: there was still one more somebody to get unstuck. It was not too late after all. No, not too late at all.

And Faith was now on her way to find her.

So, instead of going inside, since she didn't recall that was where she was headed anyway, she began wandering across the backyard, in and out of the light streaming from the mansion, stopping every few steps to squint into the dark for that certain somebody, either big or small. Finally, she found herself in the side dirt-road alley, saw the nice, bright streetlight on Old Waco Road in front of the mansion, and headed for it.

"Mother?"

Ah, there she is, Faith thought, hearing the voice as she walked into the glow of the streetlight.

"Mother?" she heard again, turning toward the sound. *"Mother!"*

"Mrs. Darling!" she heard another voice yell, lower, booming: *"Stop!"*

Faith then heard a screech of brakes and a sound of something hitting something else with a pow and thud, and she realized strangely that the "something else" was her. She felt herself falling as yet another voice above her was now screaming: "I didn't see her! She walked right in front of my car!"

The bit of asphalt of Old Waco Road upon which Faith landed was pleasantly warm to Faith's cheek. From far away, as if it were someone else's inner voice, she heard her own worried thoughts rushing through her memory litany:

My name is Faith Bass Darling . . . I live at 101 Old Waco Road in Bass, Texas . . . Today is . . . Today is . . .

Then Faith paused in mid-litany, vividly aware of herself in the out-of-body way she'd heard happened in such times, and thought:

Where's my life? Shouldn't it be flashing in front of my eyes?

Yet, as she lay in the streetlight's early evening halo, all she saw— all that seemed left in need of being seen—was a void looming over her as big as an elephant.

And it was ticking.

The emergency room curtain parted. In walked a slender, prematurely balding man in a tuxedo. Claudia stood up. She'd been sitting for an hour by the hospital gurney where her mother lay unconscious.

"You must be Claudia," he said, extending a hand that Claudia numbly shook. "I'm Dr. Peabody. Forgive the attire. My wife decided we should greet the new millennium in formal wear, even here in Bass. We were just stepping out the door for a party," he said, moving over and checking Faith's bandages. "They tell me it's only a mild concussion, but I wouldn't worry about her being unconscious. Sometimes a slight concussion makes a person pass out. Beyond that, she only has some cuts and bruised ribs. She was lucky." He looked over Faith's chart a moment, then turned to Claudia. "So, in the wake of today's dramatic escalation in her sundowning episodes, your mother chose the day's actual sundown to wander into traffic."

"Yes," Claudia answered.

He sighed, replacing the chart. "Alzheimer's patients often wander, and that's now obviously manifested itself. This is the moment that the care center with its controlled environment becomes the only safe alternative."

Claudia looked toward her mother. "She keeps saying that today is the last day of her life."

He hesitated. "Well, even though your mother has had the condition awhile, Alzheimer's patients can live on for years. That's why it's often called the 'long goodbye.' Her notion could be about the dying that's happening to her brain. . . ." Then the doctor paused.

"But?" Claudia asked.

"But I believe there's a mind/body connection, and I've learned never to say never with the elderly." He smiled. "But it's only a few hours until the day is over. She should come to herself soon. We'll move her into a room and keep her overnight for observation until she's awake and alert. Let's talk then." As the tuxedoed doctor disappeared beyond the curtain, Claudia heard him say: "Going to be a busy night, eh, Deputy?"

"You got that right."

The curtain parted again and John Jasper appeared, moving over close to Claudia to keep his voice low.

But Claudia spoke first, looking back at Faith: "They're keeping her overnight."

He settled his hands around his gun belt. "I was hoping to hang around to help till my charter, but it looks like the partying's started early. Jerry Stamper's barn is burning after his boy decided to do some target practice with a bottle rocket. And Hiram Hitt's next-door neighbor is waving a deer rifle over a bag of batteries Hiram says he stole. So the knuckleheads are calling. Sorry."

Claudia shook her head, smiling for the first time in hours. "John Jasper Johnson, there's not a sorry bone in your body." For a warm moment, she drank in the comforting surprise of this special man from her long ago and now from her long, long day. Before she knew what she was doing, she'd reached out and touched his hand resting on his belt in the exact same way she had as a teenager by her brother's car. Then she reached up and kissed him on the cheek: "Thank you."

John Jasper did not move for a splendid second. Placing his other hand over hers, he held her smiling gaze for a nice, healing moment. Then, with a last look at Faith Darling, he disappeared beyond the curtain.

And Claudia settled in for a nice, quiet, boring Millennium New Year's Eve.

Father George Fallow, careful not to stumble on the broken step in the dark, entered his church office, flipped on the light, and plopped the money bag on his desk. He'd been driving around and around, trying to focus, but he just couldn't think straight with all that money in his car seat. So he finally gave up and came back here, hoping that his parishioners were busy with personal party plans and wouldn't see the light on. He had no desire to explain why he had in his possession a big bag of cash. Dropping into his office chair, he found Jesus staring straight at him, Faith's kitschy garage sale picture still leaning against the far wall.

And the inner debate began.

Would it be wrong to do this and keep the money?

Have I no self-respect left?

But what would it hurt?

Me, that's what it would hurt.

Would it?

It would certainly hurt his pride if anybody saw him. George eyed the money bag. But what would it hurt to swallow his pride, do as she asked, keep the money, fix the step, and help the church that, after all, is the house of the Lord?

It was more than pride, wasn't it? If the issue was what was "right" for him as a priest, he could probably find such an ancient rite if he started looking. And if it was a rite, it was certainly all right to use it. If the issue was ethics, it's not like he'd keep the money without doing as she wished, no matter how useless he thought it might be.

What, then, was bothering him so much? Intent? False pretenses?

Think this through, George, old boy, he told himself, leaning over his desk to stare at Jesus. You've been saying it yourself for months now—it's just words. But that's your problem, not hers. All the woman wants is a saying of some words. Who are you to not give her such comfort?

Besides, George reminded himself, she already thinks you're going to do it. There's really no going back. And if you do it, then surely it would be all right to keep the money.

"That wouldn't be wrong, would it?" he said to the Jesus picture with those forever eyes.

Then why did it *feel* wrong?

Rolling his eyes, he contemplated giving himself a good pop upside the head. Snap out of it, George, old boy! he commanded himself. Performing the rite would truly be no different than the words you've mouthed every week for thirty-five years. *"This is the mystery of faith, we believe . . . we acknowledge . . . "*

We repeat and repeat the words.

George took off his glasses and rubbed his eyes, trying to calm all the way down. Perhaps he should think about something else for a moment, find some calm in the order of his somewhat neglected church week routine.

Putting his glasses back on, he picked up the lectionary's scripture reading sheet for the coming Sunday's services.

Then his eyes fell on the week's first passage. . . .

In the beginning was the word
and the word was with God
And the word was God.

And Father George Fallow ever so slowly fell apart.

Quiet.

Claudia sat by her still-unconscious mother in her mother's private hospital room. It was almost eleven P.M. She'd been sitting with the lights low for several hours now, savoring the quiet of the hospital, away from the growing frenzy of the emergency room on New Year's Eve. Away from surprise garage sales and empty mansions and God-hearing mothers and the sudden old intimacy of hometown friends. The silence had been heaven, smooth shelter from the chaos she'd driven into just this morning, a lifetime ago.

For the last quiet hour, she'd been summoning the words she needed to say to her mother when she woke up, rolling them around and around, wanting to get them right this time.

Having listened to the cadence of her mother's breathing for hours, Claudia was absently thinking about breath itself, the Zen belief that we are the breath—that we take the breath and move from life to life according to our karma—when she suddenly realized she was breathing in sync with her mother. Claudia all but snapped to attention, consciously breathing her own breath, to her own cadence. *Her own.* And with that, unable to wait a moment longer, all the summoned words began to spill out:

"Mother, I don't know if you can hear me," she began, staring hard at her sleeping mother, "but you cannot die yet—not until you see me. I am almost forty years old and I have to let all this go. I just have to put it to rest and get on with some sort of life that isn't so hard. I don't know what life is for. Honest to God, I don't, but it sure can't be for what both of us have been doing." Claudia breathed in, out: "There's too much to rehash, but there's one thing I *need* another chance to tell you: Grandmother Belle's ring—Mother, it's been here all along. I believed you loved it more than me, so, yes, I took it but then I hid it. In the rolltop. The stupid child I was thought I could just drop you a note to tell you, when I was good and ready. I wanted to hurt you and I don't want to do that anymore. And for that one thing I hope you'll forgive me." Claudia closed her eyes. "Because you didn't read the letter and now the ring's gone and you're all but gone . . . and there's nothing I'd rather do right now than give you back that ring."

"What ring?" Faith blearily murmured.

Claudia's head popped up. As her mother's words registered, she felt as if something were slowly crushing her chest. She might as well have said, "What daughter?"

Her mother was saying something else: "You're too big to be scared of the dark, Claudia Jean." Taken back by the sudden soft timbre of her mother's voice, Claudia held her breath as her mother turned groggily toward her to say: "If you want, I'll move the elephant clock into your room. How about that, young lady?"

When the sob she'd been holding in for twenty years came rushing to the surface, Claudia strode out the door, down the hall, through the hospital's automatic doors, and into the December night air.

Faith Bass Darling sat up and looked around.

Where am I?

It looked like a hospital room. "But, these days, you never know," she mumbled, blinking, especially since she wasn't alone. The room was certainly crowded with all these distant family members standing all around. *Very distant,* she suddenly realized, seeing they were all dressed quite old-fashioned.

They were all saying hello.

"Hello yourself," Faith said to the whole bunch standing there looking exactly like they did on her foyer's portrait wall. "It's good to see you," she went on, "although you'll excuse me if I don't get up and/or call you by name. You see, I can't recall them. I seem not to be able to place names with faces anymore. And right now I cannot place your names at all. But never mind. I'm so very glad you've come to see me off. Such a nice gesture. Forgive me for selling your things. I always called them mine, but they were really yours. You'll have to ask God why I had to sell them." She frowned. "Now I have to go. I'm rather sure what's supposed to happen is not supposed to happen here." She looked down at her paper hospital gown. "And definitely not dressed like this. My goodness."

Faith winced, discovering her bandages. Her eyes shut momentarily with the pain, and when she opened them again, she was alone.

And for the second time in one day, she was certain she heard her name called like soft lightning . . . and it was coming from the direction of her home. . . .

Finding her sundress, Faith took off her hospital gown and pulled her dress painfully over her head. Then she smoothed it down, scooted into her shoes, and stepped out into the hall where she saw a door marked "Emergency Exit." Since this was certainly an "emergency exit," she headed straight for it.

John Jasper cussed.

The cherry bomb landed on his boot heel and exploded, making Deputy John Jasper Johnson jump where he stood in the big middle of the impromptu pasture party watching Jerry Stamper's barn burn. The knuckleheads—stuffed in the junkers and pickups jamming the farm road as far as he could see—all had pockets full of firecrackers and hadn't been afraid to use them. His gun hand actually jerked to his holster, and, as itchy as he was feeling, he had a good mind to pull it out and make a few knuckleheads jump for a damn change.

Instead, he fumed, then checked his watch: 11:14. He'd thought he'd be long gone by now, prepping for his midnight charter flight. But word had spread as fast as the fire. By the time John Jasper finally made it out to join the other deputies, half the teenagers in the county had already arrived, riding their pieces of moving junk all at the same time in the same direction down the same main two-lane county road: Texas Farm Road 3237. Things only got worse after the fire spread to the Stamper boy's stash of fireworks in the neighboring shed. The result was a display that the people in the next county saw, a display that might even surpass the town's big show still scheduled at midnight. And the crowd was the kind that was going to have to clear itself out.

He checked his watch, fuming again: 11:15. He'd been late to the scene. He'd made up some lame excuse to tell the other deputies and didn't like himself for doing it, because he'd been late for one reason—he hadn't taken the shortcut from town they all took, the old river bridge road. Instead, he'd taken his usual detour around it and gotten stuck in the redneck gridlock. Any other night, avoiding the old bridge road would have been fine. It had been fine all these years—nothing in the world more important than not going down that road past the scene of the accident, past ClaudeDamnDarling's oil lease. Past his goddamn past.

But he'd been stuck out here too long. Now he had a big problem, a time problem, and he couldn't decide what the hell to do: it was take the old river bridge road or miss the charter. Either five minutes over the old bridge road or God-knows-how-long through the maze of the Texas farm road gawker-parade in reverse, because the knuckleheads were all now turning their moving pieces of junk around to go back to town for the downtown party, creating gridlock the opposite way.

He checked his watch: 11:17.

He had to move.

Move.

Cussing himself now, he strode over to his cruiser and got in, grabbing up his long-dead buddy's moldy half-deflated State Champs football from the passenger seat. He hadn't been able to leave it at the Darling mansion. He'd tried—it was beyond saving, the ruined pigskin ripped and rat-chewed along with any good memories still attached. Yet on his last check of the mansion before heading out here, he hadn't been able to resist the force of old habit, and he'd scooped it up from where he'd left it in the grass. Now he sat in his cruiser squeezing the ruined old football, thinking hard. He had to go—he had to *go*! Just five minutes down the road, he coached himself. Five minutes and twenty years, his mind finished the thought.

For a moment, he seriously considered living without the big chunk of money from the charter group, which made him instantly disgusted with himself. He gritted his teeth. Life's 640,000 hours long, he thought, and I've wasted hundreds of them right here. And he was just goddamn sick of it. Dropping the ball into his lap, he put the cruiser in gear and drove the half-mile to the old road's turnoff.

Then slowly, ever so slowly, he turned down the dark old road.

Within a mile, he had passed the entrance of the oil lease property. In the moonlight, he could see it was abandoned, nothing but a rusted cow grid gate and rotting equipment. He stopped anyway, just to wait a minute. Because as bad as that was, it wasn't the scene of his nightmares. That was just ahead: the curve ClaudeDamnDarling missed, before the bridge, before the water. Less than a quarter mile ahead. Less than the distance he used to run faster than anybody, greased lightning on a stick, his feet barely touching gridiron grass.

He rolled the patrol car ahead until the curve was in headlight view. Hearing the flow of the river, he steeled himself against what his mind was hearing: the screech of truck tires . . . the swoosh of his body soaring as the truck flipped them airborne . . . the thud of silence that followed . . . the kind of silence that comes with the last silence, a silence he shouldn't know about . . . a silence he'd believed all these years was a part of this place as surely as earth and water.

That was the silence he was about to drive through, right now, the car his only shield against it. He took a deep breath.

Easy as pie, he told himself.

Just five minutes out of 640,000 hours.

On your mark.

Set.

Go.

But he could not take his foot off the brake.

John Jasper slammed the car into Park and sat back, disgusted at his gimp-kneed weakness. And as the old blood-rushing rage took him over, he began to furiously pound the steering wheel, throwing his entire body into each blow—over and over and *over*—breaking a sweat, gasping, heaving, drained to his very soul from all the years of being stuck.

Right.

Here.

For a moment, he sat in the silence. Then, grabbing up the old football, he got out.

"No more," he muttered, striding toward the curve and the bridge beyond.

Not-one-goddamn-second-more—

He moved into a trot, tucking the ball in, feeling the weakness in his ruined leg and spirit, the constant threat of them both giving way.

Then he sucked in the sorrow—and began to sprint.

When his knee finally let go, when he hit the ground hard enough to force a rolling curse right out of him, he was past the curve, on the bridge, over the water, with the ball still in hand.

Then, propelled by the last burst of his own inner fireworks, John Jasper Johnson forced himself up on his good leg, took two steps back, and let the half-deflated, ruined football fly into the black Brazos River flowing by. He didn't breathe until he heard the sound of the ball splashing through the shimmering surface below and flowing, deeply, darkly, finally, away.

Meanwhile, in the private dark of the town's hospital parking lot, Claudia blew her nose, heaved a last big sigh, and leaned against her Volkswagen. She was finally all sobbed out. So, wiping her eyes and wadding up her last tissue, she composed herself and headed back inside, back through the hospital's automatic doors and back into what she thought was her mother's room.

The bed was empty. "Mother?" she called. She checked in the bathroom. She checked the closet—her mother's sundress and shoes were gone. She went into the hall and checked the room number. *"MOTHER!"*

Ten minutes later, after checking every wing, every empty room, every public bathroom of the small hospital with the spotty help of the elderly security guard, she finally stopped in the lobby to catch her breath and let the old guard catch up to her.

"Want us to call the sheriff?" the security guard wheezed, wiping his forehead with the back of his sleeve. "She ain't in the building."

Claudia ran both hands over her face, took a calming yoga breath—in, out, hair to toenails—and concentrated, trying to decide what to do. She glanced at her watch: 11:29 P.M.

"Maybe she's gone home," said the guard. "It ain't that far."

Claudia turned all the way around to look at him.

"You're Mrs. Darling's daughter, Claudia Jean, ain'tcha?" he said.

"I'm sorry." Claudia paused. "Do I know you?"

The old guard waved that silly question away, it being a small town and all. "I'm just sayin', if I were her, that'd be what I'd do."

So Claudia rushed out to her VW and roared from the parking lot to begin scouring the streets, from the hospital to the mansion, streetlight to streetlight, squinting hard for signs of the wandering Faith.

✍ PROVENANCE

19TH-CENTURY MANSION

Two-story historic Queen Anne on two-acre plot in
quaint small Texas town • Century-old sycamore and
oak trees • Well cared for until very recently

Circa 1880   *Value: $750,000*

*In 1880, on the eleventh anniversary of the opening of the Brazos Valley
Railroad line between Austin and New Orleans, a shipment arrived in
the prospering railroad town of Bass, Texas, consisting of lumber from a
pine forest in Bastrop and a cypress forest in Louisiana, factory-made
nails from Chicago, and pricey original plans from famous Austin architect E. B. Bose. It was all loaded onto wagons and hauled by horses up
Waco Road to a spot on a small rise chosen by the town's namesake and
Bass Bank founder, the wealthy James Tyler Bass.*

*By 1882, workers had finished building the Queen Anne–style man-
sion, with a downstairs foyer, parlor, library, and dining room, six upstairs bedchambers, a wraparound porch, a widow's walk balcony, a
turret, a grand half-turn staircase, nine fireplaces with mantels, and a
detached kitchen. Inside, the architect added plaster cornice moldings,*

wood floors, brass fittings, elegantly paneled woodwork, and hand-carved front double doors. Then a brick walkway was laid down to the road with a popular wrought-iron "lawn jockey" hitching post marking the address.

By the end of the year, the railroad had delivered the last of the fancy furniture that turned the mansion into the showplace of the county, and the first generation of Basses moved in.

In 1905, the kitchen and toilets were added to the main house by the second generation.

In 1925, the house's oil lamps were converted to electricity by the third generation.

In 1963, the wrought-iron lawn jockey's black face was painted white and the air-conditioning unit was added to the kitchen area by the fourth generation.

In 1981, the mansion and its grounds began to fall into gentle disrepair.

In 1999, in the last minutes of its second century, the mansion's contents were emptied onto the sloping, overgrown lawn for a yard sale.

And as the seconds ticked toward its third century, the mansion awaited its fate at the hands of the Bass family's final generation.

Faith Bass Darling stumbled along neighborhood streets toward the mansion, the habit of a lifetime showing her the way home, as small-town revelers lined the town's main street anticipating the big moment—the sounding of the thudding old clock over Buford Drugstore that would signal the volunteer fire department to set off the county's biggest fireworks blowout ever.

As the seconds ticked toward midnight and bottle rockets warmed up the night air for the big moment's display, somebody down Old Waco Road set off a long string of whambang jumbo firecrackers right as Faith shuffled by.

BLAMMM Ratttertatttttttttt

Faith, though, barely heard it. Oblivious to historic countdowns, she was unaware of the cars driving by or the blocks she'd walked or the houses she'd passed. She felt nothing but her own motion and the throb of her own ribs against the warm whirl of the night wind. Despite the faint sound of the antique elephant clock *tick*s without their *tock*s still in her ears, time wasn't a thing for her. It might have been a minute; it might have been an hour. It didn't seem to matter anymore to her mind, which was now its very own place, connecting to something beyond such things ruled by time.

Then her foot landed on her mansion's lawn and she felt it like a whambang firecracker all its own. Suddenly, inexplicably, she was aware of the earth turning, a hint of something spinning under her feet and inside her skin. The dizzy jolt brought her back once more to herself, standing now on the sticky, dead St. Augustine grass covering the only bit of earth she was still attached to. The next thing Faith felt was the dead grass sticking right up her nose. Blinking and groggy, her chest searing with pain, she pulled herself to a standing position and gazed around her, more than a little confused, wiggling a stubbed toe and holding her bandaged, aching ribs.

She headed up her brick walkway to her house. Whispering, shuffling, scurrying noises were coming from the alley's hedgerows as she went, but she registered the ramification of this with barely a blip of annoyance.

I need some tea, she decided, wincing with each step. Instead of going in the front doors, up all those steps, she headed around to the side screen porch and into the kitchen—the door of which was wide open. And the ramifications of that did not register at all.

Inside, Faith forgot about switching on the light. She weaved around the piles in the streetlights' faint glow streaming in the windows, found and lit a cigarette, and then forgot about it, setting it down in the ashtray on the counter, along with the burning kitchen match she also forgot. As they both lit up a nice little unseen flame, she walked over to the stove and turned on the right front burner to make some tea, *clickclickclick*ing the pilot light to make the flame come on. In mid-click, though, she forgot why she was standing there and walked off before the pilot light ignited, leaving the unlit gas burner on.

Just then, the air conditioner's sputtering thermostat clicked off, the unit buckling to a halt with a resounding *whoomph* like a fist slamming down on wood, and jolted Faith back to the moment. Frowning, she tried to remember what she was doing.

Oh yes. Tea.

So she reached over the right burner—on but not lit—turned on the left burner—*clickclickclick*—and then forgot it, too.

Faith eased down on the counter stool directly under the round white wall clock, its hands moving ever closer to midnight, and reached for the ashtray's cigarette. Then she forgot about that as well and just sat there, not moving at all.

Six blocks away, Claudia pulled her car over to the curb. Her mother couldn't have gotten this far already. Could she?

Glancing every few seconds at the clock's green digital numbers in the dark, she numbly watched them change: 11:41. 11:42.

Revelers whooped by her, swerving, honking, bouncing off the curbs before screeching away. She could just see her mother wandering into the street now; all she'd have to do is step off the curb at the wrong time and she *could* die tonight. Claudia pushed her mind past that fear and it flipped over right into anger: "It is not going to end like this, Mother!" she yelled. "Where the *hell* are you?"

Inhaling slow and furious, she started once again to call her mother's name. But, just then, the car's green digital clock changed again: 11:43. And the sight made her all but despair. This is not happening! she thought, jerking the wheel and floorboarding her VW toward the mansion.

Within seconds she was in front of her childhood home, but there was no sign of her mother. Not one light was on. She decided to quickly take the block before going inside to check the dark mansion.

Claudia rolled her car down the side gravel road and then turned onto the dirt street at the back edge of the mansion, creeping along, squinting, the nearest streetlight too far away to be much help. She slowed the car to a halt, waiting for her eyes to adjust. The only gap in the back fence along the property's border was a slight one around the base of the big old oak tree. The tree was as mammoth and magnificent as it was when she was a kid. Claudia stared at it, a smile surprised right out of her, as a wonderful childhood memory came flooding back: her oak-tree-hollow hiding place.

Despite herself, Claudia's smile grew as her eyes quickly scanned for the hollow right at the roots along the fence that she'd made into her little hiding place when she was small enough to crawl inside. It had been her own little "house," where things could be hidden and broken and dirty and just hers and hers alone a world away from uptight mothers. And there was a time when she'd loved it even more than the mansion.

There it is, she realized, craning her neck for a better look.

But before she could enjoy the sight for even a nice nostalgic moment, she heard something odd.

It sounded like . . . a ringing cell phone.

Claudia checked around the car, her big-city street smarts expecting someone lurking near. As far as she could tell, though, she was totally alone.

Turning off the ignition, she eased out of the car and waited.

There it went again: a muffled ringing cell phone. And it seemed to be coming from *inside* the tree.

She crept close, until she was just inches away from her old tree hollow. Leaning in, she cocked her ear toward the opening.

There it went again: *definitely* a ringing cell phone.

"What the hell?" she said under her breath. Then she remembered her mother. With a flustered peek through the fence gap at the still-dark mansion, Claudia checked her watch again: 11:45. "I don't have time for any new craziness!" she groaned and pivoted to hurry back to her car.

But then her oak tree hollow "rang" again.

Claudia stopped in her tracks.

Throwing up her hands at the universe and all the madness whirling around her the entire day, she stomped back to the VW and fished out a flashlight. Then she got down on her hands and knees by the tree trunk's root hollow and flashed the beam of light into the opening that now seemed impossibly small and ridiculously grungy.

But as the beam of light landed on her forgotten little-girl treasures, something inside her melted. As a small thrill rippled through her, Claudia couldn't help but feel she was coming all the way home—as if she were once more entering the wonderful little world she'd created and then, one day, without a thought, left behind. She could only see parts of the hollow's interior even with the flashlight, but it was enough for her memory to fill in the rest. With glimpses of the jar of buffalo nickels and the rusted stadium seat frozen in time, she might as well have been six years old in her tree-hollow world rearranging her snitched treasures.

Then the cell phone rang again, startling her back to her wild-goose detour.

Just one more minute, she told herself, *that is absolutely all I'm giving this.*

Claudia tried to push her head in far enough to see, reaching in with one hand and holding the flashlight steady with the other. But that didn't quite work. So dropping the light, she just thrust a hand in, trusting memory, recalling without a bit of surprise exactly where she'd placed every piece of her precious little-girl collection. Pushing aside the stadium seat, her fingers stretched past the unseen things (including, she hoped, any creepy crawlers) toward where the ringing sound seemed to be coming from—the hole's "special" gnarly root area. Her fingers found the headless naked Barbie who'd always made the gnarly root her home and Claudia pulled it out just for the pleasure of seeing it. Leaning Barbie against the tree, she wiped the dirt from her hands and reached in again.

But instead of finding a cell phone, her fingers wrapped around something else nestled in the gnarly root dirt . . . something small and boxy and round-cornered and velvety . . . and as familiar as her own skin.

For the most vertigo of moments, the world spun off its axis while her brain tried to make sense of what her fingers told her they'd just found.

What it seemed to be.

What it could not be.

Sitting back on her knees in the dark, her fist full of something completely beyond impossible, Claudia fumbled for the flashlight and aimed the beam directly at her palm. What she saw in the halo of the light sent chills roaring up her spine and down every last nerve ending of her body.

Her fingers hadn't lied. Forgotten was the now silent cell phone; forgotten were the headless Barbie and the jar of nickels and the tree-hollow world. Forgotten were the countdown to midnight and even her wandering mother. All that existed for that moment was her hand, her eyes, and the worn black velvet ring box in her palm that, even covered with tree grunge, she'd recognize anywhere. Claudia sat frozen to the spot for fear that any movement might scare away the vision or wake her from a dream. It was as if all her wishing had made the velvet ring box materialize, as if she'd performed a magic trick by some accident of longing and desire and regret. Her heart was pounding so hard she thought she was going to choke on it. She sat there, stupidly staring, waiting for her mind to catch up with what was happening.

Is this really happening? she had to wonder. Trembling, she pushed her hair back out of her face, leaving a streak of dirt on her cheek, trying to calm down. Because now she was fighting a stone-cold case of dread at what might or might not be inside the little box.

Claudia placed the flashlight between her teeth. Carefully, nervously, she took the worn little velvet box in both hands, and, steeling herself, she snapped the little box open. . . .

And it was *there*: the heirloom antique wedding ring—the seed pearls—the gold-filigree setting—the huge pear-shaped diamond—*there*—sparkling in the flashlight beam brilliant enough to blind her.

Blinking wildly, Claudia Darling burst out laughing, dropping the flashlight from her teeth.

Scooping it back up, she aimed the light beam squarely back at what she still didn't quite believe she was seeing. For a fine moment of mystery and wonder—feeling at the center of something incomprehensible—she drank in the remarkable ring. Then, needing to touch it, to see its *Love Eternal* inscription, she positioned the flashlight on a root aimed her way and gingerly removed the ring from the box. And, as her fingers began to convince her eyes, her mind started working on all the begged questions:

Why is it here? How did it get here? Who put it here? And *when*?

She had no idea what to think. Hadn't she just given up the ring as gone forever? Hadn't she just made herself finally let it go?

And now here it is in my hand, she thought, like an incarnated second chance. Claudia could see all the plans for the future that had brought her back home rolling out in front of her again. If she wanted the fitness club partnership and the sane stability it would offer, she could have it.

"Just like that," she said to herself.

If she didn't know better, she'd call this karma of some sort. If she believed in such things, she'd think it a miracle of some sort. But do such things happen if you know better and you don't believe? And her mind quickly dismissed the notion of it being luck or some colossal coincidence. But there was something she couldn't dismiss: even if this were the biggest coincidence in the cosmos, even if she were at that moment the luckiest person on the planet, even if it were karma or a little miracle served up just for her, she couldn't shake the overwhelming feeling that she'd had to let the ring go before it could come back to her.

The wording of that thought made her finger close around the ring. And she felt her heart sway. In that instant, Claudia knew she would never sell it because it *did* come back to her. Then she paused to gaze back toward the dark mansion beyond the fence. "No," she said quietly, correcting herself. "Come back to us."

BLAMMM Ratttertattttattt

Claudia jumped, the ring almost jiggling right out of her hand as revelers whooped down the side street hurling whambang jumbo firecrackers. But the ring was definitely still there—squeezed so hard it left an imprint in her palm. Quickly, she placed it back into the velvet box and snapped it safely shut.

Then she checked her watch: 11:56.

Jumping to her feet, she shoved the ring box into her jeans pocket in the exact way she'd done at seventeen. And with a last glance at the oak tree hollow, she sprinted back to her car, hand hovering protectively over her pocket. Mysteries will have to wait, she thought, her mind still racing over the "who" and "how" and "why" of it all.

But a nice little revelation of her very own halted Claudia Darling in mid-stride: Who *cares*? I have the *ring*! she suddenly wanted to shout.

As Claudia felt herself moving beyond the need for answers or questions, the inexplicable Zen riddle from that morning popped back into her mind—*What is the answer? What is the question?* And for a moment, just a moment, she realized she was dangerously close to understanding it.

With another touch of the lost and found ring in her jeans pocket, Claudia hopped into the VW and careened around the property fence line toward the mansion as the seconds ticked away.

Inside the dark kitchen, several minutes had passed for Faith Bass Darling, who found herself near the kitchen stool under the round white wall clock. She was thinking fondly of the elephant clock, since she was still hearing it in the distance—that and the fact she could now see it on her little daughter's bedroom mantel, having no thought of how doing so was possible, considering she happened to be in the kitchen. Faith smiled as she watched its trunk sway and its hands move from 11:56 to 11:57, listening to its eternally soothing *tick-tock, tick-tock*. For some reason, she was hearing both its *tick* and its *tock* just fine now—and it was music to her old ears.

Then she knew why:

The kitchen door opened and there stood her daughter. As Faith groggily watched, Claudia pushed her way into the kitchen, coughing, blinking, gasping at the smell, rushing toward where Faith lay, cheek to tile, beside the kitchen stool.

But Faith was not seeing Claudia. She was seeing little Claudia Jean. She watched her little rascal of a daughter screw up her button nose. When she felt her little daughter's touch, Faith patted her arm.

"Hello yourself, Claudia Jean," she murmured. "Where have you been hiding, young lady? I've been looking all over for you. You see, I've changed my mind—all is forgiven. I'm not going to spank you. After all, a ring is so small compared to an elephant."

Clearing that up made Faith Darling feel so good that she reached out to pat her little daughter's head. But instead, she felt her daughter grab at her sundress and tug. And she was tugging with surprising strength for a six-year-old. "No, no, I can't stay," Faith pointed out, flipping a wrist as if in mid-conversation. "A deal is a deal. I can't be Mr. Frudigger, I won't—" she went on, as a daughter's hand much too strong for her age slipped into hers and tugged quite hard. "So, please, dear, *please*, *please*, you must let me go."

Faith felt her eyes close for what seemed only an instant. She heard a slap of a screen door, felt a breeze on her face and heard crickets and rustling leaves and tree bark digging into her back. The hand holding hers seemed bigger now. But she was still sure whose it was and it felt nice to hold it, although it was quite clear her daughter needed to use hand lotion. A good expensive cream should do the trick, if she'd listen to her mother.

"Mother! *Mother!*"

Faith, struggling to open her eyes, turned her head toward the muffled voice. And without a bit of warning, Faith's old eyes sprang open—truly open—some lost, lucid part of her briefly awakening. She blinked once at the sight before her.

And her eyes grew wide:

Claudia Jean?

"Mother—wake up!"

It's really her. . . . Grown-up. Strong.

Home.

She drank in the sight of her long-lost daughter's lovely face as time waited for her to revel in it, to relax in it—all in the suddenly yawning space between the music of a single *tick* and *tock*.

Then Faith quit struggling.

And all the minutiae of all the memories of all the moments of a long lifetime came flash-flooding back to her, a thousand roiling surges of instant recall washing over her in a single huge wave, just as she'd always heard:

My name is
                    . . . Faith Bass Darling
of 404 Old Waco Road Bass Texas
born Faith Ann Bass October 3, 1929
                            . . . elephant clock tick
a Bass of the James Tyler Bass founding family
                            one husband two children
                    survived by one daughter
            one mansion
grand staircase turret parlor foyer of portraits
rooms of beautiful blessed things
Queen Anne Georgian Chippendale Louis XV Spode
Wedgwood Louis Comfort Tiffany highboys lowboys love
seats sideboards wardrobes hope chests bureaus wingbacks
four-posters china silver crystal porcelain banker rolltop,
grandfather clock mother's elephant clock
                            lamps lamps lamps

from all the dearly beloved lifetimes

James Tyler Bass married to dearly beloved Belle 1879

James Tyler Bass Jr. married to dearly beloved Zelda 1902

James Tyler Bass III married to dearly beloved Pamela 1927

Faith Ann Bass married to not-so-dearly beloved Claude Angus Darling 1955

son Michael Bass Darling born 1959

daughter Claudia Jean Darling born 1962

                                    . . . elephant clock tock

son Michael died, Dragoon 1977

God my God The Lord is my Shepherd I Shall Not Want

Husband Claude Angus died, 1977

                              I confess I did not do my duty

                    God Where oh where were You?

Faith Ann Bass baptized May 1, 1942 and the Lord bless you

Today is . . . Today is

The Lord bless you keep you

The Lord make His countenance to shine upon you

  and give you peace

          give you peace give you

                  peace

Then as floods do, they all flowed away as suddenly as they came. And in the way the truly finished things can be truly forgotten, Faith Bass Darling then forgot all the living that got her here, all the pain, the regret, the sins, the desires, the longings, the anger, the tragedy, all the questions, all the confusion, the wrong she'd done and the wrongs done to her. All the waiting, the listening, the unanswerable questions stacked up over years and years like stone walls, all the demands for reasons behind everything. None of it mattered anymore. It was all gloriously gone. Washed away like water.

No longer did she hear the *tick-tock*ing of the elephant clock, because no longer was there any time to tick away.

She was surprised to find a nice young woman she did not recognize holding her hand with the most concerned, confused, yet loving look on her lovely face. But before Faith could ask what was wrong, she heard . . . for the third and final time . . . the soft special lightning of her own name in her ears just as she had twenty-four hours ago.

This time, full of final hope, she turned her head toward the Wordless Words: The Still. Small. Silent. Thundering. Fireworks-Sound of the Midnight Almighty. Saying Hello.

"Well," she said. "Hello Yourself."

Then, relatively certain there was one more thing she was supposed to do if she could just remember, Faith concentrated: Now, what was it?

Ah, yes. She had to let go.

So she closed her old eyes and let her ears fill with the new Sweet Silence meant only for her.

And through her mind wandered these last wordless words of her own:

My name is Faith Bass Darling. Today is Today is Today is
Today

A thousand feet above town, John Jasper Johnson was making lazy circles over the town for the entertainment of his paying New Year's Eve revelers, eighty-seven-year-old Harvey and Louise Thistlewaite and their bachelor son, sixty-five-year-old Harvey Jr.

"Happy New Year!" Harvey Sr. wheezed.

Harvey Jr. checked his watch's illuminated dial: 11:57. "Not yet, Dad."

They had already begun partaking of the bottle of 1969 vintage Dom Pérignon brought with them for this once-in-a-lifetime party and were oohing and aahing at the aerial beauty of the town's lights transforming their earth-bound, dirt-plain world below into a wonderland.

"Mmmm, Dom Pérignon!" sipped bent-over Louise as she ogled.

"Happy New Year! Happy New Millennium, old girl!" crowed Harvey Sr., dentures clattering, as he planted a kiss on his wife's cheek.

"Oooo-ooh!" went the gurgle-happy response from the bent little woman.

"Happy New Year!" Harvey Sr. went on. "Happy New Year!"

"Not yet, Dad!" griped Junior, checking his watch again.

The more champagne they drank, the more they checked their

watches against John Jasper's dependable panel clock, itching to start the countdown to the historic moment spent in the heavens, yet hard-pressed to take their eyes off the twinkling lights surrounding them, the stars above and the town below.

Two of those lights below, headlights of an old Toyota streaming down Old Waco Road, turned off past the Darling mansion, moved down the side gravel alley, and went dark.

The Toyota deposited Father George Fallow by Faith Darling's backyard once again—away from view, he hoped. He'd chosen this exact moment knowing it upped his odds of not being seen. The rector began pulling vestments from a sack, anxiously glancing toward the house across the street from the mansion, praying that Maude Quattlebaum's eyes were glued to all the millennial reveling on TV. Sweating already in the warm night, George threw on his vestments as he scurried for the cover of the hedges. Then, entering the backyard, he chose the shadow of a nice dark tree to stand in. He was going to perform the rite because he promised to, but he was not going to trespass inside the dark mansion on this night of all nights. Out here will do just fine, he reassured himself. So he turned toward the house, flicked some holy water at it from a baggie he'd stashed in his pants pocket, pulled a book and a flashlight from his other pants pocket, then straightened his vestments, took a deep breath, and began to quietly read:

"'I exorcize all influence and seeds of evil that they may be bound fast with chains. . . .'"

A thousand feet directly above, Harvey Sr. gulped his champagne, gurgling: "Ten! Nine!"

"Not *yet*, Dad!" snapped Junior.

Below, Father George Fallow continued to read: *"'. . . I lay upon them the spell of Christ's holy Church. . . .'"*

Inside the Darling mansion, as the priest mouthed ancient words, as John Jasper and his revelers circled above, as the townspeople readied for the countdown to either the future or Y2K apocalypse, something was happening. Behind the closed doors of the kitchen where Faith had forgotten to turn off the unlit burners, the faulty thermostat of the temperamental old window air-conditioning unit—enveloped like the rest of the room by now with nothing but pure natural gas—began its old rattling, rolling, clicking start-up, each click creating more and more of the electricity needed to create the magnetic arc spark that would restart the air-conditioning unit's motor.

Downtown, the revelers held their breaths.

Up above, Harvey Jr. gave the signal: "NOW, Dad!"

Under the oak tree, the priest continued reading: "'. . . *casting into outer darkness . . .'*"

And the countdown began:

10 !

"'. . . *until the day of their repentance and restoration . . .'*"

9 !

—the electricity built—

8 !

"'. . . *that they trouble not the servants of God, I exorcize thee . . .'*"

7 !

—the arc leaped—

6 !

"'*Visit, O Lord, we beseech thee, this house and drive from it all the snares of the enemy . . .'*"

5 !

—the spark sparked—

4 !

"'. . . *let Thy holy angels dwell herein and may Thy blessing be upon us evermore.*'"

3 !

—the flash hit the gaseous air—

2 !

"'. . . *Amen.*'" Father George lowered his flashlight and breathed a sigh of relief. "Okay, that's it."

1 !

And the whole kitchen side of the Darling mansion blew itself to kingdom come.

"God Bless AMERICA—" gasped Harvey Thistlewaite, Sr., gawking at the explosion out the plane's left window just as the town fireworks exploded out the right. People all across Bass, Texas—Dr. Peabody in his tuxedo, Hiram and Geraldine watching Dick Clark on their television, Bobbie and Juanita and Angelina and Moon along with every other downtown reveler—turned in unison toward the surprising sound, while Maude Quattlebaum levitated right out of her bed.

In a spectacular display of echoing homemade thunder, the mansion's rows of windows nearest the kitchen then blew outward, one by one, from back to front—followed by the tinkling shower sound of glass, hitting like sharp rain onto the front porch.

"Now, that's what I call fireworks!" howled Harvey Thistlewaite, Sr., high above, slapping the gaping John Jasper on the back. Then all three Thistlewaites, complete with champagne, sloshed into each other's laps as John Jasper pulled the plane hard toward the blast.

Father George, vestments billowing, came running around the side of the mansion. There under the big tree, aglow with the reflection from the fire, he saw Faith Darling and what looked like her daughter, who was pulling herself upright from where she'd been knocked sideways by the blast, blood beginning to trickle from a cut to her temple. Faith, though, was limp, deathly limp, lying unnaturally against the singed sycamore.

As the priest scurried toward them, Claudia, still holding her mother's hand, gazed in shocked wonder at the space where this side of her family's mansion used to be—glass dust filling the air like glitter—as pieces of wood, linen, wallpaper, mattress stuffing, and bits of unfound paper money rained down upon them in the gaseous glow.

When Claudia finally looked back toward Faith at the other end of the cold hand she was squeezing so hard, she paused, stunned at how still her mother was. So still. Too still. Claudia slipped wordlessly up on both knees to watch the stillness. And she felt suddenly enveloped inside a small and silent space within the world of noise, the present noise around them and the years of noise between them. While sirens sounded, and fireworks burst overhead, while volunteer firemen rushed toward their fire engines and John Jasper circled above, Claudia felt the sensation of time slowing to a stop. As if the earth beneath them had also paused . . . and a universe of silence for that one final moment was theirs and theirs alone.

Slowly, reverently, she pulled the black velvet ring box from her pocket, opened it, and placed the heirloom ring back onto her mother's finger, closing her hand around Faith's one last time. And as she felt herself being pulled back into the noise, Claudia leaned toward her silent mother in the glow of the burning mansion and kissed her gently on the forehead, letting her go.

January 1, 2000

✧ FUTURE PROVENANCES

As the new day of a new year, a new century, and a new millennium begins, all the things at Faith Bass Darling's sale have moved on, each possession passing into new hands, their stories beginning all over again.

Father George Fallow will spend most of New Year's Day in his office, sitting and thinking and occasionally gazing at the large kitschy picture of Jesus with the following eyes still leaning against the wall by the door. Tomorrow, he will decide to give Faith Bass Darling's money bag back to Faith's daughter. But today he will stare at Jesus staring back at him until he will decide to take down the Currier & Ives print he hung above his desk to replace the little water lily oil painting so long ago. In its place, he will hang Jesus, deciding he'll leave it there until his parishioners notice it above him, looking their way.

Then, as he turns back to his desk, his eyes will land on his copy of *The Book of Common Prayer*. As the day begins to fade, he will slowly flip to the Evening Prayer section, something he has not done in a very, very long time, and he will sit down and spend the rest of the evening alone with its words.

Four blocks away, the little water lily painting will spend the day in the Hitts' den locked safely once more inside the old rolltop. Geraldine and Hiram, having dodged Y2K, will read in the newspaper about an Austin stop for the PBS's *Antiques Roadshow*. Leaving a scoffing Hiram at home, Geraldine will take the little painting to it, and there she'll be singled out for the on-air spotlight segment, just as she knew she would. Cameras rolling, she'll smugly announce, "I found it at a garage sale in a valuable antique rolltop I paid twenty dollars for." Her heart will skip a beat when the handsome expert removes it from its frame, flips it over, and says: "What we seem to have here is an original work by the famous Impressionist Claude Monet." Then, as the camera zooms in, he will go on: "But it is a student copy of a Monet masterpiece, a student coincidentally named 'J. Claud.' We can tell this by the once traditional student signing of such works seen here: 'J. Claud de Monet,' which means 'J. Claud of a Monet,' to be exact. Thousands of these museum masterpiece copies went home with American tourists in the early twentieth century. Our viewers now know how to spot them. Thank you for bringing it in."

Afterward, on the way home, Geraldine will stop at the Episcopal church's rummage sale donation box around the corner from her house and chuck the little painting inside.

In the Darling mansion's backyard, the mighty oak tree, barely singed by the New Year's Eve blast, will begin its third century. There it and its little-girl-sized tree hollow will stay long after little girls go wherever all little girls go, outgrowing its secret world and all the precious things hidden there. However, one day a decade or so in the future, the biggest storm of the new century will blow through, causing a few branches nearest the mansion, weakened by the gas-blast fire, to finally come crashing down. A worker with a chain saw will find among the tangled limbs a blackened and busted old pistol, its long barrel and chamber now in pieces. He'll study them for a moment, and then pitch them into the trash along with the charred wood on its way to the county landfill.

Long after that, long after Faith Bass Darling's legendary last garage sale has disappeared from local memory, the mighty backyard oak tree will inevitably die and be chopped off right at the level of the hollow, and some new owners of the property will uncover all the things left in its tree-trunk hollow as a sort of time capsule of the twentieth century. Along with, among other things, a jar of mint-condition buffalo nickels, a device once called a cell phone, a tarnished silver music box, a pristine Walmart plastic bag, and a yellowed manual for something called Y2K, they will find the over-sized Deluxe Family Bible, its dingy gold-trimmed white leather cover disintegrating, its fancy family tree insert smudged beyond reading. And from it will flutter the tattered remains of a piece of paper money. The new owners, thinking it only a piece of child's play money, considering the ridiculous $10,000 denomination it bears and the obviously fictitious U.S. president on its front (*Salmon P. Chase?*), will leave it behind, with a chuckle, when they carefully bundle up the rest of the potentially valuable artifacts to take to a dealer for appraisal.

. . .

But all of that is very much in the future, into another generation. Today is still the first day of the new century and millennium. And by sunset, as the light begins to fade, Juanita Lopez, who has spent the day making her Tiffany lamp of beauty shine, shine, shine, will turn it on and sit down in the glow of its holy, musical, magical light.

All across Bass, Texas, the same thing will happen. In double-wide trailers, bungalows, and tract houses throughout the little run-down Texas town, forty-three other garage sale customers will turn on their bargain authentic Louis Comfort Tiffanys as day turns to dusk. And Bass, Texas, will once again bathe in the exquisite antique light bought to reflect James Tyler Bass III's true love for Faith's mother, Pamela.

Then, as the new millennium begins to settle in along with the ash and dust at the damaged mansion on Old Waco Road, Claudia Darling, Bobbie Blankenship, and John Jasper Johnson will begin to look forward instead of back.

John Jasper will begin to feel a geographical freedom he has not felt since high school, driving anywhere without a thought, avoiding neither the old river bridge road nor Old Waco Road. And when he passes the Darling mansion, which he'll feel compelled to do several times a day that first week, he will find he is no longer thinking of ClaudeDamnDarling at all. Instead he will think fondly of Mike and, more than not, Mike's kid sister who's decidedly not a kid anymore.

Bobbie Ann will also find herself driving by the mansion that first week, but she will be mourning it as anyone would a half-blown-up dream. Until, that is, she realizes that she—Bobbie Blankenship, Expert Bungalow Rehabber—is just the one to partner with her good friend Claudia Darling to save it. She will plan to suggest that very thing when Claudia Jean calls her about the elephant clock, as Bobbie knows in her heart her good friend soon will do.

As for Claudia, she will fill the first few days of the new millennium performing the things of this world that must be done when a loved one leaves it, spending the nights inhabiting the parts of the mansion unaffected by the blast. At her request, she will do it alone, staying a little while on her own—to think and not think, to let all her questions find their own answers—comforted only by the glimpses of a familiar police cruiser disappearing around the corner, morning and night, like clockwork. Until, one bright January morning, she will wake up wishing for the sound of a familiar tick-tocking in her ears and she will pick up the phone to call Bobbie.

When she does, before the sun hits the noon sky on that day of new days, Claudia, Bobbie, and John Jasper will leave Bass, Texas, on a mission. They will take flight in the four-seater propeller airplane bought by Claude Angus Darling's gun collection, heading due south toward Houston.

To rescue an elephant.

ACKNOWLEDGMENTS

When an idea sticks over miles and months and calendar years, and you find yourself spending more time in its sticky, expanding universe than out, you start to wonder what the heck's got ahold of you. That's when you realize it's trying to tell *you* something, whether or not it's ever shared with another soul. That it got to do both is the minor miracle performed by two crazy-gifted souls named Dorian Karchmar and Amy Einhorn, and I'm one lucky soul to have found myself in their brilliant corner of the publishing universe. (Who knew that both my agent and my publisher could have senses of humor more overdeveloped than mine? That kept the joy alive through it all, a precious thing, you two.)

To all that was prelude, the life support of any writer's too-stubborn-to-die literary dreams: artistic organizations that primed: Sewanee Writers' Conference, The Ragdale Foundation, Illinois Arts Council, Community of Writers at Squaw Valley, Atlantic Center for the Arts, Writers' League of Texas; academic communities that nurtured: Randy Albers and the gang at Columbia College Chicago's Fiction Writing Department, Amanda Boyden's MFA fiction workshop at the University of New Orleans, David Guest and Austin Peay State University; doggone pals who one by one snoozed under my rolltop while I dreamed: Baylor, Brazos, and Blanco; far-flung family and friends who've seen the good, bad, and ugly; and especially the long-suffering college sweetheart who had no idea what he was getting into when he married a writer-to-be, I say simply, warmly, humbly:

Thank you all for helping me keep Faith.

READERS GUIDE

Faith Bass Darling's Last Garage Sale

1. On the first few pages of the novel, we learn that Faith Bass Darling is fighting a losing battle with Alzheimer's but has not told anyone. After receiving a midnight message from the Almighty, she decides to put her house in order. Even Faith is skeptical of the message, but decides it's "rather prudent to obey." What would you think if you got such an inspiration? Would you be like Faith and follow the instructions? Or would you be like Father George, who, when Faith asks him whether he believes God talked to her, answers, "No. But I'd like to," and choose to disregard the command?

2. The role of memory is a theme often touched on in the novel. Faith asks: "Without our memories, who are we? Doesn't the soul have a memory? If not, what's all this living for?" What do you think? Would you still be "you" if you didn't have your memories, or do your memories make you the "you" you are now? How can our past experiences shape what we do later in life and inform our future decisions? Do we ever actually change completely as the years go by, or do we always hold on to our true selves because our memories have formed who we are?

3. The novel also asks, "Do our possessions possess us?" Several of the main characters grapple with this question. Who do you think struggles with it the most, and what conclusions does this character come to? Faith and Claude, for instance, both put their faith in

material possessions. We all know the famous biblical reference to the camel going through the eye of a needle, warning of the dangers of material wealth, so what is it about our possessions that makes us happy?

4. Faith and Claude's daughter, Claudia, is convinced that her family's possessions could very well keep her from ever being happy. Can a person feel weighed down by material goods? Why or why not?

5. The novel opens with the short provenance of an antique elephant clock that went from the French Revolution to a yard sale in Texas. Have you ever thought about the antiques or heirlooms or any passed-down possessions that you own and the lives they had before they "knew" you? Think of such objects now. How can they make history come alive and give you a personal attachment to the past?

6. If you could buy a priceless antique lamp for one dollar—knowing that the person conducting the sale was not of her right mind—would you or wouldn't you? Why is this such an ethical problem for Bobbie? Have you ever been faced with an opportunity that has caused you to judge your own moral character?

7. Humor plays a big part in the telling of this tale. Do you see it as a funny story? If not, what is the role of humor in the book? Is it always possible to find humor during painful times?

8. Racism also plays a significant role in the story. Do you think the novel effectively portrays the modern learning curve of the average small town and its inhabitants? If so, in what way? If not, why not?

9. Every main character—Faith, Claudia, Bobbie, John Jasper, Father George—confronts his or her own demons on this single day at the

end of the millennium. What are they? What is it about New Year's Eve that elicits introspection?

10. Claudia struggles with family obligations, guilt over her family's tragedy, and a childhood mansion haunted with memories. She has made a mess of her life trying to run from all of these. Was she justified in leaving? When she returns, does she make peace? Or is it just the hope of peace?

11. What is it about mother-daughter relationships that makes them so fraught? Is it inevitable that they are more complicated than other family relationships? One could argue that Faith was unsupportive and critical of Claudia—and the same could be said of Claudia toward Faith. At the end of the novel, is there real rapprochement and forgiveness, or are they simply tired of fighting?

12. Claudia pointedly rejects the countless antiques and heirlooms that have long been valued in her family—except for the ring. Why does it have such a special place in her heart? Do you possess an object of comparable importance? What does our relationship with our most-prized possession say about our personality? Is gauging someone by what he values most a suitable way to assess character?

NOTES